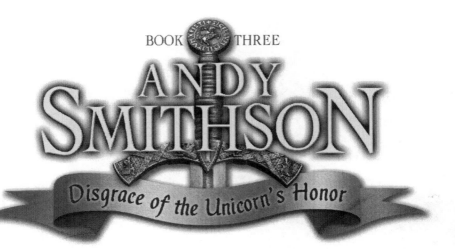

BOOK THREE

ANDY SMITHSON

Disgrace of the Unicorn's Honor

L.R.W. LEE

ISBN 10: 1500673773
ISBN 13: 978-1500673772

Createspace Independent Publishing
North Charleston, South Carolina

Dedication

In memory of my father, Paul Woodgate

Acknowledgments

Thanks to my husband who supports my efforts even though he would be the first to admit middle-grade fiction is not his favorite read. What a guy!

Thanks to my daughter, Kirstie, for her constructive comments that served to strengthen the story line.

Thanks also to my mentor, Jonathan Lee, from whom I learned many philosophies that changed my life. I have woven these throughout the story line in hopes of helping others experience a more peaceful and satisfying journey through life, as I have.

Thanks to my editor, Amy Nemecek. Because of her, you can enjoy a more engaging tale.

Table of Contents

The Land of Oomaldee

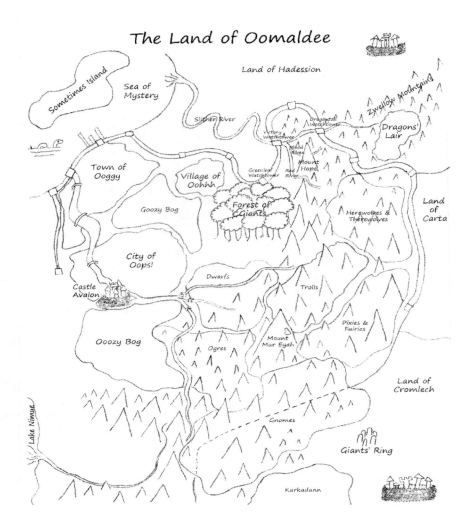

CHAPTER ONE

Inverted Polarity

A ndy sat on his bed with his arms circling his knees, cradling his face. Even a week later, his mind continued to swirl over that conversation. He felt as though his world had been turned upside down. It all began on the way home from the natural history museum after returning from his second visit to Oomaldee, clothes tattered and body bloodied. Dad had uttered nine simple words: "It's time we tell him. He deserves to know."

Mom had opened her mouth as if to object, exchanged a knowing look with Dad, then slowly nodded.

A knot had usurped control of Andy's stomach. A villainous taskmaster over the last several days, it now constricted further as he remembered the family conference that followed.

Mom had closed their bedroom door over Madison's protests of, "I'm part of this family, too, ya know!"

"That's enough," Dad had warned. "And don't let me catch you sitting outside our door eavesdropping."

Andy heard Madison stomp down the hall as he sat on his parents' bed. Dad cleared his throat as he settled into one of the dark leather chairs in the alcove of the bay window and watched Mom approach. She stopped briefly to open the top drawer of their dresser before joining them; Andy couldn't tell what she pulled out. She sank into the leather chair next to Dad and revealed her prize. The instant Andy saw the envelope, he gasped. It was gold.

Dad's eyes pivoted to Andy. "You've seen this before?"

Andy shook his head. "But I've gotten notes in gold envelopes just like that. They always rhyme."

Mom's eyes jetted to Dad and he reached his hand over, gently placing it on her arm, before beginning. "Your mother and I wondered when this day might come. I guess the best place to begin is before your birth."

Andy started jiggling his foot.

"Dad had just started his business and money was tight, but I wanted another child. I hadn't said anything, but the next thing I knew, this envelope arrived."

Mom passed the letter to Andy.

"Imagine my shock when I read the note inside."

Andy read the addressee:

To Emmalee, Favored One

Andy felt his body stiffen, and he struggled to ask, "Who?"

"We don't know who sent it, Son," Dad chimed in. "Your mother found it on her pillow."

Mom nodded, confirming.

"Open it," Dad encouraged.

Andy's brain shifted into overdrive before accelerating to warp speed. With shaking hands, he pulled out a single page of parchment and read:

Five hundred years have passed,
And a king has come forward and asked,
An heir, yet unborn, to stand fast,
'Til the curse be lifted at last.

The requirements of the law allow
A descendent by means of a vow
To bear the chosen one

And raise him as her son.

Teach him responsibility,
And to love civility;
Train him in obedience,
Instill in him great diligence.

For when the time is come,
Your son will not succumb.
These virtues he will command,
And wield them to deliver the land.

Your name, it will be known
As Favored, for you have shown
Love for the husband of your youth,
In word, in deed, and in truth.

Andy reread the letter several times before looking up. When he did, he saw his parents' faces etched with worry.

"I know it's a lot to take in, Andy," Mom tried to reassure. "It was a lot for me when I first read it."

"Is this letter saying what I think it's saying? That King Hercalon is…is my father? How's that even possible?"

"He's alive? You've met him?" Mom questioned.

Andy nodded.

"How is he?"

"Fine."

Andy couldn't read Mom's expression.

Dad ran his hands back and forth his on his pant legs. Trying to keep the conversation on track, he continued, "We don't know how this is possible, Son. But what your mother told you is true."

The facts struggled to register. So many times Andy had hoped the king was his grandfather. Now though... *This seems too good to be true. But what about Dad?* Andy thought.

"Andy? Honey? Dad is not your biological father, but he's still your dad."

Awkward silence filled the room like a fart wiggling free in a library. Dad shifted in his chair.

"Your necklace," Andy managed to get out a minute later.

Mom tilted her head to one side and pulled the pendant from inside her blouse. She stared at the stone dangling from the chain until the light of understanding rose on her face and she smiled. "Do you know what the Stone of Athanasia is?"

Andy nodded. "It's what keeps King Hercalon alive."

"Mermin's brother, Merlin, was able to get a piece of it before he sent me here." Mom's expression told Andy there was more to the story, but it would wait.

"I guess you're not forty-three then?" Andy asked, squinting an eye and tilting his head.

Mom smirked, then added, "I'm 508 years young."

As the truth sank in, Andy blurted out, "Is that why you get your hair dyed?"

Mom laughed, releasing some of the tension. "My hair is completely gray. If I didn't get it colored regularly, I'd look 608!"

Andy thought another minute, then questioned, "Dad, is that why you're always so hard on me? Why I feel like anything I do is never good enough?"

"I can't control what you think, Son, but yes, that's why I demand much from you concerning your behavior." He paused before continuing, "Before Mom and I married, she told me her whole story—that she had been a servant in the house of a king, about falling in love and marrying the man. She told me about the uprising and Merlin helping her escape from Oomaldee and the stone that keeps her alive. As you can imagine, at first I didn't believe her. I thought she had changed her mind about marrying me and was trying to break up."

Andy tried to picture it. It wasn't hard.

"Your mom finally convinced me her story was true."

"That was no easy task," Mom intoned. She exchanged a look with Dad, coaxing a smile to his face.

"I'll bet," Andy replied.

"When Mom received the letter, neither of us knew what to think; the news was too 'out of this world.' But within a couple weeks she knew she was having a baby."

Mom reached over and patted Dad's arm. Her expression revealed the strain the situation had placed on their relationship.

"It took me awhile. I just couldn't believe what was happening. But I finally came to grips with the situation. Thankfully, she forgave me for how stupidly I acted."

Andy had never heard Dad admit to weakness, and he allowed the resentment he usually felt toward him to evaporate and be replaced by pity. He didn't know what to say. He'd never wondered what Mom had seen in Dad— they were his parents. Perhaps hidden beneath his commanding exterior there was a softer side to Dad that he allowed only Mom to see.

"We committed to raising you to embrace responsibility, civility, obedience, and diligence, as the letter instructed. I feared we would not prepare you well or soon enough and you would suffer for it."

Andy heard passion in Dad's voice and the pity he'd felt rapidly morphed into respect. He and Dad had never seen eye to eye, but for the first time Andy realized Dad's love for him had guided his actions all along.

Maybe Dad could love me a little less and we'd get along better? Andy pondered before tuning back in.

"So when you started telling stories about being transported to strange lands, we couldn't tell whether it was just your overactive imagination. When you flooded the kitchen a year ago and we found you wearing strange clothes, we knew something was going on, but you were so young. We didn't want to believe. Then when I saw you this afternoon at the museum and you wore those clothes and you told me your story…" Dad let the thought finish itself.

Now, a week later, Andy wiped tears from his eyes and sniffled on his bed as he continued thinking. Since he'd learned the news, the thrill of knowing the King was his father had been extinguished by the realization that if he broke the curse, not only would he lose the King and Mermin, but he'd also lose Mom. The thought was almost more than he could bear. He felt like an executioner and hated himself for it.

"Why me? Don't make me do this!" he pleaded with the ceiling. "Mom and Dad don't understand. They can't."

He glanced over at the nightstand where he had placed the pouch he usually wore around his neck. The belt with holster, empty except for Methuselah, was on the floor next to the nightstand. He hadn't touched either since the conversation with his parents. It felt as though picking them up meant he accepted the inevitable, and he wasn't ready for that.

"Andy, would you come here, please?" he heard Mom call from downstairs. He wiped his face and blew his nose before walking out his bedroom door.

He found Mom in the kitchen staring blankly out the window. "You called?"

"Oh, Andy."

"Are you okay?" Andy questioned.

Mom nodded. "I was just thinking about the King."

"Do you want me to tell you about him and Mermin?"

She hesitated.

She looks as though hearing more might further complicate her life.

"Please," she finally responded.

"This must be really weird for you," Andy speculated aloud. "Mom, the King has changed a lot since you knew him. He's a kind and loving man."

"The man I married was kind and loving—although perhaps a bit ambitious." She smiled, remembering. "Why do you say he's changed?"

"He told me what he was like before the curse. He said he loved power—his words, not mine. Honestly, the way he described himself was hard to believe."

"Really? I don't remember he loved power so much as he loved his family. Did you know his sister was murdered?"

Andy nodded.

Mom continued, "He shared with me the experience and how devastated he was by her loss. He knew, once his father passed, he would now be responsible to rule." She paused and stared into Andy's eyes. "He so wanted to rule well, and the responsibility weighed heavily on him. He said his parents couldn't handle the loss. Apparently, when he tried to comfort them, they asked him to leave for a time so they could grieve alone. He felt as though they rejected him, and it hurt deeply. But he respected their wishes and left the palace, never returning until after their deaths. It's a very sad story."

"He told you that?" Andy questioned, the truth not aligning with Mom's narrative.

"Yes. So when a rumor circulated that he was the one who had killed Imogenia, I was furious. He had been through enough. Sometimes people can be so cruel. He was worried for my safety. I think he didn't want to risk having anything happen to me, like his sister."

Andy didn't know what to say. Clearly, Mom didn't know the truth. *I guess that's a good thing, because I'd hate to think she married a man she knew was a murderer*, he thought. *Should I tell her and ruin her ideal of a man she loved, especially when that man no longer exists?*

"Andy?"

"Sorry, what were you saying?"

"That's when he sent me here." She paused and studied Andy. Her furrowed brow told him she was unsure how he was coping with the recent revelations. She pulled him close in a hug.

After a minute, Mom completed her sharing with, "Well, I guess I better do some work. Oh, and Andy, would you go get the mail for me?"

"Sure."

Andy headed out the front door and down the walk. His mind was still preoccupied, but as he reached the mailbox, on the ground to the right of its base he saw a wooden chest, a miniature version of the one in the attic. He picked it up. Two buckles held it closed and he unfastened them to find a single piece of parchment inside. The note read:

Andy,

I hope you are readjusting well. We all miss you, especially Alden and Hannah.

It's nice feeling like myself again. I didn't get to tell you before you left, but thanks so much for all you did for the King and me. We are most appreciative. I've heard much positive gossip around the castle about you since then.

By the way, Hans was wondering if you would kindly return his ring since you didn't have the opportunity before you left. If you put it in this chest and then move the chest to the left side of your mailbox, I'll know it's ready and bring it back.

The King sends his love. We're looking forward to seeing you again.

Warmly,

Mermin

After the week he'd had, Andy couldn't help laughing. *Well, at least he didn't send Sir Gawain and Alexander to deliver the note this time.* He glanced at the front yard. Dad's grass was not yet close to looking like its former self.

He buckled the straps and returned the chest to the right side of the mailbox, not yet ready for Mermin to claim it. With the note and the mail for Mom, he headed inside, his mood lighter.

Back in his bedroom, he reread Mermin's letter. *The King sends his love.* Despite what Mom believed about the King versus what he knew to be true, Andy was certain the change in the King since his youth was real, and revelations of the monarch's status as his biological father had only deepened Andy's love for him. The situation with Dad not being his real father still felt weird and would take longer to get used to.

He looked at the pouch on the nightstand that held Hans' ring, hesitated briefly, then finally reached for it. *Everything will work out,* he told himself. *I'm not sentencing Mom to death.* He wanted to believe it.

He extracted Han's ring and scribbled a quick note to Mermin and another to Alden and Hannah before taking everything out to the front yard. He placed the small chest on the left side of the mailbox as instructed and stepped back to wait for something to happen. Within five minutes the trunk vanished, and as it did, Andy couldn't help smiling. He now had a way to communicate with everyone in Oomaldee when he wasn't there.

Two weeks later, Andy found the miniature chest back in his front yard. A note from Alden read:

> Andy,
> This is great that we can write each
> other. Sure beats last time. My mom says

hi, and Hans says hi and thanks for getting his ring back to him.

I'm feeling much better. My arm's back to normal size; I just have this nervous twitch. Kidding. But really, I have two cool fang marks. Mom hates seeing them. I think they're awesome! Hannah won't say what she thinks.

The King decided to finish the Oscray season even though you're not here. He figured you might be awhile. I hope you don't mind. BTW, we won! We're amazing, no thanks to you. The team said to say hi, too!

Mermin said the King replaced the pinnace we destroyed. I guess the owner was honored we used his boat as part of restoring the King and Mermin back to health. But he was also thankful to have a new one. They're not cheap.

I'm back to practicing for this Fall's Festival. Optimistic is so good. I hope we win again. I got Hannah to try out for the Tower Chase this year, so she and

Veracious have been practicing, too.
They're pretty good.
I hope you're doing okay.

Your friend,
Alden

Andy glanced down at his arm. The mark from the bellicose was still clearly visible. He thought about the trip with Alden and about seeing Razen meet with Abaddon. He remembered the dragon's demand that Razen kill the King once he figured out how to get the Stone of Athanasia to change its loyalty. Andy ran his hands through his hair, letting out a long breath. *Nothing's happened yet or Alden would have said something,* Andy reassured himself.

Promising Abaddon you'll kill the King... He trusts you. You're...you're such a piece of shriveled fruit, Razen!

Andy penned a reply:

Alden,
    It's great to hear from you! School
started again. My sister, Madison, loves it
(she's such a brown-noser). Me, not so
much. I started sixth grade. The only
good thing is I have all new teachers. I'll
have to tell you about it sometime.
    I don't know if you'll get this letter
directly from Mermin or if anyone else
might read it before you, so I'll be

indirect. Do you remember where we were going to explore? I took a look when you were occupied and found something very interesting. I recommend you check it out when you can. Be sure to look under everything.

Have you seen shriveled fruit doing anything troubling?

Your friend,
Andy

He thought about telling Alden all that had happened since he'd returned, especially about the King being his father, but finally chose not to. That was a conversation he needed to have one-on-one with the King, and he would not risk leaking any information should someone intercept the letter.

After placing the chest on the left side of his mailbox and seeing it disappear, Andy wandered back inside, passing the study where Dad sat hunched over his computer, staring it down and furiously pecking at keys. Dad's back was toward the hall. *I better not disturb him.* He found Mom and Madison in the kitchen preparing to leave.

"I need to take Madison to her piano lesson. We'll be back in an hour and a half. Why don't you find something to do upstairs. Dad's preparing for a big meeting on Monday." Mom kissed Andy on the top of his head and she and Madison left through the door to the garage.

It had been awhile since Andy looked in the trunk in the attic. Now seemed like as good a time as any. As usual, he quietly opened the door at the end of the upstairs hall and mounted the steps. He flipped on the light and looked around. Nintendo 64, check. Gamecube, check. Playstation 2, check.

Games, check. Assured everything was as he had left it, Andy slowly opened the lid of the trunk. *Huh? What's that laying in the upper tray?*

CHAPTER TWO

Diligent Deduction

A ndy quickly scanned the attic for intruders but saw nothing unusual, so
he returned his attention to the newest mystery. Between the black
leather holster with the King of Oomaldee's purple family crest and the
unsigned note Andy had once disobeyed lay a small parchment scroll. *How'd
that get in here?* he wondered.

He unrolled it and immediately recognized several of the Oomish letters
Baruti and Fronia had translated for him at the Library of Oomaldee. It was a
decoder of the Oomish language into English, and where there wasn't a direct
equivalent, explanations were offered in English!

"Score!" Andy pumped his fist.

Andy moved the upper tray aside and looked at the fifteen scrolls
populating the second level. He'd studied them many times but never knew the
full extent of their mysteries. The scrolls were put in this trunk for a reason, but
why?

Andy selected several of the manuscripts and spent the next twenty
minutes translating their titles. Several times during the process the King's
voice filled his head: "Responsibility, diligence, and dignity are the keys to
success." Diligence was definitely the right word. It would take forever to
translate all the scrolls.

Among the titles were page-turners such as *Antiquity of Methuselah*,
History of King Abaddon, *Lineage of the Kings of Oomaldee* (this was the
family tree he'd studied before), and *Prophecy of Deliverance,* to name just a
few. They all sounded interesting, but two scrolls in particular peaked his
curiosity. The first was titled *Alchemy: Transforming the Inanimate into
Metals*. He remembered seeing Max, Henry, and Oscar at work in the Goldery

changing straw into gold thread. *Are these the directions for how it's done? Wow!*

The second scroll troubled him—*Alchemy: The Power of Transforming the Animate.*

Animate? puzzled Andy. *That means living things. This can't be good.*

Andy retrieved notebook paper and a pencil from his bedroom, then unrolled several feet of the parchment. He laid it on the attic floor, putting five of his old Nintendo 64 games across the top to hold it open. It was a long scroll, and he remembered seeing all the calculations and equations throughout the text alongside drawings of animals. The first time he'd seen it he'd thought it looked like someone had experimented with turning one animal into another. One drawing of a black and white Holstein cow was followed by an arrow pointing to scribbled mathematical equations before another arrow indicated a dappled rabbit.

Below that someone had drawn a scary wolflike creature, then an arrow pointing to more formulas and resulting in what Andy recognized as a the pug-nosed, large-pawed herewolf he'd seen carved on the headboard of Mermin's bed. Mermin had told him herewolves descended from werewolves, but he'd begun to wonder if their lineage was natural or the result of some mad science experiment.

More troubling still, farther down the document he'd seen the drawing of a man. Formulas followed the crude renderings, but it was clear the result had not been successful. He'd always wondered why anyone would want to transform one animal into another, but *people?*

Andy felt his shoulders tighten. *Well, I guess I'll finally find out what happened.*

* * * * *

Thanksgiving vacation found Andy continuing his work deciphering the cryptic writing on the scroll. The more he translated, the more disturbing the clues that emerged. Just this afternoon he had read notations about reducing a being in one form to its base character to release energy for another purpose. It didn't make any sense to him, but he determined to struggle through it. He kept reminding himself that these particular scrolls had been given to him for some reason, and although he didn't yet understand why, he had a feeling he would be tested on them and he wasn't about to fail this exam.

As a sculptor chiseling the form of a terrible monster, that night Andy's dreams began shaping an alarming hypothesis of what the scrolls might mean. Andy saw himself walking alone. He held his arms up, trying to shield his face from the dust whipping at him as he took step after struggling step across the charred and barren soil. The smell of sulfur assaulted his nose and made his lungs burn. Over the whistling of the relentless wind, Andy could hear the sounds of baying wolves and other beasts he hoped to avoid. He walked for what seemed like hours.

When his feet began to stumble and he felt as though he couldn't take another step, through squinted eyes Andy saw a dark castle take shape on the horizon. A sense of trepidation gnawed at his stomach as he approached; while he rejoiced that salvation from the elements was in sight, it took every ounce of willpower to resist the fear he felt licking its lips, ready to devour him. He stopped in front of the massive black walls and withdrew Methuselah from its holster. He knew he stood before King Abaddon's castle fortress, and the blade reassured him he held the power to sever evil from good.

Approaching the gates, they mysteriously opened, and he strode through unopposed by the three dozen burly, well-armored vulture-men he passed. It seemed as if he was a ghost. The massive compound intimidated. Everywhere he looked he saw vulture-people: hardened vulture-warriors squawking orders; older vulture-boys practicing sword fighting much as he and Alden had done with the stone knights; raggedy adolescent vulture-beings pummeling rocks with sticks they'd found. He passed grumpy vulture-women stooping over meager, steaming cook pots and hissing at grimy vulture-children who fought over scraps.

He eventually reached a tall, shiny stone edifice. Gargoyles and other types of ugly, bewitched beings stood as ornamentation both on and around the building. A pair of rough vulture-men finished placing the statue of a husky man on a pedestal directly outside the imposing front doors. The statue's clothing was chiseled in the fashion of Oomaldee and its right hand was raised, the fist clenched in protest. As they dusted off their hands and waddled away, Andy thought he overheard the vulture-men grumble, "Serves you right."

He approached and studied the statue. Somehow the man looked familiar, although he couldn't immediately place him. Reaching the bejeweled stone doors, these too opened and admitted him. As he took his first glance around the shadowy interior, a sense of horror overwhelmed Andy. Around the perimeter statues of men, women, and children stood on black stone pedestals. All were dressed in Oomish styles, and every last one posed in outrage.

He awoke gasping. In the instant it took him to remember where he was, the disturbing images mercifully vanished. He lay in bed, breathing heavily. He glanced at the floor by the nightstand and in the orange glow of his alarm clock located the belt and holster with Methuselah. He grabbed it and brought it next to him under the covers. Only after reassuring himself the sword remained in its rightful place did Andy begin to calm down.

*****

Christmas vacation had come and gone when Andy, bundled in his winter jacket, sat in the attic one Saturday afternoon. He had been working on deciphering the troubling scroll when he decided to take a break. As he headed down to the kitchen for a snack, he glanced out an upstairs window and saw the regular biweekly note from Alden materialize. He walked past Mom and Dad's office and saw his parents hard at work through the French doors. Madison had gone to a friend's house for the afternoon. He crept out the front door and retrieved the small trunk.

Mmmm. The smell of fresh baked chocolate chip cookies assaulted Andy's senses as he opened the lid. *Yes! Thank you, Marta!* He stowed the still-warm treats in his coat pocket and pulled the note out. A cold blast of winter wind bit him as he opened it, and he decided to read it inside.

Enjoying his third cookie back in his bedroom, he read:

Andy,

As you know, I've been studying shriveled fruit for a while now. The prized eggplant is fine, no worries. But yesterday, when I checked the storeroom where the shriveled fruit is kept most of the time, I found something I think you need to know about.

There were wrappings with instructions about how to cure a certain damaged and charred tomato. I don't think shriveled fruit has figured it out yet, but something's up. Said fruit has also been more snippy than usual.

Also, the King got a report yesterday that Abaddon's goons have been terrorizing citizens by turning them into vulture-people. It's not widespread, just one or two here and there, but the randomness has folks really on edge not knowing if they might be next. Don't ask how I know, but trust me when I say it's true.

Your friend,

Alden

Andy thought aloud, "The King's fine, that's a relief. But Razen's been researching how to cure Abaddon. I wonder what injuries Methuselah inflicted this time, beyond blinding him that is. And Razen's more annoying than normal. Good, sounds like he's on edge. Serves him right! But Abaddon's thugs transforming people—?"

Andy gasped. The dream! As the thought registered fully, Andy suddenly felt dizzy. The cookie didn't taste good anymore and he set it down on his nightstand.

*****

May finally arrived and the end of school neared. Andy wanted to feel excited about starting middle school, but instead he felt antsy. The terrifying recurring dream coupled with more discoveries from the scroll and Alden's regular updates made him long to be back in Oomaldee defending the people. *When will I get to go back?* he wondered for the umpteenth time.

Andy noted today's date on the calendar above his desk: Saturday, May 31. *Just ten days until we go to Schlitterbahn Water Park to celebrate my birthday. I can't wait!* No sooner had that thought cheered him than concern erased it. *But I don't understand why I haven't heard from Alden. I should have gotten a letter from him a week ago.*

Andy met Mom in the kitchen making breakfast.

"Have you seen a package arrive for me in the mail?"

Mom looked up from the cook top at the kitchen island after flipping four pancakes. "No, honey, I haven't. What's it look like?"

"It's a small wooden chest. I've been writing to my friends in Oomaldee all year. Mermin sends the trunk every two weeks with a letter from Alden, but it's a week late."

"Really?" Mom clarified.

"Yeah, he always lands it next to the mailbox." It was nice to be able to talk about it now that he knew his parents understood his situation, at least in part.

"I'm sorry, Andy. I haven't seen it."

After finishing his breakfast, Mom suggested, "Why don't you go outside and play. It's a beautiful day!"

He didn't want to, but having nothing else to occupy him, he nodded and meandered out the front door. He looked toward the mailbox and disappointment struck once again. *I hope everyone's okay.* He spotted a rock in the flower bed and kicked it, ran and kicked it again. He pretended to be a football kicker and booted the rock all the way into the backyard and through the open window of the abandoned wooden playhouse. "Score!"

His celebration cut short when he caught sight of a small wooden chest in the grass next to the garden gnome he'd tried making come to life nearly ten months ago. The box was painted royal blue but looked identical to the missing trunk in every other way. He hastily opened the buckles, pulled out a note, and read:

> Andy,
>
> I was concerned about you since we did not receive a response back from the trunk I sent a week ago with the gold envelope. Please respond as soon as possible as we are anxious to hear from you.
>
> Mermin

The trunk last week? A gold envelope!
"Madison!" Andy bolted for the back door.

Since the conversation between Andy and his parents, Madison incessantly pestered him. She knew her parents wouldn't put up with further questioning as they'd firmly told her, "Maddy, we will tell you what we discussed with Andy when we feel you need to know." This, of course, completely frustrated her and she let her dissatisfaction be known in a myriad of ways.

"All right, where is it?" Andy demanded, barging into Madison's room.

"Where's what?" she replied, an evil smile emerging.

"You know what!"

"Tell me."

"The chest! The small wooden chest that arrived a week ago!" Andy waved his hands as he spoke.

Madison slid from her bed onto the floor and raised the bed skirt. "Oh, do you mean this chest?"

Andy glared at her for a second before snatching it. He stormed out of her room and down the hall. At least she hadn't opened it. With his bedroom door closed, Andy lifted the lid. Sure enough, a gold envelope lay on top of a note.

He picked up the gold envelope. The address read:

Andy Smithson, Prince of Oomaldee

Prince? Wow! Yeah, I guess I am a prince. That sounds weird. I'm really glad Madison didn't open this. I'd never hear the end of it.

He ripped open the envelope, pulled out the single piece of parchment, and read:

Son of the King,
Heir to the throne,
Concern for your people
You have shown.

Sufficient study you have done,
Time for action now has come.
Respect of the people you have earned,
To trust you they have learned.

Your tools make ready,
For your flight that is steady.
Your return to the land,
An entrance unplanned.

But when it will happen? I hope I didn't miss the window of opportunity because of Madison.

Returning his attention to the recovered trunk, he pulled out the biweekly note from Alden.

Andy,

Nothing new to report on the produce front, but the King asked me to let you know he had Hans implant the Stone of Athanasia under his skin. It's in his side. You can't tell anyone though. Only you, me, Hans, and Mermin know.

Yeah, he visited the Library recently and ran into Glaucin. Apparently he got the idea when he learned about Glaucin's trident implant. Right after that trip he decided it would be a good precaution.

Mom sends her love and, as usual, cookies. Hope to see you soon.

Your friend,
Alden

Cookies? Did Madison eat his cookies? Had she read the note inside the gold envelope?

Andy decided he couldn't worry about what Madison might have done. He found a piece of notebook paper and penned the following response:

Alden,

Great to hear from you! I'm fine. My annoying sister hid the chest for a week. I just figured out what happened when Mermin sent the blue trunk today. Sorry if I caused concern. Please tell Mermin thank you for me! Maybe he can beam them into my bedroom in the future.

It looks like I'll be back shortly. The gold envelope in the box said it was time to return. What a relief.

See you soon,
Andy

He took the two chests back out to the front yard and placed them on the left-hand side of the mailbox. Within five minutes they both vanished.

* * * * *

Andy found it hard to focus on anything over the next week. His thoughts kept returning to the most recent note in the gold envelope, and he hoped he didn't miss his ride back to Oomaldee.

The school year mercifully ended and Andy's birthday arrived the following Thursday. While the big celebration would be coming Saturday at the waterpark, his parents gave him a cake and presents to mark the occasion of his turning twelve. He would never forget Dad's speech as he opened his gift from the two of them.

With his hand resting on Mom's arm, Dad cleared his throat and began: "Andy, Mom and I want to congratulate you on completing elementary school. You'll be starting middle school in the fall, and we know that's a big step. We wanted to give you a gift to remember this time."

He handed a wallet-sized package to Andy.

After tearing the ornate wrappings away, Andy found a cell phone with his name engraved in the shiny black back.

"Yes!" Andy exclaimed, pumping his arm, as Madison rolled her eyes.

"You've shown increasing responsibility over the last few months and Mom and I thought you could handle this." Dad paused and ran his hands through his perfect hair before standing and walking over to Andy and giving him a hug.

I wish he'd just say he's proud of me.

* * * * *

Saturday, the big day, arrived sunny and warm. Andy was out of bed, dressed, and ready to go in record time. It took the rest of the family an hour to catch up to his pace, but they finally did and set off for the water park. Andy felt the lump in his backpack that was Methuselah with its holster next to his swimming trunks, towel, and sunscreen. Madison sat with him in the backseat drooling over her most recent book boyfriend.

Disgusting!

After staring out the window at the open fields and the umpteenth cow, Andy rummaged in his backpack and pulled out his new cell phone—the compass app fascinated him. They headed east. After playing Angry Birds for several minutes, he glanced out the window to see they'd made it to the loop skirting the northern part of San Antonio. According to the compass, they'd shifted direction and now headed northeast.

"How much longer?" Andy whined.

Mom smiled and said, "It'll be twenty minutes once we reach I-35. Maybe you can watch for the exit."

Andy began his vigil, scouring the boring landscape for any sign to I-35. Their path shifted to east by southeast just before he spotted the green highway marker.

About time!

Pacified only a little, Andy stowed his cell phone in his backpack and started jiggling his knee. He glanced back out the window and saw white fluffy clouds overhead. One looked like the head of a dragon. He thought about Daisy, the dragon he and Alden had rescued on his first trip to Oomaldee, and smiled. A long way off, between the clouds, flew a gray bird. It was so small he almost missed it.

"We're nearly there. Just five minutes," Mom informed from the front seat.

Andy fastened all the zippers on his backpack and prepared to escape the confines of the backseat.

An hour later, he and Dad stood next in line to ride Dragon's Revenge, a wicked water coaster. Mom and Madison had gone to buy bottled water. He couldn't wait to experience the dragon screen tunnel that was supposed to look like a dragon chasing you, about to blast a stream of fire.

I'll be the judge of how real it is, Andy smiled to himself.

Just before the operator allowed them to board their log car, Andy noticed a park security officer running past the ride.

"Move up," the attendant instructed, bringing Andy's attention back.

The attendant released them, and a minute later Andy and Dad felt themselves chugging up the ramp, propelled by one of the nine blaster pumps on the ride. Water sprayed everywhere and Dad hollered, "Woo-hoo!"

After rounding two curves, Andy noticed a large shadow cross over the chute their log car floated down. He looked up, but whatever it was had vanished. Water shot at his face as he and Dad entered the dragon screen tunnel. The walls lit up orangey red and Andy heard a rumbling noise. Andy flashed back to the fight he'd had with the yellow dragon in Oomaldee and reflexively felt for Methuselah. He laughed at himself, remembering he'd secured the sword in the locker they'd rented.

Another jet of water hit him in the face. Dad looked over and laughed. "Real enough for you?"

Andy didn't reply. *You've no idea.*

Their raft bumped gently into the dock and they climbed out. Other riders pushed them to the attraction's exit where Andy caught sight of a dozen park security officials holding spectators at bay and barking orders to stay back. He rushed ahead, leaving Dad to fend for himself as he sought out the source of the commotion. Andy rounded a corner and froze. A gray dragon sat in the path.

"Everything's okay, folks. Just a publicity stunt I'm sure," an officer shouted, convincing neither himself nor the gawkers.

"Wow! How'd they do that? It looks so real!" a boy next to Andy exclaimed to his mom. She probed the growing crowd for an escape route.

Andy walked closer, studying the creature.

Andy! There you are!

Andy looked around. No one looked at him or talked to him.

It's me. Daisy. I've come to take you back to Oomaldee, the dragon said telepathically.

"Daisy?" Andy questioned, snaking his way through small openings in the mass of people.

He reached the edge of the crowd. An official held his arms wide, blocking his way. Andy ducked under and ran toward the beast. "Daisy!" he shouted.

"Stop, son! Stop!" the man yelled.

A collective gasp went up.

"Andy!" Dad called after him.

Andy reached Daisy and gave her large neck a hug. "It's so good to see you again! Wow, you've grown!"

As have you, Andy. Are you ready to go?

"I just need Methuselah. It's in the locker. Can you help me get it? Our locker's over there. It might be quicker than me trying to get through this crowd by myself." Andy pointed across the peopled path to a hut-like structure housing several hundred storage lockers.

I'd be delighted to, Daisy replied with a snort, causing a lady close by to shriek.

"Oh, wait! I need the locker key!"

"Andy! Come here! It's not safe!" Dad scolded as he broke through the blockade of officials. "That's my son!" Dad declared to the officers, worry etched across his face.

"Dad, this is Daisy. I'm going back to Oomaldee! I just need to get my sword."

Never before had Andy seen Dad at a loss for words.

"I need the key to the locker."

Dad stared vacantly, as if in a trance.

"Dad! The key!"

Dad robotically removed the elastic bracelet the locker key hung on and handed it to Andy.

"Stay back, folks!" another official yelled, trying to sound calm. He turned to Dad and added, "Sir, I need you and your son to move away from that thing."

Andy rushed back to Daisy and hopped on as Dad snapped out of his unplanned meditation. His eyes found Andy and he yelled above the noise, "Go, Andy! Do what you've been called to do!"

Andy nodded. *Dad believes in me…* He hoped his expression communicated all he felt, for words escaped him.

"Sir! Now!" the officer demanded.

The dragon took several slow deliberate steps so as not to step on anyone, sending another ripple of panic through the crowd. When she reached the lockers, she lowered her head and Andy slid off her back, causing yet more panic from onlookers. Andy retrieved his backpack and remounted as police officers arrived, bearing weapons.

"Shoot the thing!" someone in the crowd yelled.

"They can't or they might hit the boy!" another replied.

Daisy unfurled her wings and took flight as more shrieks erupted.

Once airborne, Andy could make out Mom and Madison in the crowd below, carrying water bottles toward the dragon ride. *I've got to find a way to save her.*

The noise of the crowd grew faint as Andy and Daisy flew.

I'm gonna see the King, Mermin, and everyone else again! Wait until I tell the King he's my father!

Your father? Daisy questioned.

"Yeah. Oh, wait! The letter. I need the letter! Daisy, we need to stop by my house. I need something."

As you wish. Which way?

"You don't know where my house is?"

I was asked to find you and bring you back to Oomaldee from wherever you might be.

Andy held on with one hand and located his cell phone in his backpack with the other. Reading the compass, he instructed, "We need to go west, that way." He pointed.

Moments later Andy spotted his house far below.

"That's it! You can land on the driveway and I'll run in and grab the envelope."

To say the neighbors were shocked would have been an understatement. As he slid off the dragon's back and bolted for his front door, he noticed their nosy neighbor across the street grab her cell phone and begin dialing madly.

Andy ran into the house and grabbed Mom's gold envelope from the drawer of his nightstand. Glancing out an upstairs window, he saw Daisy waiting patiently, so he took a couple extra minutes to change out of his swimming trunks and into his black T-shirt and blue jeans. He put on the belt with Methuselah's holster and stowed the pouch with the gold key under his T-shirt. From the last several minutes in flight he knew it would be chilly flying, so he grabbed a sweatshirt on his way out the door.

By the time he made it back to his ride, police cars raced down the street, sirens screaming. Daisy danced nervously and Andy could hear her working up her fire bladder.

"Let's get out of here!" Andy yelled over the commotion.

CHAPTER THREE

Dreams Do Come True

A ndy looked back and saw his house and neighborhood now looking like the old Matchbox set he used to play with. Police cars and emergency vehicles littered the street. *I feel like a convict running from the law. I wonder if they'll send a helicopter after us?*

No point in worrying about it. We'll deal with it if the time comes, Daisy reassured.

Five minutes later, Andy saw the buildings of downtown San Antonio sail by off to his left. To his right, the distant skyline of Austin grew smaller with each mighty flap of Daisy's wings. He breathed a sigh of relief. No one pursued.

Andy pulled his cell phone out of his backpack and checked their direction. They headed northwest. *Where are we going?*

Toward Denver, Colorado. Ever been?

Mom had mentioned Denver many times as he was growing up. She had lived there at one time.

No, but I'd love to see it!

We'll be flying over, not stopping, but you can get an aerial view.

Andy immediately realized the wisdom of not stopping based upon the hullabaloo they'd just left.

Have you been to my world before, Daisy?

No, this is my first time.

Then how'd you know where to find me?

You have a very distinctive smell, Andy.

What? But I took a shower yesterday!

Daisy shuddered a laugh before continuing. *It's not that you smell bad, you just have a distinct odor. I remember it from the first time we met. Dragon's have a very sensitive sense of smell. The one who asked me to get you told me roughly where I might find you and my nose took it from there.*

Who asked you to come get me?

I can't say, Andy. I never saw them. I received a message this morning on the whisper stream. It sounded important, so I left immediately.

Whisper stream? What's that?

Yes, I guess you wouldn't know anything about it, Daisy divulged. *The whisper stream is a network of messages. Don't take this the wrong way, Andy, but higher-level beings use it to communicate telepathically—dragons, centaurs, unicorns, griffins, the sphinx. Humans haven't made it on...yet.*

Andy wasn't sure how to take that, so he let it pass.

Wow, there's that many creatures that can talk telepathically?

And more, Andy. There are many more.

Andy thought about this revelation for a minute before responding. *But you and I are communicating telepathically. You're reading my thoughts.*

Yes, Andy, I'm reading your thoughts, but you can't read mine. I'm pushing my thoughts to your mind. It doesn't flow both ways between us.

Andy tried to picture the whisper stream. *It sounds kinda like the internet, but with thoughts.*

I'm not familiar with your internet, so I couldn't say, but the whisper stream is a flow of thoughts between beings that has existed for thousands of years.

Andy pondered for several more minutes until his stomach announced dissatisfaction at its empty condition.

Getting hungry, Andy?

Yeah. I ate breakfast awhile ago.

They had been flying for two hours according to Andy's cell phone. The land they crossed at the moment was barren and largely uninhabited except for a farm here or a herd of grazing cattle there.

There's a town not too far ahead, over there, Daisy announced. *I'm a bit hungry myself. It took me five and a half hours to reach you. I saw some large pigs a minute ago. Perhaps I'll have some pork chops on the rare side while you scrounge up something to eat.*

Andy didn't know much about the eating habits of dragons, but given the area of Texas they flew over, he guessed the pigs Daisy had seen were feral and dangerous based on TV shows he'd seen.

As Daisy circled for a landing, Andy saw a sign: "Welcome to Lubbock, The Giant Side of Texas." She found an open field on the outskirts of the city with a row of trees separating it from the highway. A cozy diner stood on the far side of a scarcely filled parking lot, six hundred yards away.

Andy felt in his pocket. He was glad he'd grabbed the twenty from his allowance as he left. "I'll meet you back here in half an hour, Daisy. Be careful. Those pigs are wild and vicious."

Thank you for your concern. I'll be careful.

Right on schedule and with a full stomach, Andy broke through the trees lining the open field, but Daisy had not yet returned.

She must still be hunting, Andy thought.

I've nearly rounded up these pigs. I'll be with you shortly, came Daisy's telepathic reply.

Andy smiled. Communicating with thoughts definitely had its advantages. *I wonder how far away you can be and still have it work.*

Andy sat down with his back against a tree. He didn't have long to wait. Within five minutes, terror-filled squeals shattered the calm as three huge feral boars came barreling from behind a substantial clump of trees in the middle of the field. Andy bolted up. He saw the glint of the sun off gray scales as Daisy emerged in pursuit.

The tusked hogs rushed forward, and Andy turned and scrambled up four feet to the lowest branch of the tree. From experience, he knew Methuselah would not extend, for it only did that in Oomaldee. He looked out, estimating the time to impact. Daisy scooped up the unlucky beast closest to her and two bites later resumed the chase. The next boar succumbed seconds later. The fastest pig charged like a bullet toward Andy's tree. Andy searched for branches to ascend higher but knew the twigs further up would never support his weight.

That thing's at least four feet tall and has to weigh over 400 pounds! he estimated, bracing for impact.

Daisy put on a burst of speed and nabbed the beast just five feet from Andy. He breathed a sigh of relief then nearly retched as he watched her consume the creature up close.

WTMI, he thought. *Way too much information!*

Daisy belched loudly. *Sorry. Serves me right for eating too fast.*

Andy cracked up, releasing the tension of terror he'd felt. *Nothing like waiting til the last second.*

Daisy chuckled. *You need to trust me, Andy.*

Two hours later, towering snowcapped mountains rose to their left and Andy checked his compass. They'd changed to a northward course.

How much longer?

Andy's behind and inner thighs grew sore from the constant rubbing against the dragon's tough scales, and his teeth chattered. Even though he wore his sweatshirt, it didn't repel the wind, and the constant gusts had chilled him to the bone.

If you lift the scale in front of you a bit, it should shield you from much of the breeze.

He did so and the tempest slackened considerably. That combined with heat from the dragon's body began to warm him up. He couldn't see what approached this way, but the ride became bearable.

So much better! Thanks!

That's Pueblo, Daisy narrated twenty minutes later as they flew over a city. The rays of the sun began to lengthen.

How do you know?

That's what the sign said.

They flew over Colorado Springs fifteen minutes later, and Daisy told Andy, *Denver's just ahead.*

He peeked over Daisy's scale and saw an army of skyscrapers standing at attention as they approached. They passed over a golf course; the people playing looked the size of grasshoppers.

They crossed a busy highway and Daisy veered left toward the mountains. A passenger jetliner passed close by, preparing to land at the nearby airport. Andy could see the eyes of the pilot and co-pilot grow large. He smiled and waved.

Five minutes later, an ice-covered mountain towered in front of them. Daisy continued forward, not altering her course or her pace.

Uh, Daisy, shouldn't you turn so we don't crash?

Daisy didn't reply but kept flapping her mighty wings.

Not satisfied, Andy tried again. *Daisy? Shouldn't you turn?*

Still no response.

Andy pounded on the skin under the dragon's scale. *Daisy! You need to turn. We're gonna crash!*

Nothing.

Yards from the sheer face of the mountain, Andy screamed, "Turn, Daisy! Turn!"

He braced for impact, but the collision never came. Daisy continued beating her wings, and brown and gray rock replaced blue sky. The farther they flew, the darker the tunnel became.

Wha… What just happened?

Daisy roared with laughter that reverberated off the hard walls and assaulted Andy's eardrums.

Welcome to Oomaldee, Andy.

Oomaldee's inside the Rocky Mountains?

Not inside them, through them. At least, that's one entrance.

Whoa! This is wild!

Daisy chuckled again. *Like I told you before, you need to trust me, Andy.*

Andy thought about that.

Not much longer now, Daisy reassured ten minutes later.

Sure enough, Andy saw light at the end of the pitch black tunnel and moments later Daisy flew out into dense, foggy skies. He couldn't see the dragon's head.

Yep, this is Oomaldee alright, he thought, then yelled, "I'm back! I'm really back!"

No sooner had he celebrated than Andy heard a familiar voice, like Dad's, in his head: "Gotcha!"

Huh?

"Headquarters found out about your coming and dispatched me," replied Andy's inneru.

Oh, it's you.

"Of course. You know I'm duty bound to rejoin you when you're in Oomaldee."

Are you going to introduce me? asked Daisy.

What? You're telling me you can talk to my inneru? You said humans aren't evolved enough to be part of your whisper stream.

They're not, but innerus aren't human. And yes, they communicate in the stream.

Oh, bother! You're telling me you hear everything innerus think about humans?

That's right.

"It's very nice to meet you, Daisy," announced Andy's inneru.

Likewise, Daisy replied.

Would you two stop! Andy objected.

The inneru and Daisy shared a snicker.

"I got a quick update from your conscience, Andy," the inneru continued. "It told me you're maturing some. It said you've started respecting your dad. That's commendable."

Thanks, I guess.

"It also reported you're very concerned about saving your mom from what you perceive as injustice."

Well, it's not fair! My mom didn't do anything wrong, and unless I can find a way to prevent it, she's going to die if I break the curse.

"Andy, these thoughts and feelings are welcome news. You're growing up."

They flew on in silence for several minutes.

You do know where you're going in this fog, don't you, Daisy? Andy questioned several minutes later.

What did I tell you earlier, Andy?

Andy saw the outlines of shop roofs through the fog and the sun's fading rays as Daisy circled for a landing several minutes later.

Where are we?

We are in the city square of Oops. The message this morning told me to bring you to meet the King. He's here. I smell him.

He's here? But I've never seen him outside the castle. No sooner had Andy thought it than understanding dawned on him. *Of course! He's got the Stone of Athanasia. Now he can go anywhere. Awesome!*

Andy could hear heavy barrels being scooted across wooden walkways and bells on shop doors jingling as merchants closed up for the night. Although it was hard to see, it had the same feel as the square in the town of Ooggy, but bigger. Just before they touched down a woman screamed as she caught sight of them through the haze. Several other shoppers echoed their alarm, and Andy and Daisy found themselves quickly surrounded by a garrison of the king's soldiers with swords drawn.

"Freeze!" came a gruff command.

Andy and Daisy complied.

A beefy officer dressed in the blue uniform of the Oomaldee army stepped forward and questioned, "What's the meaning of this? Who are you?"

Andy remembered the skirmish he'd had with army officers the last time he arrived in Oomaldee and hoped to avoid the ordeal.

"I'm Andy Smithson, sir, and this is Daisy. She brought me—" Andy stopped himself as he remembered the added trouble he'd gotten himself into the last time when he told the truth about coming from his world.

"I'm supposed to meet the King here," Andy corrected.

The soldier shifted his weight and his eyes darted to the door of a tavern a stone's throw away. Clearing his throat, he growled, "Why would you think the King's here? Who are you anyway?"

"I told you, I'm Andy Smithson, and Daisy tells me he's here. She can smell him. She's got a good sense of smell, sir."

The man was clearly at a loss for words. How do you contradict the sniffer of a dragon?

Andy interrupted the officer's thoughts. "If you'll just tell him I'm here, I'm sure everything can be easily cleared up."

"Sergeant Goodman!" the officer rumbled.

"Yes, sir!" responded a wiry uniformed youth, bounding over.

The beefy man turned his back toward Andy and Daisy and whispered orders to Sergeant Goodman. The junior officer bobbed his head, eyeing them as his superior gave instructions. When the huddle broke, the wiry soldier cut through the circle of fellows and headed straight for the drinking establishment.

Butterflies took flight in Andy's stomach.

Nervous? Daisy inquired.

Yeah, a little. This is the first time I'll see the King since I found out he's my father. He doesn't know.

Five minutes later the King dashed from the tavern with Mermin at his heels.

"Andy!" the King boomed, stopping next to Daisy. As usual, he wore faded blue jeans and a long-sleeved black T-shirt with the sleeves pushed up to his elbows.

"Your Majesty! Please, it's not safe!" the beefy officer objected.

"It's fine, Major," the King countered, looking up at Andy still seated on his mount. "That's a fine dragon you've got!" He patted Daisy's shoulder and smiled. "I must say, you pick unusual methods to enter the land, Andy."

Andy grinned. "Yeah."

"This dwagon looks familiar," interjected Mermin.

"This is Daisy. We rescued her when we were looking for the red dragon scale, remember?"

"That's why! Vewy good. She looks healthy. The new colony must be agweeing with her."

Mermin held up his hand asking for silence and looked Daisy in the eyes for several minutes, nodding periodically. Andy couldn't hear anything, but he remembered learning that Mermin had studied dragons for many years.

Finally Mermin exclaimed, "Is that wight?" and laughed.

Mermin turned back. "She was telling me about your twip. A little wowwied about a big pig and cwashing into a mountain, eh?"

Andy felt his face grow warm. *Thanks for keeping that our little secret, Daisy.*

The dragon shuddered a laugh.

"Well, what say we get you some dinner?" the King suggested, helping Andy down from Daisy's back.

Andy paused. *Thanks for the ride, Daisy. It's good to be back.*

My pleasure, Andy. If you need help, just call me in your thoughts.

I will, Andy assured her.

"Stand back, everyone!" the King commanded.

With that, Daisy stretched out her gray scaly wings and lifted off. Andy heard several soldiers shuffle and gasp.

The King put his hand on Andy's shoulder as they walked toward the tavern. RAPSCALLION read the sign hanging above a weathered, wooden door that complained as they pushed it open.

They entered the half-full establishment, and Andy noticed a mix of townsfolk and vulture-people. He followed the King to a table littered with unfinished bowls of porridge, a platter of meat, and two leather tankards of ale. The King waved his hand, summoning a maid.

She hurried over, curtsied, and blushed before asking, "What can I get for you, Your Majesty?"

"Maerwynn, let's get Andy his favorite: chicken and dumplings."

"Yes, Your Majesty. And to drink?"

"I'd like some moonberry honeybeer, please."

Maerwynn again curtsied and hurried toward the kitchen.

While he ordered, Andy had noticed a well-fed, older gentleman amble toward the huge fireplace and nest in a stuffed leather chair to the left of the stone hearth. He was dressed in a modest red and green striped tunic with a somewhat rumpled white shirt underneath and green leggings. Several patrons had turned their heads to watch the man.

The King drew Andy's attention back as he exclaimed, "It's great to see you again, Andy! Your arrival always surprises me."

"When Daisy landed and told me she smelled you here, I was surprised," Andy commented. "You're out of the castle. That's great!"

"Yes, Mermin and I have visited every corner of the land since you've been gone. It's so good to be released from that prison. You've no idea."

At this, Maerwynn arrived with Andy's drink.

"I propose a toast," the King suggested. "To you, Alden, and Hannah. I am forever grateful!"

"As am I," Mermin chimed in.

The three clanked mugs.

Andy leaned in. "Alden tells me you had Hans implant the stone under your skin."

"Indeed I did. A great idea Glaucin gave me. No sense in taking chances." He smiled and patted his side.

"So, do you come here often?" Andy questioned.

The King glanced quickly at Mermin, then leaned in closer to Andy. In a voice not much above a whisper, he explained, "There's been a rash of townsfolk turned into vulture-people over the past four months. That's why we're here, doing a bit of investigation. Nothing like spending time with my people to uncover the truth. We're trying to determine whether it's Abaddon's doing, and if so, piece together why so many in such a short time."

Andy felt himself inhale quickly.

"The stowyteller is weady to begin," Mermin interrupted. He nodded in the direction of the fireplace where the gentleman now puffed on a pipe, slowly releasing smoke rings to the admiration of onlookers.

A storyteller. So, that's what he is.

"Let's continue this once he's done," the King suggested.

A dozen patrons scooted closer and a hush fell over the establishment.

"My name is Asher Dain, and mine has been a full and fascinating life, or so I've been told by folks not unlike yourselves."

Several in the tavern encouraged with a chorus of low chuckles.

Taking another draw on his pipe and brushing back a wayward lock of peppery gray hair, the old man surveyed his congregation of hopeful faces and nested himself more comfortably.

"I'm not from these parts. No sir, I make the world my home. I have lived many a year and have experienced more of life than the average man. Sovereigns have called me friend and knights have vowed to cleave my spirit from my flesh or pursue me through the halls of..." He pointed downward as he raised his eyebrows.

Several children squirmed and anxiously sought the reassuring touch of a parent.

"As long as the younger folk in our midst care not about unsettled dreams in the coming days, then a tale I shall impart."

Andy smiled. *This guy's good.*

The storyteller sighed and continued, "I've heard rumors of ye enduring certain afflictions of late."

Several patrons shifted on their chairs.

He cleared his throat and kneeded his generous, silvery eyebrows as he thought. He took another draw on his pipe. Maerwynn brought him a full tankard of ale and he took a sip, then nodded appreciatively.

"I believe I have something in mind," Asher spoke softly, drawing his listeners to the edges of their chairs. "Tis a tale of power, treachery, and love, so settle in and have a listen."

CHAPTER FOUR

A Tale

"**O**nce there was a land ruled by a gracious queen. As much as has ever been possible, she loved her people and they in turn loved her. Rather than lording over them, she found joy in mingling among the commoners, for she believed if she knew their problems, her edicts would help and not harm her subjects. And so this kingdom flourished for many years.

"There came a day when, as the queen visited with merchants in the market, a disturbance interrupted her conversation. A merchant held tightly to the ear of a grimy young urchin, dragging him toward her. He complained, 'This lad stole two mince pies from me, Your Majesty. What shall I do with him?' All in the crowd saw the contents smeared across the boy's face. The lad knew he had no defense and hung his head awaiting judgment.

"The queen scrutinized the boy. 'Judging by your clothing, you're not from around here.'

"The lad lifted his head and stood straight before replying, 'I'm from a land far away. My family was killed in a war and I alone survive. I came here looking for work. I never meant to steal. I usually do odd jobs to pay my way, but I was hungry and no one had work for me. I'm sorry.' At hearing this honest reply, the queen's spirit felt compassion for the youth and she took him into her home to raise as her own.

"The lad received a lukewarm reception from her husband and their three children, however, for while the queen's heart overflowed with love, her husband did not share compassion in the same measure. And while the queen held out hope her children would one day adopt her ways, at present they chose to follow the path of their father steadfastly.

"Thus the boy loved the queen. He grew and profited from the education and luxuries of royalty, but the three children became increasingly jealous. They took to tormenting the lad at every opportunity as their hearts hardened. Until one day when the child, now nearly a man, could endure their harassment no longer. He left the castle, his once loving heart broken. Love for the queen and a broken spirit could not coexist. Try as he might, his wounded spirit won.

"He returned to the streets and eked out a subsistence living. Whenever he saw the queen searching for him, he hid, unwilling to endure more from her vulturous children. Then one day a group of merciless traders raided the kingdom, taking with them all the street urchins they could capture. Parasites they called them."

A little girl Andy judged to be no more than five yelped and buried her head in her mama's lap. Several adults glanced over and smiled. The storyteller took another sip of his ale and waited for the eyes of his audience to return to him.

"The traders sold the penniless young man into a life of cruel slavery. When he could not meet the demands of his owners, they beat him until he was barely conscious. Despite his harsh situation, his thoughts fixated not on himself but on taking vengeance on his former siblings for the pain they had caused him. 'I will gain my revenge,' he vowed daily. His broken heart hardened and became as a stone: inflexible, cold, and unbending.

"One day the young man learned the queen and her husband had died. 'It is time,' he declared. 'I loved the queen and would never have touched even a hair of her children while she lived lest the pain of it consume her. But her presence no longer protects them.' He cut down his owner and escaped with not so much as a pang of guilt or remorse. His sense of mission crowded all other thoughts from of his mind.

"He found passage back to the land, and not long after the young man entered the castle and slew the heir and his two siblings, usurping power. Having no love in his heart for anyone, himself included, he enacted harsh edicts on the people. The citizens quickly rose up, seeking his demise. And so, his mission of revenge fulfilled, he found himself drifting without purpose or meaning. He reflected over his life—he remembered his family being killed and the cruelty of his life in the streets. He thought of the mutual love he and the queen had shared. He remembered how his heart had been warm and pliable. He reminisced over the outings they would take, just the two of them, when the queen made him feel loved, despite the other children. He reflected on the words she imparted to him, words he could barely remember, so long had he pushed them to the back of his mind: 'While man seeks advantage over his fellows, no one controls love. It is your freedom. It is your choice.'

"He continued thinking through the transformative moments of his life. 'When did my heart become stone?' he asked himself at last. After a long while, he finally offered an answer: 'When I stopped choosing to love.'"

A man in the back blurted out, "Are you tellin' me yer whole tale is about nothin' other than bein' lovey-dovey? Bah! And I s'pose you're gonna tell us the guy apologized to the citizens and they lived happily ever after. What a crock of manure!"

Another patron stood up wagging his finger at the storyteller. He glanced down at a vulture-woman seated next to him and yelled, "They just turned my wife! You expect me to be lovey-dovey with whoever did this to her? They should be hanged!"

The situation worsened as listeners hurled insults at Asher Dain.

Finally, a burly farmer stood. Next to him sat his wife, who dabbed tears with a hanky, and their two vulture-kids. "If you'd all be quiet, I'd like to hear how it turned out."

The crowd quieted and refocused on the storyteller, who took another sip of his ale and another draw on his pipe. He straightened his tunic and readjusted himself in the leather chair. At last he continued.

"The young man did not have the opportunity to apologize and make things right. The citizens overran the castle, dragged him out, and beat him to within an inch of his life. Had the youth's heart remained stone, he would have succumbed. But as he lay there, discarded, what he learned in his childhood took on new and deeper meaning and his heart melted."

"Did you make this whole thing up or did you see it happen?" a woman in the front interrupted.

Asher smiled. "Dear madam, I saw it happen, for I am the boy."

Murmurs rumbled through the room.

"So what's the point of your tale?" another patron interjected.

"We're supposed to love no matter what happens to us? That's a load of rubbish!" someone in back shot out.

"No, we're supposed to love having our family turned into vulture-people!" another heckler crowed.

The crowd tossed out other suggestions, arguing over the meaning of the narrative. Andy saw two children, eyes wide, leave their seats and run to their mother for reassurance.

Andy couldn't take anymore and he climbed up on his chair. The King and Mermin both looked up at him, raising their eyebrows. "The point of the story is that we have choice!" Andy yelled above the roar.

Townsfolk paused, looking for the source of the outburst. The crowd observed the King and Mermin giving their attention to a boy standing on a chair and quieted.

"You're missing the point," Andy continued. "Our storyteller's trying to say we have choice. In most areas of our lives, this isn't the case. But we"— Andy thumped his chest—" *we* control whether we love or not, no one else. If we choose to love, our hearts stay warm and open to give love. If we choose not to love, our hearts grow cold and we lose the ability to love. But each of us has the choice! When so many have been attacked and everyone's nervous, wondering when it might be them, now is not the time to be fighting. Now is the time to come together and choose to love. We are as strong as the love we choose to share."

Silence grew loud, saturating the room.

A smile sprouted and blossomed across the King's face, and he began clapping slowly. Others joined in until nearly everyone in the tavern applauded. Andy felt his face warm.

"Well said, Andy!" The King beamed.

Andy looked down at the King from his perch. "I couldn't stand everyone fighting over the meaning of a tale about love."

While the castle staff knew Andy's role in restoring the King and Mermin to health during his last visit, word had not spread to the communities. "Who is that kid? And why's he dressed like the King?" someone across the space bellowed.

The King stood. "I'd like you to meet Andy, a youth wise beyond his years. Now, if any of you disagree with what he suggested, I invite you to question politely." Andy noticed the King did not elaborate further on his identity.

No one voiced opposition, and several folks stood and shuffled forward, murmuring thanks and dropping coins in a bowl situated before Asher Dain.

Andy hopped down from his perch and resettled himself, finishing the last bites of the delicious chicken and dumplings Maerwynn had brought while the storyteller wove his tale.

Once the tavern emptied, Andy watched the King approach Asher Dain and engage him in conversation. *I suppose they have some things in common.*

"We need to get to the bottom of this," Mermin voiced, interrupting Andy's thoughts.

"How many people have been turned?"

"No telling. We're still twying to detewmine that."

Andy couldn't help but think of the scroll he'd studied and his terrifying dream. *Why would Abaddon do that? What purpose would it serve?*

The King rejoined them several minutes later. "It's late and you're probably tired, Andy. Our earlier conversation will keep until tomorrow."

Maerwynn showed the King, Mermin, and Andy to their respective rooms. Soldiers followed each to his door. Andy watched one of them turn and stand guard outside the King's before a beefy soldier closed Andy's door behind him. After washing up, Andy climbed into bed and fell asleep almost immediately.

Andy saw himself walking alone once again. As always with this particular dream, he held his arms up, shielding his face from the dust whipping at him as he took step after struggling step across the charred and barren soil. The smell of sulfur again assaulted his nose and made his lungs burn. Over the whistling of the relentless wind, Andy heard the sounds of baying wolves. He stumbled as he took several more steps, finally stopping in front of the massive black walls of King Abaddon's castle and drawing Methuselah.

Passing through the city gates, he again came upon the tall, shiny stone edifice housing Abaddon's throne and noted the gargoyles and all manner of hideous beings standing as ornaments on and around the structure. He passed the statue of a husky Oomish craftsman waving a clenched fist directly outside the imposing front doors, then continued on into the shadowy interior.

He could never shake the sense of horror he felt glancing around the perimeter where more statues of Oomish citizens stood on black stone pedestals. He made his way toward the far end of the room where, for the first time, the mist that usually obscured his sight lifted and he saw a seven-headed dragon slumped on its throne. Its once red scales had turned to a deathly mix of gray and mauve. Each of his heads had a bandage over its left eye. The creature struggled to speak to the translucent image of a young woman wearing a white dress, hovering nearby.

"The boy is back," the lady hissed.

Andy moved closer to hear the beast's reply.

"Can you not see my condition? Are you completely daft?"

"He must be stopped! If you can't do anything, at least get your bellicose back on his trail."

"Discover how to heal me and I will consider it."

A vulture-warrior approached the throne and bowed. "My liege, do you need an infusion?"

The seven heads drifted in a nod and the vulture-man waddled from the room. He returned momentarily, followed by a shuffling line of eight bound men, women, and children, their heads slumped in defeat. A host of accompanying vulture-warriors wielding swords reinforced their sense of helplessness.

Andy shivered as he heard their whimpers. *What's he going to do to them?*

A vulture-warrior separated the first man from the group and forced him to stand before Abaddon.

"Kneel and pledge allegiance or be turned to stone," the warrior commanded.

"Never!"

"Fine. Your choice."

Andy saw a bright flash and he closed his eyes. When he opened them, the man stood unmoving.

"Get him out of here!" the vulture-warrior demanded.

Andy nearly threw up as he saw two bird-men lift the statue and carry it off.

Soldiers next dragged a young woman before Abaddon.

"Kneel and pledge allegiance or be turned to stone," the warrior commanded.

The lady sobbed and fell at Abaddon's feet. "Please, don't do this to me," she begged.

"Then pledge allegiance to King Abaddon."

Through a torrent of sobs the woman quaked, "I pledge my allegiance."

Another blast of light lit the room and the woman, now with long arms, bulging eyes, and beak-like nose, crumpled to the floor.

"Tag her!"

A vulture-warrior scurried over with a circular disc and red hot branding iron, grabbed the woman's right arm, pushed up her sleeve to expose her bare shoulder, and applied the mark. The woman let out a shriek that pierced Andy's core. No longer able to control his angst, he puked.

"Not one word to anyone about this, is that clear?" the warrior warned the woman. "You have been tagged and we will know if you say anything. If you do, you've seen what will happen to you."

The woman wobbled upright, clutching her shoulder, and nodded through a stream of tears.

"Get her out of here!" Abaddon demanded.

Andy saw the scene repeat itself, this time with a child.

Andy screamed, but to no effect. Only gritty resolve kept him watching as two more captives were turned to stone and the rest limped off to an existence most fowl. When the horror finally ended, Abaddon sat tall on his throne, his scales again red.

Abaddon looked at the translucent young woman who had watched it all with a pained expression. "If only this treatment lasted longer," he droned.

"Treatment?!" Andy protested to no effect.

"At this rate I'll need another infusion by sundown. They don't last as long as they used to. Find me a lasting cure and we'll see about defeating the boy."

"But he's the one who did this to you! With that sword!"

"His time will come," Abaddon's seven heads sang in unison.

Andy woke with a start, soaked in sweat.

Andy recounted the nightmare to the King and Mermin the next morning over breakfast in the tavern. Both men listened in horror. When he'd finished, no one wanted anything more to eat.

After several minutes of contemplative silence, the King said, "While I fear your dream revealed the truth of the situation, we need to verify to be sure. I suggest we split up and question several townsfolk. If everyone refuses to speak with us, we will know."

Andy and Mermin nodded their agreement, and the three headed out of the Rapscallion into the fog-covered city square. The sun's glare against the white clouds made seeing any distance painful. Andy squinted and his nose picked up the unmistakable stench of an apothecary.

No doubt someone will seek a cure there.

GALLIPOT'S APOTHECARY indicated the sign above the door as he entered. While still early, several folks waited in line to be helped. Most gave him strange looks, which he assumed was because of his T-shirt and jeans. One couple stood protectively near a bird-child who looked to be maybe eight or nine, whispering encouraging sentiments and hugging the girl. Another family lingered by a wall of jars that included fairy dust, weather root, troll hair, spiderwort, wormwood, and other equally disgusting remedies. The wife kept hugging her bird-husband, trying to reassure herself as much as him. Similar situations repeated themselves throughout the shop. The healer looked to be doing the best she could, but she wasn't used to such demand. She glanced at Andy with an apologetic look.

A whiff of rotten eggs wafted from the back of the establishment and Andy regretted choosing this store to question folks. He wheezed and moved away from the odor, then passed a putrid barrel with a sign declaring its contents to be dragon dung. *Are you kidding me?* He finally stopped next to a couple in which the wife bore unmistakable fowl tendencies.

Andy lingered uncomfortably, not sure how to start a conversation about such a traumatic event. At last he decided he had nothing to lose and addressed the husband. "I'm not from around these parts. I just arrived in town last night. I've got a problem with my arm, nasty mark I can't seem to get rid of. What are you here for?"

"That's a little personal, don't ya think?" grumped the man, turning his back.

"I'm sorry, I didn't mean to offend."

"If you must know, my wife was turned into…into…*this*," he spat out. "Since you're not from these parts, you wouldn't know, but lots of folks are getting turned. My wife's so upset she won't talk about it."

"I'm sorry. How long ago did it happen?"

"Yesterday."

"I'm so sorry to hear that," Andy mumbled.

At a loss for anything else to say that might console the man and his wife, he moved on to a family of three who were clearly here for the same reason. The child, sporting bulging eyes and a beak nose, kept accidentally knocking over colorful containers of weeds and herbal remedies with overly long arms that he had not yet adapted to.

"I overheard you talking to them folks over there," the father leaned over and remarked to Andy. "My son was out playing yesterday morning, and next thing I know, he's missin'. We searched everywhere for him. Imagine how relieved I was when he finally turned up late last night, even though he looks like this now."

The bird-boy looked up at Andy and large tears welled in his eyes.

"I'm sorry," Andy choked out. "Did he say what happened?"

"Nope. Every time we try to broach the subject he clams up and starts crying. When I get my hands on the one who did this to him, they'll wish they'd never set foot in these parts," the man growled.

Andy patted the man on the shoulder. "I'm so sorry."

He had seen and heard enough, maybe too much. He left the apothecary and returned to the Rapscallion, where he found the King waiting.

After Mermin rejoined them, they compared conversations, quickly concluding Andy's dream was, in fact, reality.

"Abaddon's declared war on us. We must answer," the King affirmed.

"I'm going after him!" Andy resolved.

"Andy, you'll be turned like everyone else," cautioned the King. "We'll need to take troops, but I don't want them turned in the process."

ANDY SMITHSON: DISGRACE OF THE UNICORN'S HONOR

Andy paced and thought, thought and paced, around and around the table as the King and Mermin conferred. *There has to be a way to stop him. There has to.*

Suddenly Andy exclaimed, "Wait a minute!"

Mermin and the King glanced over.

"Remember when Abaddon took over the castle during my first trip here? He turned everyone in the cavalry who was outside, but he couldn't touch the staff inside. That's it, sir! How much you want to bet the Stone of Athanasia protected everyone from being turned?"

"I don't know, Andy," Mermin flagged. "I think you are making a big leap. You don't know it was the stone that pwotected us."

"No, but I'd be willing to bet that's what saved everyone."

"It does make sense," the King replied, stroking his chin.

Undeterred, Andy continued, "Since you have the stone, we can go together and defeat Abaddon when he's weak. He won't be able to turn anyone."

A grin took root and spread across the King's face. "Your idea is just crazy enough to work, Andy."

Mermin shook his head.

Andy, the King, and Mermin adjourned to their respective rooms to pack. While there, Andy pulled his holster from his backpack, buckled it on, and extracted Methuselah's hilt. As expected, the silver blade immediately extended and he took several practice swings. *Yes!*

Even though he had practiced swordplay with a video game as well as with Methuselah's hilt in the garage while no one else was home, the weight of the sword fully extended felt different.

I hope I can still win a fight with it, he thought, his mind calculating the probability of meeting the bellicose.

Andy rejoined the others and the King joked, "What, no dragon to ride?"

"I can call Daisy if you really want me to," Andy joshed back.

The King laughed. "No, that won't be necessary. It's not far. It's a fine day and the walk will do us all good."

And with that they headed toward home, accompanied by a contingent of armed soldiers numbering no less than fifty.

Not long into the walk, however, a large beast with onyx fur covering its torso, a cat-like nose, piercing yellow eyes, the hands of a man, and hindquarters like a panther stumbled out from between two buildings.

I guess the probability of meeting the bellicose is 100 percent!

CHAPTER FIVE

Just the Facts

"**N**o, you fool! You're in no condition!" screamed a shrill disembodied voice.

Andy, the King, Mermin, and the soldiers froze and looked about.

Like a cat after too much catnip, the bellicose staggered toward Andy, its eyes swirling randomly. It bumped a warrior as it wobbled erratically. The man dropped his sword and grabbed his arm, yelping in pain.

No one in the party knew quite what to make of it, but Andy instinctively grabbed for Methuselah and took his ready position. *What's happened to it? I've never seen it behave this way.*

The King rushed forward. "Stop that thing!" he commanded his troops, snapping them from the spell the sight had cast. The soldiers hastened to comply and rushed the bellicose. Despite its weakened condition, the beast managed to thrust out one palm and create a force field that the warriors crashed into, forming a mound of squirming flesh as they fell.

Andy braced as the beast drew closer. *This could be a trick,* he warned himself. *Stay focused!*

The creature stopped three yards away, dagger in hand, and assumed a position confirming its lack of readiness. Its arms vacillated, and Andy watched it twitch its cheeks and squint its eyes, trying desperately to focus.

Despite its vulnerability, Andy waited for the bellicose to make the first move, determined not to get caught off-guard. Several soldiers untangled themselves from the pile and rushed again.

"Stop! You'll get hurt. I've got this," Andy warned the men as the beast lunged forward. Andy easily sidestepped and the creature teetered past, ending in a lump on the ground, its back toward him.

"Kill it!" several men roared.

I'm no coward. I can't kill it when its back is toward me.

Andy waited for the creature to stand, turn, and face him. When it finally did, it thrust its knife above its head, exposing its midsection, and swayed forward.

Andy let the bellicose get within four feet before he slashed Methuselah's blade horizontally through its midsection. Instantly, the beast crumpled to the ground and transformed into a pile of black dirt. Without warning, a fierce wind arose, stirring up dust and scattering the mound. Everyone drew an arm up to cover their eyes.

"Imbecile!" the high-pitched voice screeched. "Kaysan, you are no rightful king! The boy will pay with his life and it will be on your head. Call it a small repayment for what you've done to me. Mark my words!"

When the zephyr finally blew itself out several minutes later, everyone stood in stunned silence. Where the creature had fallen, the ground was now bleached as if the evil exuding from its form had forced all color from the ground.

"I can't believe it's gone," Andy broke the quiet, replaying the contest in his mind. *That was too easy.*

"Don't overthink this. You were skillful with your sword," Mermin rationalized.

"I've never seen it act so out of control. It's always been quick and I've had all I can do to defend myself. I don't get it."

"Perhaps it was weakened from the injuries you inflicted during past fights. Like Mermin said, I wouldn't overthink it, Andy. It's gone."

"Maybe you're right," Andy replied, giving the King a weak smile. *I'm not buying it,* Andy told himself and began inventing scenarios concerning what might have happened to the bellicose and what he might anticipate in the future, none of which cheered him.

"Men," the King called his soldiers to attention, feeling the need to explain the disembodied voice. "Many have skeletons in their closets. I have a ghost."

Andy noticed the eyes of several soldiers grow large, despite their discipline that kept them at attention.

The King held up his hands. "Please do not be alarmed. This is an issue between myself and the ghost and does not concern any of you. You need not be afraid, for I can assure you, it will not harm you."

Andy watched several men exhale.

"The kingdom is already on edge with all that is going on. It does not need more fuel added. I ask each of you, on your honor as men and warriors, not to speak of these events."

The man closest turned toward the King, fell to one knee, and bowed his head. The rest of the soldiers followed.

"Thank you all!"

They reached the castle an hour later and entered to a raucous fanfare, for the King had been away three weeks and everyone celebrated his return. When the welcome party discovered Andy in their midst, the merrymaking grew louder still. Marta threw her arms around Andy and kissed him repeatedly, causing his face to turn beet red. Hans, Hannah, and Alden raced over and hugged him as well. He spotted Razen across the dining hall and locked eyes with him for a second. *Well, he didn't scowl. That's progress. Still, what's he up to?*

The castle staff knew what he, Alden, and Hannah had done for the King and Mermin, and Andy noticed the staff greeted him respectfully, nodding their heads. Cadfael and the rest of the Oscray team, of course, gave him playful grief for abandoning the season unfinished, and Merk, ever the practical joker, grabbed him around his upper arms and drew him close, making as if to kiss him on the lips with loud smooching sounds. Andy fought with all his might to avoid contact, to the amusement of everyone.

"You're just in time for tonight's match, Andy," Ox chimed in. "Score's seven matches for castle staff and ten for cavalry so far this season. You game?"

"I'd love to!"

A cheer went up from all.

When the revelry finally died down and the staff headed back to work, the King caught Andy's attention. "We still need to finish our conversation from yesterday. I've got several matters I need to address, but after that, let's you and me have a talk. It'll probably be late this afternoon."

"That sounds good, sir—" Andy stopped himself before saying more, but the King noticed and smiled, although he refrained from comment.

"I'll send for you when I'm available."

At that, the King, Mermin, and Razen convened a meeting at the long communal table used for meals.

Andy suggested to Alden and Hannah, "Let's go someplace quieter. How about my quarters? I can drop my stuff off and we can catch up."

As they climbed the stairs, Andy noticed Alden and Hannah kept stealing glances at each other. Hannah straightened her blue skirt and tucked a few stray blonde hairs back in her kerchief.

Andy opened the door to his room and glanced around. *Yep, everything exactly as I left it.* He dropped his pack, then ran over, jumped, and landed stretched out on his back among the soft billowy covers. Foggy sunlight wafted through the window next to the bed. "Ah, home sweet home!"

Hannah sat down next to Alden on the bed.

"It's great to see you both again! I'm glad we can at least write when I'm not here."

Andy looked at Alden when he received no reply. Alden's hand was close to Hannah's and creeping closer.

"So, Alden," Andy broke the silence. Alden's eyes rocketed up at Andy and he jerked his hand back to his lap.

Alden tried to cover his embarrassment. "Do you like my scar? I haven't showed it to you yet, have I?" He thrust his arm toward Andy to examine.

Andy discerned two marks, each two to three inches long and set about six inches apart in Alden's forearm.

"Pretty cool, huh, Andy?"

"Yeah, it's great."

"Boys!" Hannah declared, rolling her eyes and shaking her head. "There's nothing cool about those marks, Alden. You could have been killed!"

"But I wasn't," Alden replied with a grin.

"So, Alden," Andy tried again, now with his friend's full attention. "You said Razen's been studying books about healing Abaddon? How do you know that's what he's up to?"

"The last time I went snooping around his office, he had two thick books open. One marked a recipe called "Festering Wound Elixir," and the other was open to the chapter "Regaining Your Perfect Shape." What was I supposed to think?"

"Did you read any of it?"

"Didn't have time. Hannah gave me the signal Razen was coming. Yeah, she's been helping."

Hannah smiled.

"I see."

Andy was getting the picture, and he wasn't sure how he felt about Hannah and Alden…well, together. Something inside him felt unsettled.

"I'd like to see it. Do you suppose he's still got the books?"

"Probably. We can check. Razen should still be meeting with the King and Mermin," Alden offered. "Hannah can be lookout again."

The trio headed right and walked the length of the hall to Razen's office. They saw no one except two assistants and a man busily working, his back toward them, when they passed the tailor's suite. Andy stopped in front of Razen's door and motioned for Alden and Hannah to keep quiet. He put his ear up to the keyhole. Nothing.

"Okay, sounds like he's out."

Andy pulled the pouch he wore around his neck from beneath his T-shirt and extracted the golden key. Having never seen what the small piece of metal could do, Hannah puzzled at the sight but remained quiet. Andy inserted the key into the lock and turned. *Click.*

Andy pushed the door open slowly to its squeaky protests and surveyed the room. In a whisper, he asked, "What's the signal?"

Hannah drew her hands up to her mouth and inhaled, but Alden cut her off. "Don't worry about it. I know what her warning sounds like," Alden offered. Hannah frowned.

Andy and Alden crept into the dim office and Alden closed the door to a crack. One torch by the door and another on the wall dimly illuminated the space. A large oak desk dominated the left side of the spartan room, and two straight-backed chairs stood at attention before it. An ornate tapestry stretched floor to ceiling behind the desk, giving the room a hint of sophistication. Both boys were familiar with the wallcovering since their discovery the previous year that it hid access to tunnels running up and down the castle wall. Straight ahead, on the outside wall, a modest fireplace stood cold and unlit. A goatskin rug lay in front of the stone hearth, and wood was stacked neatly in a pile to the right of it

Andy grabbed the torch nearest him and approached the desk. Unlike Mermin's desk, which was piled to overflowing with scrolls and parchment, Razen's workspace reflected the discipline and rigor by which the man lived. Andy unconsciously felt his palm, remembering the blisters this man caused last time he was in Oomaldee. On the left side of the desktop stood a hand-carved wooden sphere on a block pedestal. Simple in its highly polished form, it rose six or seven inches, reminding Andy of pieces he'd seen when his family visited the Dallas Museum of Art three summers ago.

Modern art? Here? Seems out of place.

On the right side of the desktop sat two large books, perfectly stacked. Several markers jutted out from the page edges, forming a fringe. Andy brought the torch closer to read the spines. The bottom one was titled "The Perfect You: Maintaining Your Shape Over the Ages," and on top of that was "Self-Help Cures for Persistent Problems." *Sounds like books I've seen at the library back home. As they say, the more things change, the more they stay the same.* Andy smiled and placed the key next to the volumes.

"What's so funny?" Alden interrupted in a whisper. "Come on, we don't have much time."

"Sorry." Andy refocused and opened the top book, turning to the first marked page. He read a couple paragraphs on "How to Judge Whether a Problem Is Persistent." *Wouldn't that be obvious?*

He shrugged and turned to the next marker, continuing his search until he came to the recipe for "Festering Wound Elixir" that Alden had mentioned. As Andy worked down the list of ingredients, a sense of foreboding filled him:

One measure raw karkadann horn, ground to a fine powder

Three gnut weed thistles

Two dried Thriae, crushed

Hair from two tails of a Kitsune

One pod of milkweed

He read further:

In a small vessel, mix karkadann horn together with the gnut weed thistles and dried thriae. Heat for twelve hours over low heat, taking care not to boil. Let cool completely.

Slowly stir the remaining ingredients into the kettle. It is critical the intended recipient drink the brew as quickly as possible, for the potency of the mixture will diminish within seconds.

"Alden, the list of ingredients," Andy whispered. "Do you know what any of them are?"

"I only recognize karkadann horn and milkweed. Karkadann is like a ferocious version of a unicorn. The horn is supposed to heal anything that ails you, even poison. Karkadanns live in the land of Cromlech, where Hans is from. He told me about them once. In fact, I think that's what he used to cure you from the poison dart that time you saved my life during the Tower Chase competition."

"What about milkweed?"

"Milkweed is sweet. My mom uses it in the kitchens. The potion must taste pretty bad if…" Alden continued yammering, but Andy's attention shifted to the wooden sphere on the desk from which a wispy, translucent swirl had wafted. It rose up, forming a ball twelve to fifteen inches in diameter that hung rotating above the manuscripts. A voice spoke: "Andrew Ferrin Smithson."

Whoa! Mom?

"This isn't good. Sculptures should not emit swirls that sound like your mother," Andy's inneru warned.

Mesmerized, Andy continued listening.

"What would you give to save me while still breaking the curse?"

What? Only Daisy and my inneru know about that!

Before Andy could question further, Alden whispered loudly and roughly shook his shoulder. "Andy! I said Razen's coming. We've got to go!" Alden shut the book, silently closed the office door, replaced the torch on the wall, and grabbed Andy's arm, dragging him through the double tapestries behind the desk.

"Wh-what?" Andy queried, coming out of his trance in the tunnel.

"Shhh, come on."

They scampered down the stairs as quietly as they could in the darkness. Only when they reached the dungeon level and plunged through the wallcovering concealing the lowest flight of stairs did they stop to catch their breath. Thankfully, the dungeon appeared empty, although they could hear Sir Kay and Sir Gawain taunting each other.

"What happened to you back there? One minute I'm talking to you and the next you're zoned out," Alden complained.

"You didn't see the—?"

"See what?"

Andy told Alden all he had just experienced, omitting the question the swirling sphere had asked.

"You don't think it's the same as when the key brings stone statues to life?" Alden asked, pointing toward the one-upmanship they overheard from around the corner.

Andy shook his head. "No, this is definitely different."

"Let's go meet Hannah. She should already be back at my room," Alden indicated.

They headed back through the tapestry in the dungeon wall, up one flight of stairs, and through the sliding panel that connected the tunnel with the servants' quarters. Hannah was waiting for them outside Alden's door.

"What took you so long?" she interrogated once they closed the door to Alden and Marta's room.

Alden related everything he and Andy discussed.

"Are you kidding?" Hannah replied.

"Did you sense anything, Hannah?" Andy queried, remembering how she'd perceived the bellicose before it attacked during the Oscray match.

"Nothing more than I usually do when I'm near Razen."

"So you felt something," Andy probed.

"Everybody has a vibe. When I'm near my parents or the King or Mermin, I get a warm, almost fuzzy feeling in my stomach, if that makes sense. But when I'm around vulture-people—not all of them, mind you, just some of them—I get a cold, prickly kind of feeling. I haven't figured out what makes the difference. Razen's vibe is weird, it's a mix of warm fuzzy and cold prickly at the same time, almost like there's a battle going on inside him."

"I'm surprised you feel any warm fuzzies with Razen," Andy commented, at which Hannah and Alden shared a laugh.

Bringing the conversation back around to the mission's original intent, Andy reported, "I read the ingredients for the recipe and I have to agree with Alden. It's got to be a recipe for curing Abaddon. Unless Razen's got something wrong with him."

The second he said it, Andy paused, realizing how funny that sounded.

"I can think of several things wrong with Razen," Alden offered, launching the three into a fit of giggles.

"Well, Hannah and I need to practice for the Tower Chase. Want to watch?"

Alden and Hannah went to change and Andy made his way down to the kitchen where he had agreed to meet them. Reaching his intended destination, he grabbed a handful of chocolate chip cookies, much to Marta's delight. In no time, his two friends appeared wearing their equestrian uniforms—royal blue jackets and green riding breeches. As they headed toward the back door of the castle, a young servant boy called after them, "Master Andy!"

The trio stopped and the boy, who couldn't have been more than six, panted, "I was sent to tell you His Majesty is ready for you. He's in his chambers."

"What's your name?"

"Marcus."

Andy smiled. "Thanks for letting me know, Marcus. By the way, you can just call me Andy."

Marcus grinned before running off.

"Well, I'd best be off then," Andy said. "See you at dinner."

On his way to meet the King, Andy stopped by his chambers and retrieved the gold envelope from his backpack. He accidentally dropped it and, as he bent to pick it up, he noticed his shallow breathing. He stared at the addressee—Emmalee, Favored One—and exhaled a long breath before slipping the envelope in his back pocket.

He climbed the two flights of stairs and knocked on the door of the King's chambers.

"Come in!" boomed the King. "Ah, Andy. Please, come in, come in."

The King approached and closed the door after Andy. He motioned toward a pair of chairs situated near his desk, which stood against the wall to the left of his enormous bed. "We haven't had the opportunity to properly catch up and I thought my chambers might provide a quieter place to do so."

Andy sat in one of the handsome leather-covered armchairs and watched the King open a small, decorative wooden box resting on the upper right corner of his desk. He pulled out a stoppered vial of liquid.

"Know what this is?"

Andy smiled. "Yes, the vial of venom."

"I've kept it here since you left because I can't see that darned book to put it away for safekeeping. Let's take care of it as soon as we're done here."

Andy laughed. "No problem."

"So then," the King began, "while you've been away I visited the Library of Oomaldee, as you know. I saw the portrait you mentioned, and I agree, we look nearly identical at your age. It's uncanny." The King began to grin. "I couldn't help noticing your near stumble when you acknowledged my request for this meeting, and I'm wondering if you might have learned something more that will help explain the situation."

Andy returned the grin and reached for the envelope.

The King's jaw dropped as soon as he caught sight of the golden color.

"You told me your wife's name was Emmalee."

The King nodded, affirming the assertion.

"My mom said she got this just before she got pregnant with me," Andy said as he handed it to the King.

"No!" the King exclaimed, jumping to his feet as soon as he read the addressee. "My Emmalee!" Tears began running down his cheeks as he stared at the envelope. Then, as realization clicked, he looked over at Andy and choked out, "My son?"

Andy nodded and ran into his outstretched arms. They hugged for what seemed an eternity.

"Read the letter," Andy encouraged when they finally broke apart.

The King and Andy both laughed as they dried their tear-stained faces and blew their noses.

Seated again, the King pulled the single sheet of parchment from the envelope and read it several times. He shook his head, nodded, and cried more as he digested the news.

At last the King wiped his tears and looked up. "How is it possible she's still alive?"

"My mom wears a necklace with a slice of the Stone of Athanasia."

"Merlin! What a skillful wizard he was. Bless that man!" the King praised, then thought quietly for a minute.

"I've been wondering…," Andy started. "What should I call you?"

The King chuckled. "What do you call your father in Lakehills, Texas?"

"Dad."

"Did you have something in mind, Andy?"

"May I call you Father?"

The King locked eyes. "I would be honored…Son."

Andy beamed.

"Speaking of your dad…" The King paused, slowly shaking his head. "I find it hard to express the gratitude I hold for what he has done. It couldn't have been easy."

"He said he'd been hard on me growing up because he wanted me to be prepared if and when the time came. He feared I would suffer if I wasn't ready. I wish he hadn't been as hard on me as he was, but I get it."

"I have great respect for him, Andy. Your dad is an amazing man."

Andy smiled, and for the first time in his life, he felt pride toward his dad.

"I'd love to see your mom again, but I don't want to cause her problems or pain. She has a new life. I respect that."

"Maybe I can put in a good word for you," Andy joked.

The King smiled wistfully and seemed far away for several minutes.

"We need to throw a banquet to celebrate!" he declared when his attention returned. "We'll invite the governors and anyone who cares to join us, in a fortnight. This is a momentous occasion in the history of the kingdom. You are heir to the throne. Shall we call you Prince Andrew?"

"Do you have to? Prince sounds so stuffy. I prefer just Andy."

"Ah, you must understand, ruling well is about the people, not you. The people will want to give you an official title, a name that makes them proud when they associate with it."

"Oh."

"Those closest to you can still call you Andy, but in public, you will use your formal title."

"Looks like I've got lots to learn. How's this all gonna work with my family back home?"

"I don't know, Andy, but I'm sure your path will become clear as time passes. It always does."

Andy's stomach rumbled loudly and he covered his mouth. "Excuse me!"

The King laughed as he returned the letter to the gold envelope and handed it back to Andy. "We still have a curse to break. What say we file that vial in the invisible book before something happens to it and head down to dinner?"

The King put his hand on Andy's shoulder as they walked down the flight of stairs to Mermin's library. Andy reveled in the closeness he shared with his father.

They greeted Mermin and announced the headlines, much to the wizard's astonishment. As Mermin tried to grasp the King's news, Andy located the book invisible to all but him, brought it over to the table, cleared a spot, and opened it. The single page at the front held a message:

1. Flirt not with temptation.
2. Take care where you leave things.

What's that supposed to mean?

Andy turned the page and opened the compartment with the white loop handle. To his surprise, it held more than the six red dragon scales he'd collected.

CHAPTER SIX

Rewards of Temptation

The gold key sat on the top. *I forgot to pick it up when we left Razen's office! If he'd found it... Whoever you are, thanks!*

Andy picked up the key and stowed it back in his pouch before placing the vial of venom in the book. Turning back the page, he checked to see if the message had changed. Below the original admonitions, it now said, *You're welcome.* He breathed a sigh of relief as he closed the book and re-shelved it.

The key explains the part about taking care where I leave things, but what does "flirt not with temptation" mean?

Mermin had recovered from the shock of the news and a grin filled his entire face as he embraced the King in congratulations.

"I'm so happy for you both! And I'm so pwoud of my bwother!"

"You should be, old friend, for he's made much of this possible."

Mermin gave Andy a hug, then joked, "Pwince Andwew, huh?"

Andy raised his hand and batted the comment away while laughing. "That's what Father says, but you can still call me Andy."

The King gave Andy a wink.

Dinner became a riotous affair after the King announced the news, and normal decorum evaporated as all in the dining hall celebrated. Alden and Hannah rushed over and mauled Andy, thrilled.

"You thought he might be your grandfather, but your father?" Alden burst. "That's awesome!"

Marta's enveloping hug, Hans's firm squeeze, Cadfael's bear hug, Ox's pummeling, and manhandling by other well-wishers left Andy sore but in high spirits.

"Hey, we've got an Oscray match to win tonight with Prince Andrew!" Ox yelled above the din after everyone had eaten their fill.

With that, strong hands propelled Andy forward, down the hall, and out the back door of the castle. The throng emerged into the orange-streaked haze of tiring sunlight and the stench of cow farts. Someone thrust a set of nose plugs into Andy's hand as the crowd whisked him on toward the egg-shaped playing field.

News of Andy's identity had spread quickly, for he noticed several signs celebrating Oomaldee's new heir scattered throughout the stands, even among the opposing cavalry fans. He wasn't sure what to think. The blue-clad fans of the castle staff chanted:

No need to make do,
Cavalry can't outdo,
Castle staff will subdue,
Since we have Prince Andrew!

When Andy reached his teammates at the edge of the field, Alden grinned and shouted over the noise, "No pressure!". With all the commotion, Andy hadn't had the opportunity to change into his Oscray uniform, but no one seemed to care. Andy greeted Emmadank, the giantess, and Gwinny, the vulture-woman, who both gave him warm hugs.

Cadfael pulled Andy aside and said, "Come see me tomorrow. I've got something for you."

Merk, adorned in his royal blue tunic and leggings, ran up to Andy and head-butted his full stomach, nearly knocking the wind and his dinner out of him. He left a blue mark on Andy's black T-shirt. "Great seeing ya!" he roared.

"Thanks," Andy managed to cough.

"Thought I'd dress for the occasion!" Merk informed. From his balding head to his hairy feet, the dwarf had colored himself royal blue. Around his neck he wore a noisemaker.

All he needs is a white hat and he'd look like a Smurf, Andy thought.

Hans walked up and greeted, "Welcome back, Prince Andrew." He smiled and Andy laughed. The healer's tone turned serious. "That must mean a lot to you. I know how much you love the King." Words escaped Andy, so he just nodded.

"And speaking of the King," Hans added.

The King waltzed over to the castle staff team with Mermin in tow. "You've got your ace sponger back! That ought to make you feel good. Good luck tonight!"

"It sure does," Ox cut in, arriving just in time to start the match.

The King and Mermin climbed into an elevated spectator box not far downfield. *Cool, they're on the sidelines now!*

"If everyone would move off the field, we can start tonight's match," came a familiar voice. Andy looked up to the castle porch and saw Hannah holding the cone she always used to amplify her voice as she announced the proceedings. Next to her stood Razen, straight-faced, unmoved by the goings on.

Both teams walked out to meet Max, one of three referees, in the middle of the field for the coin toss.

"Max, Henry, and Oscar still have their jobs as refs, huh?" Andy remarked to Alden.

"Yeah, they haven't made too many controversial calls lately." Alden smiled. "Impartial gold weavers, gotta love 'em."

Max addressed Ox, refocusing Andy's attention. "Since you lost the last match, which side of the coin will you call, king or castle?"

"Castle," Ox replied.

Max tossed the coin up and it flipped several times before coming to rest on the ground with the image of the King's face up.

"Cavalry wins the toss," announced Max.

Hannah echoed the result over the crowd, producing a cheer and mad flag waving from the bright green throng of cavalry fans.

"So much for having Prince Andrew to help you!" whooped one cavalry fan.

Andy laughed and headed for the sidelines with the rest of the team.

"And it looks like Private Boingderban will be throwing the lurk to start the first game," commentated Hannah, causing raucous hooting to erupt from the green side of the field.

The private waddle-ran with the wobbly white lurk lofted to shoulder height, releasing it just before crossing the fallow line. *Looks good. He didn't cross into the egg white,* Andy translated in his head. It stirred up dust as it bounced erratically, finally wobbling to a stop nearly in the center of the flump. Again, a roar went up from fans on the green side of the field.

"Well done, Private!" Hannah complimented.

"Cadfael and I will throw the bumpers," Ox announced to the team on the sideline.

Ox, Cadfael, and the two cavalry players lined up on the edge of the field, each wielding a blue sphere the size of a medicine ball. At Oscar's whistle, the four players rushed the flump. *Before the egg yolk! Release it before the egg yolk!* Andy urged silently.

Ox and Cadfael made spectacular throws, both landing close to the lurk on the cavalry side of the field. The cavalry throws were less spectacular, landing short and nearly kissing Ox and Cadfael's bumpers.

"Yeah, we've got Prince Andrew alright!" a blue-clad fan shouted. The comment was deflected by boos from fans violently waving green flags. Andy glanced over and saw the King jumping about, cheering wildly. *He really gets into this!*

"No flags. All bumper throws are good!" Hannah informed the crowd.

Ox returned to the sidelines and appointed Andy, Hans, Emmadank, and Gwinny to throw the first round of spongs. Alden gave Andy a fist bump as he grabbed a green spong the size of a soccer ball. Cavalry team played with the red spongs tonight.

Because of the positioning of the bumpers, the eight spongers, four from each team, crowded on the castle staff side of the field. Andy jostled shoulders with two burly bird-men, one on either side. He noticed his teammates not getting the same attention.

Out of the corner of his eye, Andy saw Merk approach. His small stature didn't betray his speed, for quick as lightning, he snuck up behind one of the overly aggressive bird-men and relieved him of his leggings. *He just pantsed him! Or did he just legging him?* The guy's ferocity melted instantly with his clothing now laying around his ankles. Andy burst out laughing. In the ensuing chaos, Merk proceeded to do the same to the other three cavalry players, much to the crowd's delight or horror, depending on which side you rooted for. Merk finished his prank just as Henry blew the whistle.

At the sound, all motion around Andy slowed and he shot forward, launching his spong ahead of the others. As soon as he'd released it, action resumed its normal pace and he heard the cavalry players roar in outrage, attempting to restore their modesty. Merk rolled on the ground, laughing uncontrollably.

Andy's ball barely missed disqualification as it rolled to a gentle stop within an inch of the lurk, while the other three green spongs halted not far away. The cavalry players threw wildly after the distraction, and all four of their red spongs landed well out of contention.

It was a no-brainer, and Hannah didn't wait for confirmation before proclaiming, "And the first point goes to castle staff!" sending the wave through the fans in blue. Andy caught the King and Mermin awkwardly participating and cracked up.

And the chant resumed:

No need to make do,
Cavalry can't outdo,

Castle staff will subdue,
Since we have Prince Andrew!

The refs cleared the field and Ox appointed Hans to throw the lurk, which he did, landing it on the castle staff side of the flump.

"Nice throw, Hans!" Hannah broadcast.

Emmadank and Merk lined up on the opposite side of the field from two cavalry players to throw the blue bumper balls. At the whistle, they ran through the fallow to the edge of the flump and heaved the heavy spheres.

"Oh, there's a flag!" Hannah intoned.

Max strode to one of the bumpers thrown by the cavalry team and removed it from the field, at which boos resounded from the green-clad fans.

Andy, Hans, Alden, and Cadfael took their positions near the edge of the fallow on the castle staff side of the field. The cavalry players remained on their side this time based on where the bumpers had settled, but Andy noticed three of the bird-men stared at him rather than at the lurk. *Oh boy.*

The whistle sounded and Andy got his spong away quicker than the rest thanks to everything shifting to slow motion. As he anticipated, no sooner had he released his ball than he glimpsed three red spheres hurtling toward him. He ducked as they collided above his head, ricocheting.

"Look out!" Andy yelled, alerting his teammates.

A chorus of boos filled the air from the castle staff side, but none of the refs threw a flag.

"Refs! Did you not see that?" Hannah scolded.

"It's not against the rules," Max defended from the middle of the field.

"Point goes to castle staff. The score stands at two-zip, castle staff."

Play continued and castle staff took the first game seven-zip, shutting out the cavalry team.

To say the bird-men of the cavalry team were upset at this result would be an understatement, and they intensified their intimidation tactics during the second game. But Merk frustrated them further when he blew a noisemaker loudly behind two of their players during the fourth point, causing their throws to career off course into the cavalry fans.

The green-clad team growled ferociously as Andy, Alden, Hans, and Ox took their positions close together outside the fallow, with the score standing at four-one.

If looks could kill, I'd be dead, Andy thought after surveying his opponents. Their two best throwers locked eyes with him from across the field. *I better duck quick.*

Max blew his whistle and Andy aimed his green spong precisely, as motion around him slowed. No sooner had he released it than things resumed their normal pace. But this time a translucent tail streamed from Andy's spong as it raced toward its target. The tail slowed and swirled in place, forming a ball twelve to fifteen inches in diameter, just as he had seen a few hours earlier in Razen's office. Andy froze as his mom's voice posed the same question: "What would you give to save me while still breaking the curse?"

Andy felt the crushing impact of two spongs smash into his face and he fell to the ground, blood gushing from his nose. A collective gasp rose from the crowd and a woman screamed, "It's the prince, you fools! How could you?"

"Andy!" Hannah howled from her perch on the castle porch.

Andy grabbed his face, writhing in agony.

Hans arrived in seconds, narrowly beating the King and Mermin to Andy's side. The rest of the team quickly surrounded them as Hans pried Andy's hands away and removed his nose plugs to inspect the damage.

"It's broken," Hans reported. "Let's get him inside so I can stop the bleeding and set it."

While he didn't want to, Andy couldn't help but cry at the intensity of the pain. He felt Father's comforting hand on his back and heard his reassuring words as he stumbled into the castle.

An hour later, Andy lay in bed with his head elevated, drifting in and out. A cloth hung out of each nostril. Hans had restored his nose to its former shape and the bleeding had nearly stopped, but the flesh around both his eyes shone black from the ordeal.

"Nose injuries always look worse than they are because of all the blood," Hans reported to the King, who hadn't left his side throughout his treatment. "He's lost a lot of blood, so he'll probably be lightheaded, but he'll be fine in a couple days."

"So this is what it's like to be a parent," Andy heard the King say to Mermin just before he drifted off to sleep.

Andy woke to the sound of a rooster crowing. The King slept on top of the covers to his left, balled up in a fetal position; it looked like he'd gotten cold while keeping vigil. Andy attempted to sit up to cover him, but his head forbid it, stabbing his brain with sharp pains. "Oh, ouch," he moaned.

Father roused and slowly sat up, rubbing his eyes. "How are you feeling, Son?"

"That sounds good," Andy replied, grinning.

"I can definitely get used to it," Father smiled back.

A quiet knock came and the King instructed, "Come in."

Alden, Hannah, and Marta slowly peered around the door. "Is Andy ready for visitors?"

"I think so," the King replied.

"Hans told everyone Andy would be okay in a couple days," Marta reported. "What a relief."

"You've got two black eyes!" Alden exclaimed.

"Alden!" Marta scolded.

"What? He does."

"I can see that, but you don't need to announce it to the world! Haven't I taught you better than that?"

Alden cowered and the King laughed, adding, "I've much to learn about being a parent."

"Well, I'm obviously not a good teacher," Marta joked.

"How are you feeling, Andy?" Hannah interrupted.

"My head still hurts a lot, but I'm actually getting hungry."

"Hannah, let's you and me go get the five of us some breakfast. We'll bring it up here," Marta suggested.

"Thanks for your kindness, Marta, but I must attend to a few things. Why don't the four of you enjoy breakfast together," the King suggested.

"I'll be back to check on you in a bit, Son," the King remarked.

At this, he followed Marta and Hannah out into the hall.

"That must feel good, having the King call you *son*," Alden commented as soon as the door shut.

"Yeah, it does."

"I saved you the spong that landed you here," Alden informed, nodding toward the green ball resting in the chair next to Andy's wardrobe.

"Thanks. What a nice souvenir to remember my broken nose." Andy smiled.

"What happened to you out there on the field yesterday? You froze."

Andy struggled to reflect, but his memory started coming clear as he thought about the events leading up to the incident. "I remember throwing my spong… Oh yeah! Remember what happened in Razen's office yesterday?"

Alden nodded.

Andy described what he'd seen, but this time he included what the voice that sounded like his mom said. "You can't tell anyone. Not even Hannah. She doesn't know I'm supposed to be breaking the curse."

"I understand. Boy, I don't know what I'd do if it was my mom's life on the line. You can mess with me, but not my mom."

"Exactly."

"If it comes back, what are you gonna tell it?"

"I don't know. When I put the venom vial in the invisible book, it told me not to flirt with temptation. I assume it's referring to this. But it's my mom we're talking about. I'd give just about anything to save her."

"What would you give to save me while still breaking the curse?" Andy's mom's voice questioned once again as a translucent sphere formed from swirling vapor rising out of the souvenir spong.

"Alden, it's here again!" Andy exclaimed. This time, however, he had a question of his own: "What would you have me give?"

Before the swirling vapor could respond, Marta and Hannah returned bearing a wide assortment of breakfast goodies.

The sphere evaporated.

CHAPTER SEVEN

Golden Goose Egg

A ndy pondered the sphere's question for the better part of the afternoon between visits from Father, Mermin, Alden, and Hannah. *What would I give?* he kept asking himself. When he thought about giving anything less than his life, he felt guilty. *Surely she's worth more than things, but am I willing to give my very life to save Mom? I don't want to die!* Andy's struggle went on with no resolution. His inneru remained quiet, seemingly content to let him puzzle this out for himself.

Hans stopped by to check on his patient in the late afternoon. Andy's headache had disappeared, and except for two black eyes, a bulbous nose, and a conflicted mind, he felt much better. After a thorough examination, Hans declared, "Looks like you're on the mend. Your nose will be sore for a few days yet, so take it easy."

"Hans, what does horn of karkadann do?"

"In its powder form, it's powerful in counteracting poison. Why do you ask?"

"Do you keep track of how much you have?"

"Of course, Andy. It's very expensive."

"Have you had any shortages of ground horn of karkadann?"

"No. I keep it locked away. I'd know if any of it went missing, I can assure you. Why all the questions about horn of karkadann?"

"I'd rather not say just yet."

Hans laughed. "All right, suit yourself. I'll let you know if I find any missing," he promised as the door closed behind him.

Andy ventured out to see Cadfael in the foundry of the Cavalry Training Center later that afternoon. He heard the distinctive ringing of hammers on metal and saw a dozen men working at benches.

"Andy!" Cadfael welcomed, wiping his hands on a nearby rag. "I'm glad you're feeling better. Nice shiners you got there." He chuckled.

"Thanks, I guess." Andy smiled, then added, "At the game yesterday, you told me to come see you."

"That I did. I have something for you."

He walked to a metal chest sitting against the wall, lifted the top, and gently pulled out a bundle wrapped in burlap. He brought it over to the table he'd been working at and cleared a spot.

"Hannah told me everything that happened getting back from Sometimes Island. She said you threw every weapon available at those vulture-guys to fend them off and save her. I'm most grateful. And so I made you new weapons."

He removed the wrappings and stepped aside, inviting Andy to inspect a shiny new dagger and a practice sword with an intricately carved handle.

"They're beautiful, Cadfael! Thank you!"

"Least I could do. I tried to balance them for your size."

Andy assumed his ready position and took a practice swing with the wooden sword.

"It feels great!"

"You'll be needing to learn how to use the dagger, I reckon. I've been teaching Alden and Hannah. Why don't you come first thing in the morning and I'll give you a private lesson."

"Thanks! I appreciate it." He stowed the dagger in the holster of the belt he'd taken to wearing.

"I need to practice with my sword, too." He almost added, *It doesn't extend at home*, but thought better of it lest he raise questions he wasn't prepared to answer.

"We can exercise your sword fighting skills as well." He paused and Andy could see he had more he wanted to add. "Say, Andy, my wife and I have been talking. I don't know where you're from or why you seem to come and go so suddenly, but that doesn't matter."

Andy shifted, trying to understand where he was going with the conversation.

"You first came on Curse Day a couple years back, and now we find you are the son of the King. I've lived in Oomaldee my whole life, and so has my wife. We've seen Abaddon make trouble before. He usually attacks and then runs, but not this time. Turning citizens into vulture-people is a new twist." He sighed. "We're worried, Andy. The problem feels bigger—darker—than ever before. We have a bad feeling things are going to get a lot worse before they get better. I'm not sure how you fit into the picture exactly, but we want to help you in whatever way we can. This will be your kingdom one day, and we want to make sure there's one here for you to rule."

The frankness and reality of Cadfael's speech left Andy with a cold prickly feeling in the pit of his stomach. "Thank you, I appreciate that."

"Daddy! Daddy! Mama wants you to come for dinner!"

Cadfael chuckled, swooping down and picking up a small, energetic bundle of boy with blond hair and a beaming smile who had come barreling into the foundry unannounced. He looked exactly like Hannah but smaller.

"Andy, I'd like you to meet my son, Rohin. We call him Ro for short."

"Well hello, Ro!" Andy grinned. He knew Hannah had three younger siblings, but he'd never met them or her mom.

"Ro, tell Prince Andrew how old you are," Cadfael encouraged.

Ro made a fist and studied it intently as he slowly raised three fingers. "I'm three," the boy announced, thrusting out his hand for Andy to see.

"Well done, Son!" Cadfael cheered.

Andy joined in, chuckling. "Good job, Ro. It's great meeting you."

"Guess we better get moving before my wife sends the whole family to round me up," Cadfael added.

At the conclusion of an uneventful dinner, Hans caught Andy on the stairs as he headed to his quarters for an early bedtime. He kept yawning throughout the meal and Father insisted he get more rest. He wasn't sure he liked the situation. On his own, he'd been responsible for making choices about his bedtime, but no longer, it seemed. Yet he knew Father meant well.

"Andy, wait up," Hans called.

"Oh! Hi, Hans."

"After our conversation I went and checked my supply of ground horn of karkadann. It's short by a jigger."

"A what?"

"A jigger of ground horn is equivalent to a measure of unground horn."

"A measure?" Andy cut in, clarifying. "And I bet you were also missing a couple gnut weed thistles, some dried Thriae, and a few hairs from a Kitsune."

Hans jerked his head back and stared at Andy. "How did you know?"

Andy tapped his index finger against his lips and whispered, "Let's talk in my room."

After closing the door, Andy shared, "I have reason to believe Razen is trying to help cure Abaddon from the wounds my sword inflicted."

"Aiding the enemy? That's a very serious accusation," Hans objected.

"Which is why I haven't told anyone. Only Alden and Hannah know."

Andy told Hans what they'd found in Razen's office, including the recipe he'd memorized, to which the healer objected, "The King trusts him completely. How do you know he's not curing a festering wound of his own? Do you have proof?"

"No, I just know."

Hans raised an eyebrow. "Whoa, whoa, whoa. Stop right there. As you know, I don't completely trust Razen, but I'm not about to go accusing him of helping the enemy, especially not without proof. Your father finds no fault in him, and I will rely on my King's judgment. I suggest you keep this quiet unless you want to get yourself into a heap of trouble." The healer added a frown to emphasize his point.

Andy slowly nodded.

"On a brighter note, I will say that recipe'll definitely cure a serious wound. I've never seen any poison resist the force of horn of karkadann."

Great, so Abaddon will be cured. Then what? He didn't want to think about it, not after seeing the seven-headed monster turn citizens into vulture-people…or worse.

Andy didn't have long to wait to test his suspicions. After dressing for bed, his dreams came quickly, leading him back to Abaddon's dark castle. He stood before the menacing structure staring at three black statues just outside the ominous doors.

Two more than before, he thought.

Within minutes of arriving, Andy caught sight of a large vulture landing nearby. It transformed into a man, but not just any man. A man he despised. Razen quickly grabbed clothes out of a travel bag and dressed. He took a deep breath and then calmly waddled up the steps and into the castle, never noticing Andy.

Andy followed a few yards back. More black statues stood around the perimeter of the courtyard they passed through. Andy shivered as he did every time he saw the place. Razen showed no emotion but continued forward at as brisk a pace as waddling can take one, slowing only as he approached the dais that King Abaddon's elaborately bedecked chair stood upon.

"My liege," Razen pacified, bowing.

Abaddon sat slumped on his throne once again, listless. He motioned for Razen to approach. "This better work," he growled.

"I've done much research and believe this serum has the greatest chance for success. It seems the sword poisoned your system, making transforming into any other being impossible. This concoction will neutralize the poison."

"Spare me the details," two of Abaddon's heads replied in stereo. "Cure me."

"I'll need a kettle and flame, my liege." Razen pulled out two containers from his bag as he spoke.

"Use the fire over there," a vulture-warrior instructed, pointing.

"Very well. It will take twelve hours."

"Then get on with it," came the dragon's terse reply after which three of the heads drooped to seat level.

Another vulture-man lugged a black kettle over to Razen who busied himself organizing the other containers he'd brought, chopping and crushing ingredients at a table before the hearth.

Andy found a comfortable place to sit and wait, leaning against a pillar near the middle of the room.

Every so often, Abaddon let out a moan and his heads drifted erratically.

I'd love to kill him, Andy thought. Sadly, he knew dreams wouldn't permit it.

Andy found himself nodding off as he waited. *How can I nod off in a dream?* he wondered each time he caught himself dozing. *Time sure doesn't move the same in dreams,* he realized when, after a long and monotonous wait, Razen declared, "It's ready, my liege." *That couldn't have been twelve hours.* The bird-man poured the contents of the kettle into a tankard and handed it to a servant who shuttled it to the sickly creature.

The seven-headed beast greedily drank the potion with one mouth and with two others demanded, "How long will it take to work?"

"Under the circumstances, I am not sure, my liege. I would hope quickly."

"You would hope. You would hope," Abaddon mocked. "If it doesn't work, you will bring me that stone with its loyalties switched!"

Razen bowed. "Yes, my liege." His expression betrayed no emotion.

After a long while, the beast grew impatient and Razen's expression was grim.

Finally, Razen broke the tension by concluding, "If it was going to work it would have done so by now, my liege."

"I knew it!" the beast fumed in its weakened condition.

"My liege, we knew your case is special. No one has attempted to neutralize wounds from the sword Methuselah."

"I've heard enough! Bring me energy!"

Immediately, four vulture-warriors shoved a line of twelve bound men, women, and children toward the throne.

"No!" Andy shouted, waking himself.

Foggy sun shone through the window and Andy knew he'd slept late. He dressed and made his way down to breakfast.

"Good to see you, Son!" the King boomed, standing up from his chair at the head of the long communal table and giving Andy a hug. Andy reveled in the closeness and then surveyed the table. It looked as though the King had finished his meal.

"Good morning, Father. Did Razen taste your breakfast?" Andy questioned abruptly.

The King laughed. "As a matter of fact, he did not. I haven't seen him yet today. He's probably attending to castle operations. Why?"

"Uh, no reason. Just curious."

The King grinned, amused. "How are you feeling today? Your face is looking closer to its former shape."

"Better, thanks."

"I've got a meeting with my war council early this afternoon. I'd like you to attend."

"Really?" *Cool!*

"You're going to be ruling this kingdom one day. You need to learn battle strategy."

Andy nodded but thought, *What will happen to Mom and Dad?*

The King and Andy chatted a bit more while Andy ate his breakfast, then they scattered to their respective morning activities. For Andy, this meant a private lesson with Cadfael.

Andy approached the Cavalry Training Center and was about to heave open one of the heavy doors when he heard a familiar voice close by calling his name.

"Andy! Can you come help?"

He looked around and spotted Merk madly waving an arm, motioning for him to come. Merk had pulled the leather pouch of a giant slingshot back all the way.

"I forgot to move something out of the way. Can you hold this while I do?" asked the eccentric gnome.

"Sure."

"Be careful. Don't let it slip. I'll be in the line of fire."

I wonder why he doesn't just let it loose and then go move whatever it is? The thought flitted through Andy's mind, but he immediately dismissed it, rationalizing, *I'm sure he wouldn't have asked me to help if he could have done that.*

"Got it?"

Andy nodded, straining to hold back the tension.

Merk disappeared into the fog.

"Still got it?" Merk confirmed a second later from within the white cloud.

"Yeah."

Andy's muscles strained after holding it for more than a minute.

"You almost done?" Andy called a minute later.

No reply.

Beads of sweat sprouted from Andy's brow and his arms began to shake.

Three or four minutes later he again called, "Merk, are you almost done? My arms are giving out."

Silence. Then chuckling erupted from behind him.

"He got you good! Better you than us for once!"

Andy couldn't turn and hold the slingshot.

"Merk's inside having a cup of coffee."

Hearing this, Andy immediately understood he'd been had. He let go of the leather pouch and the projectile flew as he fell to the ground, arms exhausted.

Andy had seen Henkel and Medrick a year ago. The dwarfs directed construction of the large weapon systems Father and Mermin invented, but he'd never met them.

"I'm Medrick." The shorter, sturdy dwarf with an impressive beard stepped forward. "You must be Prince Andrew."

Andy nodded, slowly standing.

"And I'm Henkel." The slightly taller, round dwarf introduced himself.

"It's great to meet you at last," Andy intoned. "Alden told me you don't like folks interrupting your work."

"Alden would be right, but we couldn't let this opportunity go. We're usually the brunt of Merk's attempts at humor," Henkel explained, ending with another chuckle.

"Well, we best be gettin' back to work," chimed Medrick.

"See ya," Andy bade them goodbye.

Andy entered the foundry, his original objective. The coolness surprised him until he saw smoldering coals in the forge; it slumbered yet, waiting for someone to pump air into the bellows and awaken it.

Two blond-haired little girls took instruction from a woman dressed in a blue dress with matching headscarf. "Charis, put that pile of rags on the workbench over there." The woman pointed across the large room. "And Larissa, bring your pile here, please."

"Andy!" boomed Cadfael. "Good morning."

Andy walked toward his instructor.

"I'd like you to meet my wife, Lucee, and these are my daughters, Charis and Larissa."

"Pleased to meet you, ma'am." Andy bowed his head as the three ladies curtsied.

"Charis is seven and Larissa is five," Cadfael added proudly.

"Come here, Ro," Lucee called. "That's right, bring your rag here."

Ro bounded over with a big grin plastered across his face. He dragged a now-dirty rag behind him. When he reached the adults, he stood on tippy toes and handed it to his father.

"Good boy!"

"Lucee works in the laundry," Cadfael informed.

"That's right! Hannah mentioned that," Andy replied, remembering.

"My husband's told me all about you," Lucee added, rubbing her husband's muscular arm.

"Nothing too bad, I hope," Andy joked.

"On the contrary, he goes on and on about your Oscray skills."

Andy felt his face warm.

"Speaking of skills," Cadfael interrupted after clearing his throat, "I'm giving Andy a private lesson. I'm teaching him the fundamentals of fighting with a dagger. Never know when you'll need to know."

"Well then, we best be on our way and let you men get to training," Lucee concluded with a wink.

"Come children!" she commanded, and away the troop went.

As soon as they left, Cadfael turned to Andy and said, "You ready to learn how to fight with your dagger?"

"Yes, sir!"

"Let's head outside so we have more room to move."

As they did, Cadfael chatted. "Alden told me the two of you learned your sword fighting skills from some talented knights."

Andy grinned. "Yes, that's right."

"Fighting with a dagger builds on what you've learned already. What I'll teach you about fighting with your dagger assumes you don't have use of your sword for some reason. Never use your dagger before your sword. You always want to be as far away from your opponent as possible."

"Sounds good to me!"

"So, if you must engage in a fight with your dagger, I want you first to understand you *will* get cut."

"Really?"

"Really. You need to expect it, so that when it happens you don't freeze. You never win a dagger fight, you only survive one."

"Oh."

"Pull out your dagger."

Andy did so and assumed a ready position.

"This may sound obvious, but always keep your knife between you and your opponent. No need to wave it around or do anything fancy with it. Keep your moves simple."

Andy nodded.

"The hand that holds the knife I'll call your knife hand. The other hand I'll call your shield hand. Keep your shield hand in a position that protects your throat and chest. Better to have an opponent injure your shield arm than your chest. Show me."

Andy looked down at his left arm, then slowly raised it to heart level.

"Always keep your eyes on your opponent. Never look down or anywhere else."

Cadfael lurched forward, slicing Andy in the neck with the side of his rigid open hand. Andy stumbled back two steps, grabbing for his neck.

"You'd have been dead."

Andy had learned from the knights to not give an excuse for failing to do something but to remain silent and learn from the mistake.

Andy nodded and got back into his ready position, dagger in hand, staring at Cadfael as he raised his shield hand to chest height.

"With your knife, you should focus on defending yourself, not attacking like I just did. Assuming your opponent is experienced, he'll probably be proficient at blocking your attacks and shielding himself, so you won't be able to severely injure him. Focus on disarming him. Without a weapon, your adversary will have fewer ways to hurt you."

"Understood," acknowledged Andy.

"To disarm, go after one of two places on your attacker's knife arm: the forearm or upper arm, either one. If you injure the forearm, your opponent will drop his knife. If you injure the upper arm, you'll restrict how far he can move his blade toward you."

Andy nodded.

"As with sword fighting, let your opponent make the first move. He will leave himself open to a defensive strike from you. Your opponent has only two options for attacking you: from above, bringing his dagger down, or from below, bringing his weapon up, like this."

Cadfael demonstrated both possibilities. "Let's work on defending against the downward strike this morning and we'll do the upward strike tomorrow. So, for the downward strike, one effective technique to block it is crossing your forearms into an X as your enemy brings his dagger down. Your shield arm should be on the bottom, knife arm on top. Your enemy's knife should end up in the V between your arms. Try it."

Cadfael came at Andy several times until Andy got the hang of the move. Finally satisfied, Cadfael continued, "Okay, from that position, step to the side to deflect your enemy's momentum so his back is now toward you. At the same time, still in the V, bring your knife hand down, trapping your adversary's hand behind his knife. He can't get away unless he drops his weapon. Continue your momentum, pushing your enemy to the ground with your shoulder. Try it."

Again Andy imitated the moves. "Excellent!" he exclaimed a few tries later.

"You're getting the hang of it, Andy. Well done," Cadfael praised, wiping sweat from his brow. "Practice with Alden and Hannah today. We'll pick up there tomorrow morning, same time. For now, I need to get to work."

"Great! Thanks, Cadfael!"

Andy entered the back door of the castle looking for Alden. Wherever his best friend was, Hannah couldn't be far away, at least not these days. The smell of freshly baked chocolate chip cookies assaulted his nose as he reached the kitchens and stepped inside. Immediately, he saw the backs of nearly all the staff crowding around, arms raised, staring at the open window on the far wall. Ox wielded a cast-iron skillet above his head, preparing to strike as he crept forward.

"Don't hit it. What'd it do to you?" Gwinny exclaimed.

"Just shoo it out, Ox," Marta instructed.

Andy stood on tiptoe but still couldn't see over the adults. He grabbed a stool and approached. Placing it behind a shorter staff member, he climbed on top. As soon as he did, chaos broke lose. A bright flash of gold shot from the window toward him, accompanied by a honking sound. Ox swung but missed. Seconds later, the flash struck Andy, knocking him off his perch and onto the floor. He landed on his back and the gold flash landed on top of his chest, honking to exaggerate its point. Andy scrambled up, trying to get away, but a golden goose flapped and nipped at his feet despite his efforts to shoo it off.

Ox and the staff stopped pursuing and roared at the sight.

"It likes you, Andy!" exclaimed Gwinny.

Andy finally stopped swatting at the bird when it became clear it planned to stay. It honked several more times and Andy questioned, "What am I supposed to do with it?"

"No idea, but it looks like you've got yourself a friend, and a stunning one at that. Silly thing landed on the windowsill a few minutes ago and wouldn't leave," Marta indicated.

"This'll be interesting watching you play Oscray at week's end with that thing following you!" Ox added, leading a chorus of cackling from the rest of the kitchen staff.

Andy forced a smile, not looking forward to the challenge. The goose lay down on his feet but remained alert, scanning the group for movement.

"Well, look at that," Gwinny added.

Andy eased it off his feet and it reluctantly stood, but a golden egg now rested between Andy's sneakers. *Really?*

The goose looked up at Andy as if inviting him to investigate. As he reached down to pick it up, the goose hissed. He quickly backed off, much to everyone's amusement.

"Fine, then I won't pick it up."

The bird took a step toward its egg and drove its beak into the shell.

"Whoa!" several people gasped.

The egg split open, but instead of a yolk, Andy saw a folded piece of parchment. The goose stepped back, as if inviting him to investigate. Warily, he reached down and snatched the paper before the goose could connect its beak with his hand.

"How'd that get inside an egg?" Andy questioned, voicing what everyone else wondered.

He unfolded the paper and saw it was addressed to him:

To Prince Andrew, He Who Must Heed the Deliverer.

No kidding! Didn't have much choice, did I? he thought. What was that story about the goose that laid the golden egg? I can't remember.

"It's a note to me," he announced to the staff. Looks like it might be the next clue to break the curse.

"Mighty fancy messenger service!" Ox kidded. "It's definitely a step up from the pigeon post. Guess this is what happens when you're royalty!"

The group chuckled.

"Does anyone know where my father or Mermin is?"

"I saw the King heading up to the laboratory earlier," Marta reported.

Andy moved toward the doorway, trying to avoid tripping over the bird. But the goose took three running steps in the opposite direction, launched itself into the air over the heads of onlookers, and headed back out the window.

"So much for your new friend. And so pretty, too," Gwinny lamented.

Andy grabbed a handful of cookies as he'd originally planned, waved his thanks, and headed upstairs.

CHAPTER EIGHT

The Whisper Stream

Andy found Father and Mermin in the laboratory.

"Look what I just got!" Andy announced after knocking and entering.

The King smiled. "Is that what I think it is?"

Andy nodded. "You'll never guess how it arrived." He then recounted the events in the kitchens, causing the King and Mermin to chortle.

"So, what's it say?" Father finally asked.

"Before I read it, Mermin, do you remember the story from my world about the goose that laid the golden egg?"

"No, but we can look it up. Why?"

"Because the message is addressed to me, but it says I need to heed the messenger. I can't remember what that fairy tale's about."

"Let's go to my libwary and see," Mermin suggested.

Once there, Mermin headed to a section against the far wall of the large room. He slid a ladder over and climbed three rungs, stopping at several short, colorful books. He ran a finger along the shelf and mumbled titles to himself until he located his prize.

"*Faiwy Tales and Fables: A Pwimer,*" he announced, rejoining Andy and the King.

The King grinned. "I honestly don't know how you remember where everything's filed, Mermin."

"Thank you, sir," the wizard beamed. He opened the book and scanned the contents. "Here we are, chapter seven: 'The Goose That Laid the Golden Egg.'"

He handed it to Andy to read:

A cottager and his wife had a hen that laid a
golden egg every day. After receiving this gift for
some time, they questioned and supposed the
hen must contain a great lump of gold inside it.
To get the gold they decided they must kill the
hen. Having done so, they found to their surprise
that the hen differed in no respect from their
other hens. The foolish pair, in hoping to become
rich all at once, deprived themselves of the
wealth they had been assured of day by day.

Lesson: Greed loses all by striving to gain all.

"Does that mean anything to you, Andy?" the King asked.

Andy thought, but nothing came immediately to mind. "No… Is it saying I'm being greedy?"

"That's what I would understand, Son. Why don't you think on it. Something will come, it always does."

Andy nodded, frowning.

"Now then, what does the rest of the note say?" Father asked.

"I haven't read it yet. I thought I'd wait and we could read it together." Andy unfolded the note and began:

> You've two ingredients of the cure,
> The curse's ending to ensure.
> Much learning you've endured

And with it have matured.

Now the third you must pursue,
Noble, honorable, and true,
Pure of heart, full of splendor and grace
Horn of a unicorn embrace.

A young maiden's help you will need,
With the unicorn to plead.
Though unworthy, its spire bestow,
The chains of fog to overthrow.

"Sounds like Hannah will be joining us this time," remarked the King.

"Joining *us?*" asked Andy with some surprise.

"Of course, Andy. Now that I can travel, you don't think I'd leave you and Alden to face the dangers of such a quest by yourselves, do you?"

Andy smiled. "I hadn't thought about it, but having you along sounds good to me. In fact, it's more than good. It's great!"

The King raised an eyebrow and winked at Mermin.

"I hope Cadfael doesn't mind us borrowing his daughter. She went and rescued the two of you without permission the last time. I'm just glad it all ended well," the King added.

"Cadfael gave me a lesson in dagger fighting this morning, and he mentioned he'd help defeat Abaddon in any way possible."

"We'll see if that includes his eldest daughter," the King cautioned.

"No offense to Hannah, but why do you suppose it says we need the help of a young maiden?" Andy inquired.

"Because unicorns are the embodiment of honor and puwity," Mermin explained. "They will only allow humans who are closest to that ideal to come near. It is said only young ladies who display puwity may look upon or touch this magnificent animal."

"But that's not fair," Andy protested.

The wizard chuckled. "Andy, it doesn't matter if you think it's fair. You won't be getting anywhere near that beautiful animal. Neither will I or your father. We are unworthy, for men shed blood in battle."

Andy bristled. "But Hannah's killed vulture-guys before."

"Yes, out of self-defense, not aggwession."

"I'd love to see a unicorn too," the King interrupted, "but we men must accept we aren't going to retrieve that horn. It will be Hannah, assuming Cadfael approves."

Andy remained unmoved.

"Life isn't fair, as you know. Even when we want to do something, sometimes we can't. Remember I told you that after the flood you caused?"

Andy nodded, remembering.

"Do you think it was easy for me to watch you and Alden retrieve the dragon scale on your own? No. Do you think I felt it fair that two young boys were put in harm's way to break a curse I caused? Never. It should have been me out there. With every fiber of my being I wanted to join you, but I had to accept that it was not my part to play. And…I had to be okay with it."

"The 'being okay with it' is the hard part," Andy commented, pacified only a little.

"Yes, no matter our age," replied the King, smiling.

"Where do we find unicorns?" Andy inquired without missing a beat.

The King gave the wizard a meaningful look, then invited, "Ideas?"

Mermin shook his head. "Unicorns have been spotted in fowested aweas of the land fwom time to time, but to my knowledge, they don't live here. They are mystewious cweatures, coming and going as they please."

"Where do they go?"

"No one knows, Andy. It is uncommon to find unicorn hoof pwints as they twead lightly. I've only heard of sightings in marshy land. It's impossible to twack them."

"So are we supposed to wander the forests and marshes until we find one? That'll take forever," Andy chafed.

"What else do you know about unicorns, Mermin," the King redirected.

"They are gentle and docile cweatures that live hundweds of years."

"Anything else?" the King encouraged.

"The horn of the unicorn is quite powerful. It's supposed to be able to cure any illness or wound instantly, no matter what caused it."

"Really?" Andy clarified.

Mermin nodded.

Then Abaddon better not get his hands on one.

"If someone takes a unicorn's horn by force, the animal will die instantly, for the act wobs it of its dignity and honor, the essence of its being."

"What happens to the horn?" Andy inquired.

"Its power disappears and it won't heal."

"Okay, but what else? What more do you know about unicorns?" the King asked, trying to keep the conversation constructive.

"It is said that if you dwink unicorn blood you will have eternal life."

"I think we've got that one handled," joked the King.

Andy laughed as well, but a thought, not yet fully formed, began to percolate in his subconscious.

"So how is Hannah supposed to get a unicorn to give us its horn willingly?"

"If a unicorn judges someone in need to be worthy, it can offer the tip of its horn and it won't die. *That* is a gweat, gweat honor." Mermin paused, savoring the thought.

Andy and the King nodded in agreement.

"So Hannah has to make a convincing argument she's in need and is worthy?"

"That's wight."

That's not going to be easy.

"But we still need a way to find them," Andy thought aloud.

"I don't know if this will help, but they are also highly intelligent animals. The oldest and wisest are telepathic and can bwoadcast their thoughts and feelings to whomever they wish."

"Really? That's it!" Andy exclaimed.

"What's it, Son?"

"They're telepathic."

"How's that going to help us?" Father questioned.

"Dragons are also telepathic, right?" Andy clarified.

Mermin nodded.

"On my way here, Daisy told me about the whisper stream. Have you heard of it?"

Mermin shook his head.

"She said it's a network that higher-level beings use to communicate telepathically. Her words, not mine."

"Exactly what type of creature constitutes a 'higher-level' being?" the King probed, one eyebrow raised.

"She said dragons, centaurs, unicorns, griffins, the sphinx, and others use it." Then, reading Father's thoughts, Andy grinned as he added, "She said humans haven't made it to that level yet."

The King chortled. "Well, maybe Daisy, in her infinite wisdom, would take pity on us poor humans and help us out. What do you think?"

Andy and Mermin nodded in sync.

"Let me call her."

Remembering Daisy told him to call her in his thoughts if he needed her, Andy thought, *Daisy.*

The three waited several minutes with no response.

"Let me try again."

Daisy! Are you there?

Yes, Andy. What do you need?

"Daisy just answered!" Andy reported, then turned inward once more. *I have a favor to ask, but it's a secret. Is it possible to tell you without anyone else finding out?*

I better come see you if it needs to remain quiet. Where are you?

At the castle.

Give me two hours and I'll meet you behind the stables where we landed that time.

Excellent! Thanks, Daisy!

At the appointed hour, Andy, the King, and Mermin stood outside the Cavalry Training Center in the arena, waiting to see Daisy materialize through the thick fog that blanketed the area. Within minutes, Andy heard the dragon announce herself in his thoughts and then land.

"Thanks for coming," Andy welcomed.

You said it needed to be kept quiet, so this is the only way I know to accomplish that. We can speak face to face without our conversation being spread to the whisper stream. So, what's your secret?

We need to locate unicorns in the land.

Why?

It's a long story, but it has to do with breaking the curse.

I see. Well, I'm not allowed to speak into the unicorn part of the whisper stream yet. I'm not old enough. But I can listen in. In fact, we can link up and you can listen to the whisper stream through me. We can at least see if there are any unicorns in the land at the moment. If we hear any, we might get lucky and figure out where they are. Would that work?

Yeah, that'd be great! Andy filled the King and Mermin in on what Daisy suggested, and the King gave a thumbs-up.

Okay, what do I do?

Bring one of your ears up to mine and press close.

Andy scanned Daisy's head; he'd never examined it closely before. Reptilian, gray skin covered her skull. Starting just behind her jowls were coordinating scales, quarter-size at first and growing progressively larger as they reached her chest. He saw two primary white horns protruding from the top of her head and noted secondary horns spiking out of her skull below that. He also noticed tertiary horns crowding her chin, cheeks and eyebrows. Nowhere did he observe ears.

Umm.

Daisy giggled. *Missing something?*

Yeah. Where are your ears?

Daisy turned the left side of her head toward Andy.

See my largest horns?

Yeah.

Down and to the right you'll see my scales separate. There's a slit right after. That's my ear.

Oh, Andy chuckled.

Now then, press your ear into mine.

Andy stepped close. She had a unique odor about her, like the grill at home after Dad finished barbecuing. Daisy's immensity gave him pause. *It's a good thing I trust you.*

The dragon smiled as Andy cuddled close. Her ear slit measured more than half the height of his head.

Ready?

Yep.

Okay, let's have a listen and figure out if unicorns are around.

Andy heard a buzzing, much like the howling of the old shortwave radio his grandpa played with from time to time, and then he heard a very deep voice say, "I have studied the stars, Cyllarus. Draco the dragon will soon overwhelm Orion the hunter. I fear for the peace of the land."

Another equally deep voice responded, 'While we must take care concerning our interpretation, I too am disquieted, Chiron. We live in uncertain times."

"What shall we do?"

"The Fates will see to the proper end of all things."

Sounds like centaurs, Daisy cut in.

What were they talking about? A dragon overwhelming a hunter? A knot formed in Andy's stomach.

Centaurs are known for seeing over many years but not necessarily the present. I wouldn't put much stock in what you just heard.

The shortwave howling sound resumed as Daisy changed the whisper stream channel.

A voice with a British accent declared, "That scoundrel, Abaddon, shall never penetrate this mine. It is our sworn duty to protect it, and protect it we shall, with our very lives!"

"But his forces are massing again, sir! Are gold and silver worth giving our lives for?" replied another.

"Captain, we are noble creatures who shall not be overcome. Fire for fire. Claw for claw. Wing for wing."

That sounds like griffins, Daisy guessed. *Griffins zealously guard gold and silver mines.*

Where are there gold and silver mines around here?

The land of Carta. That's their whole economy. I've heard Abaddon conquered that land first to fund his conquest of the rest of the lands. Fortunately for them, the griffins are fiercely loyal and have held the mines. That beast and his minions can't get at any of it.

Alden's from Carta. He's never mentioned gold and silver mines. Neither has Marta.

Andy heard shortwave buzzing again.

"The bonds between us and our human warriors are strong, but not strong enough. We face a foe of deep and ancient dark magic. You've heard the tale of our forefather being the mount of the Greek hero Bellerophon. Together they destroyed the Chimera. Our ancestor gave him great agility to dodge the Chimera's many blows, and we must be prepared to do the same in our generation."

The talk went on, but Daisy interrupted, *And that would be the pegasi.*

Really? I know they're intelligent, but I didn't realize—

They're smarter than their humans? Daisy snickered.

Humph.

Again Andy heard shortwave screeching and then a voice that squeaked and cracked: "The trees and mountains are fair to look upon in this land. And the—"

Is that the sound of something stripping leaves from a branch and eating them? Andy interrupted.

You have good ears, Andy.

"The leaves are sweet. I would like to stay here for a time."

A sage voice responded, "I sense evil growing stronger with each passing day. We shall not tarry here beyond a fortnight."

"Where shall we go, Father?" responded another higher-pitched voice.

These are unicorns, Andy!

Excellent! Oh, but they said they're not staying beyond a fortnight. Isn't that two weeks?

It is, Andy, Daisy confirmed.

We better hurry, Andy's thoughts continued. *Where are they? Can you tell?*

Listen carefully. You may learn.

Andy heard the sound of running water and then the female unicorn exclaimed, "Oh Father, what is that awful smell?"

The creature with the cracking voice snorted. "That, I believe, would be a troll, sis."

"Let's move upwind. The stench is making me nauseous."

Trolls? That's perfect! We should be able to narrow the area down a lot from that.

Is that all you need?

Yes! This has been great, Daisy. Thank you so much for doing this.

Daisy and Mermin chatted for a few minutes before the dragon took off, instantly vanishing in the thick fog.

"Well, what did you find out?" the King asked.

Andy beamed. "There are three unicorns in the land at the moment; they're up in the area with the trolls. But I heard them say they're leaving within a fortnight. The one they called *father* said he felt evil increasing every day and he wants them out of here. The other two are brother and sister, it sounded like."

Andy informed the King and Mermin of the other three conversations he'd overheard from the mythical creatures and voiced his concerns.

"This is timely information, Son. Since it won't be long until the unicorns leave, let's plan to set out for the territory of the trolls in the morning. Oh, and Andy, please be prepared to share your report at the war council meeting this afternoon."

Having no idea what to expect, Andy questioned, "Are you sure?"

CHAPTER NINE

War Council

As soon as lunch ended, Andy joined Father and Mermin in climbing the stairs to the sixth floor.

"The war council meets up here?" Andy inquired, panting.

"It does. Most of the castle staff doesn't know the room exists. I prefer to keep our war preparations as secretive as possible to avoid leaks," the King replied.

Arriving at the landing, rather than heading left toward his chambers, the King turned right and entered an alcove. Darkness enveloped the windowless area. Father faced the wall and Andy heard him depress a stone. As with the secret doors in the rest of the castle, when they opened, the sound of stone sliding across stone filled the niche. A musty odor assaulted Andy's nose and he sneezed. He couldn't immediately deduce the room's size, for it did not echo like most.

Mermin made his way around the perimeter and lit several dozen torches, causing the room to come into view. Ornate tapestries depicting knights in combat draped nearly every inch of the walls and colorful rugs blanketed the floor. Andy saw that additional fabric lined the entire ceiling. A large conference table dominated the center of the space.

"What do you think, Son?"

"I'm not sure."

"I've taken great measures to ensure sound does not travel beyond these walls."

Uncertain what his responsibilities might be, but impressed by the honor of being invited to attend the meeting, Andy offered, "Father, would you mind if I looked behind all the tapestries?"

The King smiled. "Found the secret passages to the maintenance stairway, huh? By all means, have a good look around. You can never be too careful."

Andy grabbed a torch and ducked behind the nearest wall hanging. Feeling like a burrowing rodent, he circled the four stone walls but found no secret openings. "Nope, nothing," he announced, satisfied, at which Father and Mermin grinned.

The first council member arrived shortly thereafter. The barrel-chested man strolled into the room sporting an impeccable royal blue uniform with a crest of two crossed sabers on his left arm.

"Ragnar! Great to see you again, old friend."

The man kneeled and kissed the King's ring before standing again.

"I'd like you to meet my son, Prince Andrew."

"Yes, I heard your news. Congratulations, Your Majesty!"

"Andy, this is Regent Bellum. He commands the army of Oomaldee."

Andy bowed.

Major Cahill waddled in next, clad in his dress uniform.

"You clean up nice," Andy joked.

"That's big news, you being the prince and all," the major remarked.

Before Andy had the opportunity to respond, another council member puffed in, breathless after the exertion of the climb. The lumbering man choked out, "Your Majesty," as he bowed to the King and kissed his ring.

"Viceroy Stoneshield, I'd like you to meet my son, Prince Andrew. Andy, Viceroy Stoneshield is deputy to Regent Bellum."

The introductions continued through Major Caden and Major Magnor with the army and Regent Kayton Cronkar and Viceroy Aleron of the cavalry. Andy tried his best to remember all the names, but after the fifth officer, his thoughts scrambled. He hoped he didn't have to engage in conversation with any other of the dozen officers Father introduced, lest he show how stupid he felt.

"Looks like we're all here," the King declared at last. "Andy, would you please close the door and secure it for us?"

Andy did so and then took a seat at the opposite end of the table from Father, nearest the door.

"I've asked Prince Andrew to join us. He will be ruling this kingdom one day and needs to learn the strategies of war," the King began. "How better to learn than to listen in on our thinking and planning."

A rumble of approving murmurs rippled around the table as all eyes glanced at Andy, causing him to shift in his chair, much like when he watched a scary movie.

"Now then, we are gathered here today to continue planning for an anticipated conflict with King Abaddon. I'm prepared to update you on our progress in developing large weapon systems. Regent Cronkar and Regent Bellum will update us on the readiness of our cavalry and army, respectively. But before we present these reports, I'd like to let you know about recent events in the city of Oops. As you know, King Abaddon has, from time to time, turned a few of our citizens into bird-people. The incidents have been few and far between to this point."

Heads nodded around the table.

"We have evidence King Abaddon has recently increased the frequency of his actions, indiscriminately turning many more of our citizens into vulture-folk. Mermin and I just returned from investigating."

"What?" several officers exclaimed.

"Why would he do such a thing?" Viceroy Aleron demanded.

"We believe King Abaddon is very weak at the moment as a result of wounds received from the sword Methuselah."

A surprised chorus of "Methuselah?" hummed around the table.

Regent Cronkar questioned, "The sword exists? Are you sure?"

"The sword appeared two years ago to Prince Andrew."

All eyes shot toward Andy.

"I know, I said the same thing the first time I saw it. I have not mentioned this before now because I did not know if it would ever be relevant to our work," the King continued.

"You've battled King Abaddon?" Viceroy Aleron queried.

Andy nodded, then added, "Twice."

Several officers murmured, then cleared their throats with newfound respect for their prince.

"How does King Abaddon's weakened condition connect to his turning our people?" puzzled Viceroy Stoneshield.

"We believe King Abaddon has studied alchemy extensively. However, instead of turning objects into gold or silver, he has found a way to release energy by turning people and thereby strengthening himself."

"Horrors!" Major Magnor shouted.

"Barbarian!" Major Caden exclaimed.

"It's not right!" chimed Viceroy Aleron.

"Diabolical! He must be stopped!" exclaimed Major Cahill, standing up and waving his long arms animatedly in front of his beak-like nose.

Knowing what happened to the major, the room instantly quieted.

"Gentlemen, it doesn't matter what we think of his tactics. He is not out to win an award for congeniality. He is bent on taking what he wants, and we must stop him."

The grumbling ceased and the King continued. "How to accomplish that is the question for our meeting today," he declared. "Recent events provide more evidence that the war we face is unlike any we have waged before. I believe we need to think and act differently to effectively combat Abaddon and his forces. Their tactics are guerilla and opportunistic rather than the formal, regimented style our armies employ on a battlefield. I am hereby constituting a new strategy that combines our traditional troop readiness and large weapon systems with the flexibility and nimbleness to combat local incursions quickly and decisively. We will fight insurgent activities with rebel moves of our own."

As he spoke, heads nodded around the table.

"Because we have never fought this way, we will need to invent effective tactics. I propose we begin with a defensive approach, and as we learn more about how Abaddon and his troops fight, we will adapt countermeasures to go on the offensive."

More grunts of agreement rose from around the table.

"This is our first opportunity to devise countermeasures to defeat him," the King continued. "Our chief priority is to aide our citizens as best we can. Most importantly, they must see our efforts on their behalf, lest they become more fearful and bigger problems ensue. In this regard, I think we need to try a two-pronged approach.

"Regent Bellum, I request that you work locally with our citizens to identify farms, shops, and other facilities that should be guarded to stop Abaddon and his forces from randomly abducting people, and then make sufficient men available to accomplish this."

"Yes, Your Majesty," the officer replied. "We shall begin this afternoon."

"Second, but of no less importance, we need to encourage folks to work together and remain united. We are as strong against Abaddon as our loyalty to each other. I thought Prince Andrew made an excellent point at the tavern the night before last. Son, why don't you share what you told Asher Dain's listeners."

Andy glanced around the long table as he slowly stood. He felt a strong urge to flee. *They're all so accomplished. What have I got to say that's worthy of their listening? I think I'd rather be battling Abaddon right about now.*

He attempted to slow his breathing. "Well, ya see, there was this storyteller," Andy began. He quickly summarized the tale and concluded with, "At the end, folks argued about the meaning. I thought their fighting was stupid, so I told them when so many have been attacked, making everyone else nervous and wondering if they might be next, now is not the time to be arguing. Rather, now is the time to come together and choose to love. We are as strong as the love we choose to share."

"Well said," Regent Cronkar praised.

Andy's face flushed. "Thank you, sir."

The King pulled the focus back to strategy as he added, "We need to develop a campaign of placards and other written and spoken narratives encouraging our people to band together and support each other—neighbor helping neighbor. I agree with Prince Andrew. We are as strong against our foe as the love we choose to share."

Andy felt several eyes once again on him.

"Yes, Major Cahill," the King said, recognizing the long arm waving like a flag in the wind.

"Your Majesty, I'd like to volunteer to spearhead this campaign."

The King smiled and added, "I can't think of anyone better for the task."

"I'd like to help, too," Major Magnor voiced.

"Thank you, gentlemen. Looks like this part of our strategy is in very capable hands. Assuming these efforts are effective at stemming the problem, they should go a long way to restoring peace and confidence in the kingdom."

Several heads again bobbed.

"I like it, Your Majesty!" blurted out Major Caden. "It's a brilliant plan."

"Before we get ahead of ourselves," the King interrupted, "let's see how effective it is. If we are unsuccessful at better protecting our citizens, it won't be brilliant, now will it?"

At this the room quieted again.

"I'd like to take a few minutes to give you some perspective on our current situation based on reports I've heard recently. Prince Andrew had opportunity to gather important information this morning about what's going on elsewhere around our land. Andy, please tell everyone what you learned."

Feeling a little more comfortable this time, he again stood. "Sirs, what I'm about to tell you may sound impossible, but I swear it really happened. My father and Mermin are witnesses."

"That's quite an introduction, Prince Andrew," Regent Cronkar chuckled.

"Sorry, but you see, sir, I have a friend who is a dragon." Andy waited for chuckles of disbelief at the absurdity of his statement, but none came. Instead, the officers glanced from Andy to the King and back. When his majesty's expression remained unchanged, the men refocused their attention.

"Anyway, Daisy—that's my dragon friend—helped me listen in on conversations of centaurs, griffins, pegasi, and unicorns. The centaurs foretold from the stars that the dragon constellation would overcome the warrior. I don't know how soon. As you know, Abaddon is a dragon. I'm not sure if Oomaldee is the warrior, but if we are—"

Andy paused, expecting someone to discredit his report, but everyone remained quiet, listening attentively, so he continued. "Then I heard Abaddon is again attacking the gold and silver mines in Carta. The griffins are protecting the treasure, and it sounds like they aren't about to give up the fight. Next, I overheard the leader of the pegasi giving a pep talk. He said they faced a foe of deep and ancient dark magic. That didn't sound good. And last, I found out there are unicorns in the land right now, but their leader said he sensed evil growing stronger with each passing day and they wouldn't stay longer than a fortnight."

"Thank you, Andy," the King said, rising. "Gentlemen, whether you take stock in these reports or not, we must be prepared for what I fear will be a long, hard struggle. It will test us militarily, but I believe it will also personally try each one of us as never before. We must be absolutely committed to each other and to our kingdom."

A solemn mood fell on the room at these words. No one moved.

"Now then, let me tell you what's been happening with war machine construction," the King resumed. He gave his report and the other officials shared various updates before the meeting finally concluded.

When the group adjourned, Father informed Andy that he and Mermin would spend the afternoon planning the trip to find the unicorns. With this in mind, Andy decided to check the invisible book down in Mermin's library as was his custom before each quest, for it always gave him information he would need to successfully complete the mission.

Andy pushed open the heavy wooden door to the library, walked over to the shelf, and extracted the book. He placed it on the table, pushing aside several books and scrolls, and opened it. A portion of the message had changed. The single page at the front now read:

1. Flirt not with temptation.
2. Heed the messenger.

But it's my mom's life on the line! I'm sorry if it thinks I'm allowing myself to be tempted, but I disagree. And it's calling me greedy again. How can it say that? I don't get it.

Andy turned the page and opened the compartment with the white loop handle to see if it might hold some clue, but he saw only the six red dragon scales and the vial of venom.

Nothing new for this trip? That's weird.

As the thought lingered in his mind, the same translucent swirl he'd seen before rose up from one of the round stone paperweights Mermin used to hold down the corners of scrolls. As always, it formed a ball twelve to fifteen inches in diameter that slowly rotated above the table. Andy backed away.

"What would you give to save me while still breaking the curse?" Mom's voice asked again.

"I don't know," Andy whined. "I wish you'd stop asking me that."

"Am I not worthy of your sacrifice?"

"You are, but…"

"What is your hesitation?"

"I don't want to die."

"And you think I do?"

"No. Look, I don't know what to say."

"May it not be said that the longer you are away in this land, the less you care about me or my future."

"No! That's not it." But even as he protested, Andy wondered if it might be true, at least in part. Pangs of guilt bit down on his inneru, producing a whimper but no comments.

The translucent ball continued to spin, as if awaiting his answer. Andy slammed the book shut, returned it to the shelf, and ran out the door. He glanced over his shoulder, hoping it did not follow.

"Thank you," he said under his breath when he saw he walked alone. Still, the encounter unsettled him. He knew this was not the end of it. What am I going to say the next time it shows up?

As he descended the stairs, Andy gave way for a servant waddling upward, which brought him back from his contemplations. He needed to find Alden and Hannah. They had some serious sword and dagger fighting to practice. This wasn't going to be an easy trip.

An ominous feeling filled Andy's gut as a random thought meandered through his mind: Is the bellicose really gone?

CHAPTER TEN

Not Ducks

A ndy woke the next morning to a booming clap of thunder reverberating against the stone of his room. He hadn't slept well, for his mind ruminated on the translucent, swirling sphere, stirring up the guilt he felt for being unwilling to die in place of his mom when he broke the curse. A quick succession of three brilliant flashes of lightning lit up his dim surroundings. He gazed out the window to the left of his bed and saw heavier than usual fog forming a gloomy curtain as torrential rains poured down.

Lovely day to begin our quest.

He'd packed the bare essentials for the trip the night before: three changes of clothes, matches, and a blanket. After dressing in scratchy leggings and tunic and buckling his weapon belt in place, he added a rain poncho and his cell phone to his provisions. *Never know when you'll need a compass. Uh, right…no bars.* He checked the pouch around his neck for the gold key. *Right where it should be.* He slipped on his soft-soled leather boots, shouldered his backpack, and headed out the door.

"Off on another quest, Prince Andrew?" squeaked the two-foot-tall Sir Lancelot statue just outside his door. The miniature knight still held Clarence the barbarian under his foot as he had since Andy first met him.

"You've heard."

"Of course. Congratulations! I love it when you're around with the gold key!"

Andy smiled.

"Fare thee well, lad! Subdue those uncivilized rogues."

Andy chuckled and replied, "Okay, I will."

Andy reached the dining hall where he found several people congregated. Among them were Cadfael and Lucee with Hannah, Charis, Larissa, and Ro;

Hans, Alden, and Marta; and three men he'd never seen before. Larissa chased after Ro, trying to keep an eye on him.

"Please, everyone, sit!" Marta clucked. "You need a proper breakfast before you head out into that weather." As if to reinforce her point, the storm let loose another clap of thunder that echoed through the hall.

"So your parents are letting you come?" Andy asked Hannah, sliding into a space on the wooden bench next to her and Alden.

Hannah smiled. "My parents had a long discussion about it, but Dad finally won."

"Who are those guys?" Andy questioned, motioning with his head to the group sitting down the bench from them.

"The one in the brown tunic is Sergeant Albin," Alden responded. "The guy in green next to him is Sergeant Gavin, and the other guy is Captain Ladilas. From what I hear, the regents and viceroys put up a fuss when your father told them he would be traveling for a few days. They wanted him to take the usual platoon of fifty soldiers. As I understand it, the King refused since such a large group would attract a lot of attention. I guess these three are their compromise."

Andy was surprised at the sight of his father entering the dining hall dressed in a way he'd never seen, though he immediately understood why. A plain gray tunic came to just above his knees, and a sword and dagger hung from the leather belt that circled his waist. Black leggings and coordinating leather boots completed the ensemble. He carried a black cape over his arm.

He made his way to Andy who stood and exclaimed, "You look different, Father!"

"And good morning to you too, Son." The King pulled him close in a hug. "Are you ready?"

"As ready as I'll ever be."

Medrick and Henkel interrupted with, "Your Majesty." They both bowed before continuing. "You asked for a letter of introduction. Here you are, sir.

That should prove your identity." Medrick handed the King a sealed parchment.

"Thank you both. As I mentioned, I don't know if we'll need it or not, but since I've never met your king in person, it's best to observe proper protocol and be prepared."

"Our king is a great dwarf, fair in all his dealings. You've corresponded with him before, and I'm sure he will welcome you and give safe passage through our lands as soon as you prove who you are. He is fiercely loyal to his friends, be they dwarfs or other races," Medrick assured.

"The fact that you're here aiding our war efforts assures me that what you say is true. I'm looking forward to meeting him. And rest assured, my report concerning your work will be one that brings dignity to you and the dwarfs."

Medrick and Henkel puffed out their chests at hearing this.

"Thank you, Your Majesty. Safe travels to you," Henkel added as they turned and headed out to their work.

The King pulled a pouch like Andy's from under his tunic and added the letter.

"You're not wearing your ring," Andy observed.

"I want us to look like a group of peasants traveling, which is also why we won't be taking horses or any other beast. Should trouble befall us, my ring would betray us."

"You've thought of everything," Andy replied, smiling.

"I'm sure we'll find that's not the case, but Mermin and I did as much planning as we could. Unfortunately, this storm will make our journey more difficult. If it weren't for the unicorns planning to leave so soon, I'd wait a day until the weather clears and the woods dry. But we'll make do with the situation we find ourselves in."

Mermin entered the dining hall. He also was dressed out of character. A plain brown tunic came to just below his knees and was cinched with a leather belt about his waist. A tan cowl encircled his neck, resting on his shoulders under a coordinating brown cape that flowed behind him. He carried no weapons.

"Are you weady to be ducks out in these elements?" he joked as he approached.

"Quack, quack," quipped Alden.

Hannah giggled, to which Andy rolled his eyes. *This could get old really fast.*

Razen hustled up to the King as everyone finished breakfast.

"Sir, I have tasted all the food in your provisions. May it not be so, but should you encounter troubles, it will not be from that which nourishes you."

That's cheery, Andy thought.

"Thank you. I appreciate your efforts," the King replied

Razen glanced around at the group members. When his eyes reached Andy, he raised an eyebrow before moving on.

What's that supposed to mean?

At last, Razen declared, "I wish you all safe and speedy travels. We will be anxiously awaiting your return."

Marta stopped swooping about and came over to give Alden a long hug. Cadfael and Lucee did the same with Hannah. Andy got a hug from Marta and a bone-jarring pat on the back from Cadfael.

Hans came over to Andy and commented, "It'll be nice for you to have your father along."

Andy nodded. He'd thought about that and looked forward to spending time with him on this trip.

With goodbyes completed, the group of eight picked up their packs, now laden with food, and headed to the castle door.

"Everyone ready?" the King asked. Receiving no comments to the contrary, he added, "Then let's move out."

As he said it, a clap of thunder protested.

They walked over the drawbridge and raindrops immediately assaulted Andy's face. He pulled his poncho further up, then glanced back. Hans, Marta,

Cadfael, and Lucee stood waving from the portico between the barbican and the portcullis. Andy didn't see Razen. *What's he up to?* his thoughts accused.

Father, who walked next to Andy, pulled him close. "I'm glad we can take this trip together."

Squinting through raindrops, Andy looked up into his face and replied, "Me too."

Several minutes into the walk the group stopped under a clump of trees with dense foliage; it felt good to get out of the downpour. The King turned and addressed the group.

"I didn't want to disclose our plans until now to avoid any leaks." As he said it, the King looked up and chuckled, then added, "You see how well that worked out."

Laughter rippled through the group.

"We'll be heading toward Mount Mur Eyah. If the fog ever thins, you might be able to see it ahead in the distance. We'll travel through the land of the dwarfs. I'm hopeful we can reach their lands this afternoon. If they grant us safe passage, we should be able to get out of this downpour and walk underground. We'll travel to the southernmost tip of the troll's territory and begin a northerly trek in search of our objective: three unicorns."

Hearing this, a roar of excitement erupted, even from the disciplined army officers. "Unicorns?!"

"We have two weeks to find them and get a horn, if they'll allow it. Unicorns don't like men. They've been hunted down and killed by ruthless rogues, so it may be that only Hannah has the privilege of meeting them. She's got a big job ahead of her."

Everyone glanced at Hannah, who wore a surprised look.

"Really?" she questioned, curiosity quickly taking root.

The King looked directly at Hannah and replied, "As we journey, Mermin, you, and I will work through what we believe you can expect when we reach these beautiful creatures."

Hannah nodded, a twinkle in her eyes.

"Now then," he added, addressing the group again, "while I don't expect any difficulties beyond the challenges the terrain and wildlife will present, we must all be alert for danger at every moment."

Andy shifted on his feet and put a hand on the holster in which Methuselah rested. *Can anyone say "bellicose"?*

"The terrain is mountainous and will demand stamina from each of us. With these rains, there is also potential for landslides, so listen for rumblings."

The King surveyed the group. "We'll all be spending quite a bit of time together, so let me introduce our armed guards, Sergeants AlbinSergeant and Gavin, and Captain Ladilas."

The three soldiers each nodded in turn.

"Does anyone have any questions?" he concluded.

No one did, so the King turned and led the way back into the wet unknown.

Andy quickly realized the King's briefing had not included an explanation concerning why they would be collecting the horn from a unicorn.

As they set off, Andy watched the three officers split up. Sergeant Albin walked to the left of the group, Sergeant Gavin to the right, and Captain Ladilas brought up the rear.

The King, Andy, and Mermin took the lead; Alden and Hannah followed behind. Whether from reverence for the task ahead or the continued downpour, no one said much as they slipped and slid along the muddy path. *Squelch, squerch, squelch, squerch*, Andy's boots sounded with each step. He listened to the harmony of everyone else's footwear in the mud.

The trail looked familiar to Andy for he had walked it many times on the way to the festival when he first visited Oomaldee. Except then he had not heard waters raging off to his right.

Father noticed Andy tilt his head toward the roar and informed, "It's the Crystal River. Our path runs not far from it. With all this rain, no doubt it will be swollen."

"I hope it doesn't cause a pwoblem with the bwidges," Mermin added.

The King nodded. "I wondered about that, too. We'll know soon enough."

They approached a grove of dense trees off to their left. Andy couldn't help grinning as he spotted a herd of goats holed up, nibbling the scrub bushes. The herding-challenged boy he and Alden had encountered twice before was bundled in a tarp and sat with his back against a tree, cowering from the elements.

Andy dropped back to joke with Alden. "Look," he nodded toward the sight. "Remember?"

Alden glanced over. Smiling, he drawled, "Oh, yeah!" Then he proceeded to recount the details of their past run-ins with this boy and his goats, much to Hannah's amusement.

"Well, they won't be bothering us today from the looks of things," she commented.

The path forked--left led toward the festival grounds, right beckoned to adventures unknown. They went right. Large puddles formed in deep ruts and merged into miniature lakes as they ventured on. Pasty mud tried its best to remove their boots with each step. And still the downpour continued, punctuated periodically by a duet of thunder and lightning.

Late morning brought them to the city limits of Oops, and an hour later they arrived at the first test of their journey: Entente Bridge. The river had crested its banks and the fast-moving current spilled around the legs of the overpass, making it an island.

"The bwidge looks stable, but getting to it could be a pwoblem," Mermin observed, voicing everyone's thoughts.

"Suggestions, anyone?" Andy asked.

"I brought rope," Alden offered.

Everyone smiled at Alden as he pulled it out of his pack and handed it off.

"Good thing someone's prepared," Captain Ladilas quipped.

"I'll go first," Sergeant Gavin volunteered.

When no one objected, the group passed the rope to the soldier. He tied it tightly around his waist and handed the end to Sergeant Albin and Captain Ladilas.

"I'll secure the line to the bridge, then one-by-one you can use it to steady your steps as you cross," Sergeant Gavin instructed.

Sergeant Albin and Captain Ladilas braced themselves as Gavin stepped carefully into the raging waters. Despite his meaty frame, the force against his legs caused them to buckle. He fell backwards in the oncoming rush and the line immediately went taut. Sergeant Albin and Captain Ladilas strained to control the line in the tug-of-war against the river. Andy and Alden rushed to grab hold. As they pulled, their side of the contest slowly hauled the flailing officer from the torrent. As the weary man crawled back onto the bank, a clap of thunder boomed overhead, as if celebrating the river's victory.

"You okay, man?" Captain Ladilas inquired, checking on his officer.

Sergeant Gavin nodded as he coughed up water.

Once he had recovered, the sergeant offered, "The current is stronger than it appears and there's a hole in the riverbed that I stepped in, right there." He pointed at a spot approximately four feet from shore. "If it wasn't for that, I think I could have made it across."

"I'll try, Captain," offered Sergeant Albin.

The tall, wiry soldier tied the rope securely about his waist and stepped into the current. Sergeant Gavin, Captain Ladilas, Andy, and Alden braced themselves on shore, anchoring the line. He inched his way through the torrent, avoiding the pitfall his cohort had discovered, and soon grabbed the railing of the bridge. Heaving himself out of the water, he secured the line to the platform.

"Okay, who's next?" he yelled over the din.

"Hannah, you go," the King commanded.

Hannah bit her lower lip as she stepped toward the rope.

"Put your arm over the rope to hold on as you cross," Captain Ladilas suggested.

Hannah nodded and stepped into the current. She immediately lost her footing and let out a scream. All those on shore gasped. Seconds later, she regained her wits and began inching her way across, hand over hand, dangling from the line with her feet surfing the top of the water. The sergeant grabbed her and hauled her up, standing her on the solid structure.

"Next!" the officer yelled.

One by one the travelers made their way to the bridge at the center of the torrent. Captain Ladilas went last. As the anchor for everyone else's crossing, he now had no line to pull himself along. The group huddling on the bridge held their breath as he stepped into the rushing water and immediately lost his footing. The river claimed him and began sweeping him downstream. Thankfully, the line tied about his waist held tight. As it stretched to its limits, Sergeants Albin and Gavin, and Andy and Alden played another game of tug-of-war against the river. This time the travelers won quickly and the captain joined the rest of the party.

"Halfway there," encouraged the King, to which several gave weak smiles.

They made their way to the middle of the span. Just as they reached it, out of the corner of his eye, Andy caught sight of an enormous tree rushing toward them. He guessed its trunk measured four feet in diameter. No doubt it had stood on the riverbank for an eternity.

By the time he turned to get a better look, the trunk had neared to within five feet of the bridge.

He warned, "Look out!" as the massive log slammed into the footings, shaking everyone loose.

Andy barely grabbed the railing in time, but Hannah, who had been standing to his right, didn't enjoy the same fortune. She screamed as the impact propelled her over the side. Without thinking, Andy grabbed after her and connected with her arm. He looked down as Hannah dangled there, kicking and shrieking, trying desperately to hold on.

"Stop moving!" Andy demanded. "You're making it harder to hang onto you."

Despite his wet hands, adrenaline kicked in and Andy managed to pull Hannah up to where she could grab the railing and climb back on. As she reached safety, she looked up at Andy. Their eyes met and they exchanged a meaningful look neither of them expected. Unknowingly, they held it until Alden raced over.

"Are you okay?" he exclaimed, clearly shaken.

Hannah turned toward Alden, raising her hands to her cheeks.

"Your cheeks are flushed," Alden observed.

"Are they?" she questioned, glancing quickly at Andy.

Andy looked away, feeling his face grow warm in response.

"I suppose it's the exertion," Hannah offered.

"We need to move! This bridge can't stand against the pressure of the tree," shouted the captain. To underscore his point, the wood groaned under their feet.

What just happened?

Alden put his arm around Hannah as the three of them ran across the rest of the span and caught up with the group.

One by one they made their way to the other shore using the same method as before. Sergeant Gavin, Sergeant Albin, Alden, the King, and Mermin anchored the rope on the far shore as Andy set foot in the current. That's when he saw a second uprooted tree come barreling down the river.

"Captain!" Andy cried out.

The officer, last on the bridge, quickly untied the rope from the railing and jumped in. Both he and Andy struggled in the rushing water that seemed determined to sweep them downstream. Seconds later, the rogue tree slammed into the weakened bridge, shattering it and sending pieces sailing through the air like daggers. Andy and the captain tried to avoid the shrapnel, but with so many projectiles in flight, it proved impossible. A ten-inch fragment found its target in Andy's shoulder, and his grip faltered as it dug into muscle.

"Ow!" he screamed, pain shooting down his arm.

The anchor crew dashed down the shoreline, reeling in the taut rope.

Hold on! Andy demanded of himself, struggling to keep his head above water. He coughed and his head dunked below the torrent. *Kick! Kick!* he screamed at himself. *Ow!* The pain of the bridge fragment imbedded in his shoulder burned more intensely than any injury he'd experienced. That combined with the strong current made it almost impossible to resurface. *I'm gonna die!* His lungs felt as though they would explode. Despite willing himself to hold on, Andy's grip weakened and the wet line began slipping through his hands. His mind began to cloud and all sense of time evaporated. He felt himself become one with the fury of the river as he surrendered to it.

Sergeant Gavin somehow found his wrist and yanked, halting Andy's voyage downriver. The soldier hauled him from the torrent and laid him on the shore. Andy's mind remained cloudy and it didn't occur to him to breathe. *Where am I?* he wondered dreamily. *What's hitting my face? I really wish it would stop. It kind of hurts.*

Suddenly, a booming voice interrupted his reverie: "Wake up, Andy!"

Startled, he reflexively inhaled and began coughing. As he awoke fully, he saw Father leaning over him. Captain Ladilas lay hacking and sputtering on the shore next to him.

"Andy, you're okay!" Father exclaimed, relief in his voice.

Sheets of rain pelted the river's edge and Andy lifted his arm to shield his face.

"Eeeyouch!" he cried as pain burned his shoulder.

Andy looked over and saw a chunk of wood sticking at an angle through his rain poncho. The instant he saw it, the pain grew more intense and he yelped again. A five-inch piece of bridge protruded from the captain's arm just above his wrist. While wincing, the officer didn't cry out. *I need to suck it up and be a man,* Andy chided himself and stifled another yowl.

The sky let loose with a series of three quick flashes of lightning immediately followed by a deafening boom of thunder as if furious at its defeat.

"We'd best get away fwom this wiver," suggested the wizard.

"Andy, can you walk?" Father queried. "The dwarfs are known to be skillful healers. They can fix you up. I'm afraid if we try to remove the fragment, we may not be able to stop the bleeding. It's not far now."

Andy nodded.

The group moved back from the water and Alden cut a length of the soaked rope and brought it over. As he gently moved Andy's arm, Andy nearly yelped again, but he managed to hold back as Alden finished the makeshift sling. Hannah pulled out a spare apron from her pack, tore it in half, then gently wove it around the wood fragment to slow the bleeding. Alden made a second sling and Hannah repeated the bandaging process for Captain Ladilas.

With the dripping sleeve of his good arm, Andy silently wiped away the tears that flowed freely down his cheeks.

CHAPTER ELEVEN

A Curious Welcome

A n hour later the group trudged up a hill whose incline grew steeper with each step. Their only consolation was that with the trees being so dense, the foliage diverted some of the rain. They approached a flat clearing and saw a set of finely carved wood pillars standing ten feet apart; they looked out of place in the otherwise natural setting. Each column rose about fifteen feet and bore detailed inscriptions up and down its length. The carving of a pickaxe adorned the capital on the left pillar and a caduceus embellished the right.

"We've reached the entrance to Voluspa, home of the great hall of the dwarfs in the shadow of Mount Mur Eyah," the King announced. "You doing okay, Andy?"

Andy nodded, gritting his teeth. Each step jarred his injury and demanded his full concentration to manage the stabbing pain; he neared the point of exhaustion.

The group gathered around and the King declared, "My experience with dwarfs is limited only to correspondence with their king, Nithi XXVI, so I'm not sure what to expect. Let's proceed cautiously. Once we make contact, I will give them Medrick and Henkel's letter of introduction and we'll hope all goes well from there."

Several in the group shifted uneasily.

A path began on the far side of the pillars, so they passed through and followed it. Fifty or so paces up the trail stood a sign that looked fairly new.

As they approached, the King asked, "Mermin, what does it say?"

The wizard stepped forward and studied the strange characters, but after several minutes shook his head. "I don't know, sir."

"Well then, let's hope it's not important."

The trek grew more arduous as the incline increased. Andy found himself staggering, swaying from side to side as they advanced. Alden and Hannah moved to either side of him and steadied his steps as the climb became a blur.

No one uttered a word, and the relentless pounding of raindrops on the forest canopy drowned out all sounds except for the most adventurous animals that dared leave their dens or burrows.

"I think I see another clearing up ahead!" Sergeant Gavin exclaimed awhile later, startling the group.

The announcement broke through Andy's delirium. Then, with ten yards to the clearing, he heard a strange chorus sounding like nothing they'd encountered on their trip thus far. It didn't sound like an animal. Sharp squeaking punctuated a rising *zhhh* sound.

Sergeant Albin shouted, "Everyone, stop where you are!"

As soon as he uttered the command, all eight members of the group felt themselves rammed together and jerked off the ground. Andy's shoulder slammed into Alden and he let out a scream; Captain Ladilas moaned as the quick confinement smashed his injured wrist into the King. When movement ceased, they found themselves suspended in a rope cocoon thirty feet off the ground. It became instantly clear the unfamiliar sounds had been wheels in need of oiling and rope retracting quickly.

"Sergeant Gavin," Hannah gasped, "you're sitting on me."

"Oh, goodness. Sorry about that." The sergeant attempted to shift.

"Ouch!" yelped Alden, taking some of the man's weight as he moved.

"Don't stop there, your foot is digging into my back," informed Mermin.

"Everyone, stop!" the King declared. "We're not going to be comfortable up here. Anyone have an idea how we might get down?"

The fidgeting halted as everyone thought—everyone except Andy, that is. Glad for the reprieve from walking, he immediately dozed off despite the discomfort.

"Andy! Wake up!" Father implored, not long enough later.

With difficulty, Andy lifted his heavy eyelids. "Huh?"

"Alden mentioned the gold key might get us out of this," Father repeated. "Can you get to it?"

It took several seconds for his words to register, but Andy finally understood. Unable to look due to his confinement, he struggled to reach the pouch hanging around his neck.

"Hannah, can you move your foot?" Andy mumbled.

The request precipitated another transformation of the rope cocoon's contents accompanied by various exclamations, but at last Andy fingered the string around his neck. He slowly pulled, felt the pouch rise inside his tunic, and at last it popped out.

"Alden, can you hold it so I can get the key out?"

With considerable effort, Alden brought both hands over to the small sack and held it open. Andy's fingers finally located the key and pulled it out.

"He's got it!" Alden announced.

"Say what you need to make it work," Alden encouraged.

"Right, okay." Andy thought for several seconds before uttering a simple request: "Please get us down from here…gently."

Everyone strained to hear movement. An owl hooted in the distance and the incessant dripping of the downpour continued, but nothing more.

"Try it again," Sergeant Albin encouraged, not sure what to think about this unorthodox method of fixing the problem.

"Maybe everyone needs to believe it'll work," suggested Hannah.

"Everyone ready?" the King queried. "Okay, give it another try, Son."

"Please let us down gently," Andy repeated to the key with as much conviction as he could muster, which wasn't much at the moment.

It took several seconds, but then that distinct squeaking sound began once more and the ground slowly approached. When they stopped, the ropes slackened until the net lay flat, allowing everyone to scramble out.

Andy felt a little better after his catnap, but as they continued their trek, his shoulder resumed its war cry at the jostling of each step.

"What a cuwious gweeting by the dwarfs of Voluspa. I hope King Nithi doesn't extend any more 'welcomes,'" Mermin quipped as they climbed what had become a mountain.

"Voluspa? Nithi? Are you kidding?" Andy interjected.

"Weren't you paying attention when the King said we'd reached Voluspa?" Hannah reproved.

"I guess not."

"Why's it matter?" Alden queried.

"I read a book in school this year called *The Hobbit*. It's a story about dwarfs of the line of Durin trying to recapture their homeland after the evil dragon, Smaug, stole it from them."

Alden and Hannah stared back with blank expressions.

"I also had to write a report about the dwarfs, including where they came from, what they do, and all that stuff. Most of what I learned came from an old poem called 'Voluspa.'"

Father overheard Andy's comments and stepped back to join the trio of kids. "And where did you discover dwarfs come from?" he asked

"According to the poem, they were created by Vala Aulë, who carved them from rock. Durin was the first of the seven dwarf fathers he created, but another was called Nithi." *Could that story be true? I always thought someone just made it up.*

The King laughed. "Andy, you may know more about the dwarfs than anyone in our party. If what you say is true, you'll certainly win the trust of Nithi XXVI, which could prove beneficial in forging a strong relationship with the dwarfs as you assume the throne."

Wow, I had no idea!

The group soon came upon a pair of boulders that looked like sentinels guarding either side of the trail. As with the wood pillars, these rocks bore intricate carvings with beautiful scrollwork. One image depicted dwarfs fashioning a machine. Another showed someone wearing a crown and admiring a jewel necklace around his neck.

"Heads up!" announced Captain Ladilas. "Let's not have another welcome like the last one."

Everyone nodded and sharpened their hearing, walking slowly and deliberately for about twenty yards. They breathed a sigh of relief when nothing happened.

Fifty yards beyond that, however, Andy felt a sharp stab in his thigh through his drenched poncho. At first he thought a bee had stung him. But apparently everyone else felt the same sensation, for the other group members halted and began lifting their rain-soaked coverings.

As he investigated, Andy felt suddenly light-headed and his surroundings began to swirl. He collapsed as everything went dark.

Andy awoke some time later and could honestly say he'd never been in so much pain. His head felt as if it might explode, his shoulder kept zapping him at the slightest movement from the imbedded wood shard, his nose was still sore and puffy from its collision with the oscray spong, and every muscle ached from his battle against the river's current.

He moaned, rolled onto his side, and found himself resting on a cot.

His eyes strained in the dim surroundings and his nose picked up a decidedly musty, fecal smell. With effort he stood and peered through the iron bars that caged him. In the cell to his right Hannah lay unmoving on the cold floor.

He noticed activity in the cell beyond and glanced up to see a vulture-man staring through the bars at Hannah and then at him.

"What's your problem?" Andy called, glaring at the bulging-eyed man.

"What's yours?" a voice farther off shot back.

This comment precipitated a flurry of bird-calls and rude noises from the host of vulture inmates.

Andy's hand moved to his belt where he kept Methuselah, but it wasn't there! *The dwarfs must have taken it.* He scanned his cell. *Looks like they also took my backpack.*

Ignoring the bird-men, Andy watched Hannah sleeping. Despite his discomfort, his thoughts returned to earlier. *What happened on the bridge after I saved her? That look we shared...* He felt an unfamiliar fluttering sensation rise in his chest. He tried to dismiss it, but it persisted.

Andy roused himself and squinted. He could barely make out several more cells containing vulture-people. They stared and gestured in his direction.

I wonder why the dwarfs have all these guys locked up?

"You're awake, Andy," Sergeant Albin commented from behind him. "You've been out for quite a while."

Andy turned and looked through the bars. He saw Sergeant Albin, and Captain Ladilas in the cell beyond.

"Where's my father?"

"The King's four cells down from me."

Andy squinched his eyes but couldn't see him in the poorly lit surroundings.

"Andy! What a relief. How are you doing?" his father inquired, overhearing.

"My whole body hurts."

"I'm not surprised after all you've been through. Alden's down here in the cell to my left. He's still out."

"Where are Mermin and Sergeant Gavin?" Andy asked.

"We're here," Andy heard a duet of voices call from the cells beyond Captain Ladilas.

"What happened? How'd we get here?" Andy questioned.

"I think the dwarfs loaded tranquilizing darts on either side of the path. We must have triggered them as we passed," reasoned the captain. "I can only assume the dwarfs found us and dragged us here."

"Did you give them the letter of introduction?" Alden stammered, standing.

"Good, you're awake," sighed Andy.

"Me too," mumbled Hannah, rubbing her hands against her temples and attempting to stand.

"Since I woke, no guards or anyone else has been in here to give the letter to," the King replied.

As if on cue, everyone heard the lock click and saw the handle turn on the solid metal door of the prison. The vulture-men directed a riotous chorus of insults at their captors that increased in intensity and became deafening. A beam of light snuck in as the door opened, and Andy pulled his hand up over his eyes.

"Enough!" boomed a short dwarf in the lead. The stout fellow strutted in, wearing iron chain mail over a red tunic. A leather belt punctuated his abundant middle and black leggings covered suggestions of legs.

Two dwarfs dressed in similar livery followed close behind. Like their leader, they had meticulously groomed their abundant beards; the hair of an upper layer was drawn together in a gold ring, while the bottom had been left loose and covered much of their barrel chests.

The dwarf in front stopped outside the King's cell and commanded, "Bring him!"

His subordinates quickly complied, forcefully shackling the King even though he offered no resistance.

"Hey, take it easy with him!" Andy shouted.

"It's okay, Andy," his father cautioned.

The leader glanced at Andy and motioned in his direction. One of the soldiers walked to Andy's cell and informed, "You'll be next."

Andy swallowed, eyes wide.

They drove the King into the aisle and back out the door. The metal reverberated as it slammed shut.

"Where are they taking him!" Andy demanded.

"For questioning," Captain Ladilas speculated aloud.

"He'll give them the letter of introduction and hopefully that'll get us out of here," Sergeant Gavin added.

Hearing this, the bird-men hurled more insults. After several minutes, however, they quieted, the fun extinguished when Andy and company didn't respond.

Turtles could move faster than time at this rate, Andy thought as he lay on the lumpy cot affixed to the back wall of the cell and studied the ceiling.

After a considerably long time, Andy heard the handle on the metal door jiggling once more. "About time!" he complained as he stood.

The King did not accompany the trio of dwarf guards as they proceeded to Andy's cell.

"Where is he? What did you do with him?" Andy demanded.

They unlocked Andy's cell. "Come here," the leader called from the hallway.

"I'm not going anywhere with you until I know what you did with the King," Andy replied.

Hearing this, the vulture-men began whooping and hollering, joking that they were privileged to be held captive with royalty.

One dwarf moved past his superior and into the cell, pulling out a length of rope.

Unsure what the dwarf intended to do with it, Andy braced for the conflict, his mind spinning between, *Please don't hurt my arm!* and *How am I gonna get out of here?* His eyes darted around the cell looking for any possible escape.

Just before the dwarf reached him, the leader's expression transformed from straight-faced to smiling. "All right, Brufn, we've had enough fun!"

Andy didn't know how to react. "What?" he uttered, cradling his arm.

The dwarf trio watched Andy's reaction and burst out in full belly laughs.

The bird-men watched. Their confusion silenced them, but not for long.

"Let them out," the leader ordered. "And give them back their weapons and provisions."

"Yes, sir!" echoed two deep voices accompanied by the jingling of keys.

"Looks like that letter did the trick," commented Sergeant Albin, buckling his weapons belt. Andy shouldered his pack over his good arm.

The dwarf trio escorted the group through the heavy metal door. Its slam echoed behind, squelching the cawed protests flung at them as they exited.

Out in the hallway, Andy spotted torches hanging every ten feet or so. They illuminated the stone-lined corridor just enough to see a few feet ahead, but cast creepy shadows on the walls that seemed to come alive as the flames flickered and danced. No one said anything.

The dwarfs led them through a maze of tunnels that continually twisted and turned. Andy gave up trying to remember where they'd been. *I hope someone else remembers the way if we need to escape.* He paused, then thought, *Not that the prison is the way we'd break out. Ah, well...*

They walked for several more minutes. Andy's shoulder had started feeling better as he rested in the cell, but now it resumed throbbing with each step. *How big can this place be?* he growled inwardly.

At last they reached a narrow set of stairs and ascended single file, bookended by the guards. One flight, two flights, three flights brought them to a polished white marble hallway. Overcast natural light shone through windows that divided the apex of a domed ceiling, reminding Andy of the dome in the library of Oomaldee. Hundreds of rubies and sapphires inlaid in the walls and ceiling gave the hall a lavish feel.

The group continued until they reached a central domed atrium. A dozen hallways similar to the one they'd just existed branched off it. A white marble fountain depicting a dwarf king rose a good twenty feet and occupied the center of the space. The figure stood proudly with one marble foot resting on a mound of marble dirt. Multiple jets of water shot into a circular basin beneath. The gray light from above, the white marble, and the statue's reflection off the water combined to make it appear to move.

The group paused.

"Wow!" exclaimed Hannah. "It's beautiful!"

"I've heard of the wealth of the dwarfs, but the tales don't do this hall justice," Mermin marveled.

Andy walked around the curved walls, studying the intricate carvings of battle scenes interspersed with etched portraits. "They must have been kings," Andy guessed aloud.

"You're very astute," Brufn confirmed, puffing out his chest. "The history of the line of Nithi is preserved on these walls."

The leader smiled and replied, "Nithi XXVI enjoys his fineries, as have his predecessors."

They reached the end of the hall and the leader turned to address the group. "My name is Eero. I'm the captain of the prison guard, and these are Mazar and Brufn, my sergeants."

"Mazar, see to the care of these two," Eero commanded, motioning to Andy and Captain Ladilas.

"It shall be done, sir!" The dwarf drew his hands behind his back and clicked the heels of his boots together.

"Everyone else, follow me," Eero instructed. "Brufn, follow up the rear so no one gets lost."

Andy's eyes shot toward Captain Ladilas as the group divided.

"It's okay," the captain mouthed.

"This way, please." Mazar raised an arm and motioned toward a hallway on the opposite side of the atrium.

"We'll see you later, Andy," Alden encouraged, trailing the larger group that headed down a different hall.

"Keep up," Brufn commanded, sweeping up the stragglers with outstretched arms.

Hannah waved, but her frown betrayed any sense of calm.

Andy and Captain Ladilas followed Mazar down another impressive white marble hallway, walked under an archway with a caduceus carved into its keystone, and turned right. After passing several empty rooms, Mazar led them into one with containers lining every wall. A dwarf child played quietly with her doll on a rug in front of the fireplace at the far side of the room.

"Have a seat, and a healer will be with you shortly," a stout but kindly she-dwarf greeted them. She saw them notice the child and explained, "My daughter. She comes with me sometimes."

Andy set his pack down next to the intricately carved stone bench he and the captain shared. Mazar waited nearby. Before they'd settled in, another she-dwarf swooped into the room. Unlike her male counterparts, this sturdy lady had no facial hair, but her long brown locks had been pulled into a braid that ended at the small of her back. She wore an elaborately decorated crimson tunic and a fine white linen blouse that hung over the top of leather breeches.

"I'm Bridrika," the healer introduced herself. "This is Elganora, my assistant." She approached Andy and studied the wood protruding from his shoulder, then inspected the captain's arm.

Choosing to treat Andy first, she instructed, "Have a seat on the table. Let's get your wet clothes off so I can examine that wound thoroughly."

Andy thought he would pass out as they removed three layers of soggy, blood-soaked clothing. The bridge fragment had stapled his rain poncho, tunic, and linen undershirt to his flesh, and he cried out when Bridrika disturbed it.

"Cut the material away from the wound," the healer instructed her assistant.

With his shoulder now bare, Andy saw the thickness of the chunk of wood for the first time. Knowledge somehow intensified his pain and he gritted his teeth, doing his best to remain quiet.

"It's a good thing you didn't attempt to remove this," the healer encouraged.

That bad, huh?

"Andy, please lay down."

As he did, he felt his breathing quicken. The little girl looked up from her play.

"Elganora, Captain Ladilas, hold him still."

Andy felt hands clamp down on his ankles and his good shoulder.

"Bite down on this," Bridrika instructed, placing a piece of cloth between his teeth.

Andy's eyes opened as wide as saucers. *This is gonna kill!*

The healer placed a handful of cloth next to the wood and, in one fluid motion, yanked.

Ow! Andy screamed in his head, biting down hard and groaning.

Andy felt pressure being applied, making the pain more intense, if that was even possible.

"You can let go," she instructed her helpers.

After several minutes Bridrika let up on some of the pressure, eventually removing the cloth to inspect the wound. She shook her head and brought a bottle of what looked like wine to the table, commanding, "Hold still."

Andy saw stars as she poured it into the wound. He directed his pain into a fist he made with his good hand, smashing it down on the table next to him. Not yet satisfied she'd inflicted enough pain on her patient, the torturess found a container of foul-smelling goo and proceeded to slather it in and around the hole in Andy's shoulder. Andy winced but didn't cry out.

"That'll speed the healing," she informed. "Elganora, dress the wound while I tend to the captain."

"Okay, you can sit up, Andy," the assistant coaxed. "Slowly."

Elganora helped him to the bench and proceeded to retrieve a needle and thread. *Stitches? No!*

The little girl stared at Andy as he winced with each suture. She seemed surprised at his groaning. As the assistant fastened the eighth stitch in place, Andy wondered, *Does she think she's working on a piece of needlepoint?*

After completing ten stitches, Elganora examined her work and smiled with satisfaction, to which Andy sighed.

Andy watched as the healer treated the captain. He sat stoically on the table while Bridrika followed a similar procedure, although when it came time to extract the projectile, he declined anything to bite into. Instead, Captain

Ladilas stared fixedly at the ceiling and winced as the healer removed the wood, but that was it. *I'm such a wimp.*

When all the excitement ended, the ladies left. Andy overheard the girl ask, "Why'd that boy make such a fuss over his injuries?"

"Not everyone is like the dwarfs, dear," Elganora replied.

Andy rolled his eyes.

"Need help?" Mazar asked, bringing his attention back. "You can clean up, then I'll take you to join your king."

Andy and the captain willingly complied. Despite the dampness of their clean clothes, it felt good to be out of their filthy apparel. Mazar fitted both of them with fresh slings before exiting the infirmary.

Several minutes later, Mazar knocked on a heavy wooden door framed by more ornate carvings. A dwarf servant welcomed them into a large but cheery room with a roaring fire in the stone hearth.

"Your king is enjoying tea with His Majesty," the servant stated, looking from Andy to the captain.

"Thank you, Montag," replied Mazar, handing off his charges.

The servant escorted them down the corridor and knocked twice.

"Enter!" a deep voice boomed from inside.

CHAPTER TWELVE

Male Bonding

"Andy!" The King hurried over and hugged him. "I'm glad to see you're doing better."

"Where is everyone, Father?"

"They're freshening up. They'll join us before dinner. Speaking of which..."

The King turned.

"Please pardon my lack of manners, Your Majesty, but this is my son, Prince Andrew."

The portly dwarf nodded and smiled from where he reclined, sipping a cup of tea. "No apology necessary. I would do the same."

The dwarf king wore a long-sleeved tunic of fine red linen trimmed with luxurious embroidery and topped by a sleeveless surcoat of linsey-woolsey. A glint of silver chain mail peeked from under a pepper-gray beard that covered his chest and abdomen. Black leggings, leather boots with silver buckles, and three rings on each hand sparkling with sapphires and rubies enhanced the regal ensemble.

That's quite a beard. Looks like that's where all the hair from his head migrated, thought Andy, noticing the sovereign's shiny noggin. Andy approached and bowed. "Your Majesty."

Captain Ladilas followed.

"Please, take a seat and have some tea," Nithi invited as he dismissed Sergeant Mazar with a wave. "Your father and I were getting acquainted. We've corresponded previously but never met. He tells me you know a thing or two about dwarfs of the line of Durin."

"That's right, Your Majesty," Andy confirmed even as he thought, *I hope these are the same dwarfs.*

Another servant appeared bearing a tea service. He handed Andy and Captain Ladilas each a steaming cup and a plate of biscuits. Much had happened since Andy last ate, and he bit into a warm biscuit with enthusiasm, drawing a chuckle from their host.

"Well, I'd be interested in swapping stories if you're up to it."

Andy smiled between bites and replied, "Sure." He glanced at Father who grinned encouragement.

After consuming thirds, Andy began, "What I know starts with Thorin Oakenshield and a group of dwarfs of the line of Durin going on a quest to regain their homeland, Erebor. It had been stolen from them by the dragon, Smaug." He recounted as many details as he could remember, hoping he'd put them in the right order.

Throughout his telling, Nithi nodded, but Andy couldn't decide whether it meant he agreed with the story or whether he was acknowledging he listened. *Surely this isn't new to him.*

When Andy finished, Nithi asked, "Do you know how the dwarfs began?"

"Yes, sir. It all started when Vala Aulë—you call him Mahal—created the dwarfs. He was a smith who worked metal and earth; he formed the dwarfs from the ground. Then Ilúvatar, the master creator, gave them life. Sorry, I'm probably not pronouncing their names correctly."

Father raised an eyebrow.

The dwarf king smiled. "No worries, Andy. I'm impressed. King Hercalon, you seem surprised that the boy knows so much about dwarfs."

Father laughed, "This is all new to me."

"And what else do you know about dwarfs, Andy?" Nithi probed.

"Well, I know Mahal created seven dwarf fathers. Durin was the first. Nithi...I think Nithi was the third."

"Very good," the dwarf encouraged. "Prince Andrew, how did you come by such knowledge that your Father does not possess?"

Andy locked eyes with Father, who raised an eyebrow slightly, before
replying, "I read about it in the Voluspa. It's a poem."

"Indeed it is, lad. And it is why this place is called Völuspà, home of the
great hall of the dwarfs of the line of Nithi, in the shadow of Mount Mur Eyah."
He added the proper dwarfish enunciation as he spoke.

"I thought it might be!" Andy exclaimed. Before the dwarf king could
probe further, he added, "Would you tell me about your line, Your Majesty?"

"That was the deal, wasn't it?" King Nithi beamed as he began. "Mahal
gave Nithi dominion over Lower-earth where the deepest and purest veins of
jewels and precious stones are found. The line of Nithi multiplied and took up
mining to trade with the peoples of Middle-earth. Peace and prosperity
prevailed throughout the rule of Nithi I until Nithi III.

"But during Nithi IV's reign, in the late Third Age, we were drawn into the
War of the Dwarfs and Orcs and sustained major casualties. When we were
weakest, a dwarf calling himself the Whitehearted Potentate rose up. He was
convinced the dwarfs of Lower- and Middle-earth had become overly greedy
and obsessed with their jewels and hoards of precious metal. Believing dwarfs
were held in bondage to their desires and not truly free, he vowed to wipe out
all the lustful dwarfs and start over, if it came to that.

"He invited a trove of dragons to join him on his quest, for he knew no
one could win against these beasts. The dragons were perfectly suited to this
task. They're smart, and they hid their greed from him. The Whitehearted
Potentate waged a violent and ruthless campaign against his fellows, usually
ending with dragon's fire wiping out whole villages. After each victory, he
would then dispatch a single dragon to watch over the treasure cache.
Eventually, the Whitehearted Potentate ran out of available dragons and his
fight came to a brutal end, but not before virtually all the dwarfs of Lower-earth
had been wiped out. And, I would add, the dragons refused to give up the
treasure they guarded, even though the Potentate's campaign ended.

"During the slaughter, some dwarfs escaped, tunneling into Oomaldee.
They sought permission from your ancestor, King Matillis II, to establish a

home here. The king accepted their request and granted them mountainous land not suitable for farming. Since that day, we pay an annual tribute to your kingdom."

"Tunnels connect Lower- and Middle-earth with Oomaldee? Cool! Do you know where they are?" Andy quizzed.

"It's my understanding they were blocked off long ago to prevent dragons or any other crusader from following. Needless to say, dwarfs are not fans of dragons."

"I can see why," Andy replied. *I wonder where Daisy's line started?*

The dwarf king rose and announced, "It's nearly time for dinner. I'd like to freshen up, and no doubt you'd be interested in seeing the rest of your company."

Father, Andy, and Captain Ladilas stood as the king excused himself.

Before Montag returned for them, the King commented, "Well done, Son. You've done much to extend the congenial relationship we share with the dwarfs. Dwarf friendship is hard to earn but strong once it's won. The difference between an acquaintance and a friend among the dwarfs is about a hundred years."

"A hundred years! But I won't live that long."

"Don't worry, Andy. Some of the strongest friendships are those between human and dwarf, as long as the human ancestors were on good terms. I consider myself a friend of Nithi XXVI, and I believe it's mutual."

"I hope you're right, Father."

Montag rejoined them and escorted them down several halls, finally entering a suite with shiny marble floors, a circular common area, and half a dozen chambers branching off. A round marble fireplace inlaid with rubies and sapphires blazed with a roaring fire and served as a focal point for the space. A blue rug spread out in front of it, and cushy chairs and a cozy sofa invited the trio to sit a spell.

Hannah and Alden, who had been enjoying the fire while conversing with Mermin, rushed to greet Andy.

"How are you feeling?" Hannah queried.

"Okay, I guess."

The captain joined the pair of sergeants off to one side of the couch and shared his experiences before the trio rejoined the rest of the company several minutes later.

"If you'll excuse me, I'm going to go change before dinner," the King interrupted the chatter.

"Oh Andy, you really missed out!" Alden began. "Fendrel, he's a miner, took us on a tour of the Corundum mine."

"It smelled damp," Hannah informed, wrinkling her nose, "but it was still amazing!"

Alden continued, "Yeah, the mine went down so far I couldn't see the bottom! They'd run strings of torches up and down the walls where miners hung at various points."

"Fendrel led us down rickety scaffolding that wobbled as we walked. I looked over once and wished I hadn't," Hannah added.

Alden laughed at the memory.

For his part, a fluttery feeling again crept into Andy's chest as he watched Hannah recount their adventures with exuberance. He tried to refocus as she demonstrated how the miners carefully chiseled away at the rock, making sure no sapphires fell into the abyss.

"Oh, I almost forgot." Alden walked over to his backpack and rummaged in the front pocket. "This is a piece of sapphire for you. Fendrel gave one to each of us." Alden pulled out a small stone, returned to where Andy and Hannah sat, and handed it to him.

Andy brightened and held the stone up in the firelight. "It's beautiful! Thanks!"

"Fendrel said there are only four types of precious stones: emeralds, diamonds, rubies, and sappires. Other stones are considered semiprecious. They mine both rubies and sapphires here," Hannah reported.

"So this is worth something. Excellent!" Andy responded as Father rejoined the group.

"What's worth something?" the King asked.

"This," Andy replied, showing him the jagged blue pebble.

"Very nice!" Father acknowledged as Andy added his new treasure to his pouch.

Montag interrupted the chatter. "Excuse me, but dinner is ready and your presence is requested. Please follow me."

In no time, the group of eight entered Nithi's family dining chamber. The sovereign greeted them with arms open wide. "I thought we'd eat in here tonight rather than in the main hall. It's more private and certainly more comfortable."

A long wood table with a dozen carved wooden chairs occupied the center of the paneled space, over which hung an ornate forged chandelier with no fewer than thirty candles flickering from its six branches. A marble fireplace behind the head of the table added light and warmth to the room, as did the sconces along the walls.

"I'd like you to meet Catrain, my wife."

The queen curtsied and nodded as everyone filed by. "My husband has been telling me about your little group."

"All good, I hope," Father joked.

"Most assuredly. He is particularly impressed with you, young man," she added, locking eyes with Andy.

Andy smiled and bowed. "Thank you, Your Highness."

Father beamed.

Another dwarf servant interrupted, "If you would all take your seats we can begin serving." The stout little man directed Father to a chair on the left of Nithi, who commanded the seat at the head of the table. Andy sat next to Father, and Alden and Hannah took seats to Andy's left. Catrain invited Mermin to occupy the seat of honor to her right, across from Andy. Captain

Ladilas, Sergeant Albin, and Sergeant Gavin filled empty seats toward the far end of the table.

Once everyone was seated, Nithi raised a golden goblet and declared, "I'd like to propose a toast."

Everyone lifted their drinking glasses high.

"To friendships new and old. May they be blessed with lasting peace, and may our enemies wither under our strong bonds of cooperation." As Nithi spoke, he glanced from Andy to Father and around the rest of the table, ending with a wink to his queen.

Over dinner, Andy discovered some foods were similar to those at Castle Avalon, fairly basic and plain. Others were much different, even spicy.

After indulging in a particularly large portion of one offering that had a bright orange hue, Andy dabbed a napkin on his moist brow and declared, "This meal is delicious, Your Majesty. I love spicy food!"

Father forced a polite smile as Andy fanned his glowing face.

Nithi nodded and put on an amused look. "I'm glad you like it, Prince Andrew! We used to trade with Cromlech for spices, including many varieties of peppers, which is probably what you're tasting. But with the devastation there, we've begun trading with Miramon, a land to the northwest of Lake Nimue."

They trade?

The magistrate noticed Andy's surprised look and grinned. "Oh yes, we trade with many partners since we don't farm."

"You don't farm? Really?"

"We trade for fruits, vegetables, wine, fish, and meat with the farmers and fishermen of Oomaldee. From the Ryersk, peoples south of Lake Nimue, we trade for cotton, silk, indigo dye, kermes, and textiles. And we get other ingredients like salt, tea, nutmeg, cacao, and cloves from either Cromlech or Miramon."

Andy felt a strong draft and heard hushed whispers from the door behind him. He turned to see a footman arguing with a dwarf clad in chain mail who gestured animatedly. The servant wagged his head from side to side and refused to admit him, but the damage had been done.

Out of the corner of his eye, Andy caught Captain Ladilas and both sergeants instinctively reach for their weapons.

"Captain Terrin," Nithi boomed, motioning him to approach.

"Pardon the interruption, Your Majesty," the dwarf warrior apologized as he drew near his sovereign, then leaned in and began whispering into Nithi's ear. Conversation around the table respectfully quieted.

"Three more?" the dwarf king queried.

Captain Terrin continued his briefing, standing up only after he appeared satisfied his message had been fully received.

Andy caught bits and pieces of the information even though he knew he shouldn't eavesdrop.

"Thank you for the update. You may go," Nithi dismissed.

The captain stood up straight, jammed his arms behind his back, and clicked his heels.

That must be their salute, Andy reasoned, having seen the gesture once before.

With everyone curious but pretending not to be, Nithi glanced at his wife then around at his guests and explained, "The captain informed me they just brought in three more zolt that were caught in our traps."

Everyone but the queen wore a puzzled expression, so the regent explained, "Zolt are short men with bulging eyes, beak-like noses, and arms that extend to their ankles."

"Oh, we have those in Oomaldee, too. We call them vulture-people," Andy chirped.

The sovereign shook his head and frowned. "Yeah, they're bird-like all right. They've been making quite a nuisance of themselves since their scheming commander paid us a visit a couple months back."

"What happened?" Father asked.

"I won't go into details, but suffice it to say their diplomatic mission, if that's what you want to call it, failed miserably. We found these men to be untrustworthy and utterly contemptible. Since then we've set traps to capture their spies."

"Is that why your prison is full of them?" Captain Ladilas queried.

"It is. My apologies that you had to encounter two of our traps."

"It made for quite an adventure," Father added.

"We would never treat friends that way. Had I known you would be coming, I would have sent out an escort. Which reminds me, we heard of your pigeon post and will be opening a branch within the next couple months, so further communication should be easier. As I understand it, they're working to train the birds now. Imagine that, trusting birds to carry important messages. What will they think of next?" The magistrate grinned.

"These guys transform into vultures, I've seen them," Andy added matter-of-factly.

Nithi, who was just biting into a biscuit, stopped mid-bite. "Excuse me, but did you say these foul spies transform into vultures? As in, large flying scavengers?"

"That's right, sir," Andy confirmed, nodding. "Alden and I watched one land in bird-form. We followed it behind a tent and saw it become a beady-eyed, long-armed man."

"It was wild!" Alden chimed in.

"I see," added Nithi, frowning.

"Your Majesty?" Alden questioned.

The royal lifted his eyes and rested them on Alden. "Yes, young man?"

"You called them *zolt*. What does that mean?"

Nithi laughed. "That's the expression we use for disreputable sorts. Literally, it means 'dung eater.'"

At hearing that, everyone chuckled.

"I like it!" Andy exclaimed. "I'm gonna start calling them zolts. It fits!"

Alden and Hannah laughed, and Sergeant Albin added, "Sounds appropriate to me!"

After the giggles subsided, Mermin inquired, "Excuse me, but you mentioned their commander paid you a visit wecently?"

"Yeeesss." The king drew out his word. "He called himself King Abaddon. I had never encountered him before." A shiver rocked Nithi's form and he grasped the queen's forearm. "A dragon with seven heads and four wings. He filled me with dread. It appeared he was unwell, though. The left eye on each of his heads was bandaged."

"We're intimately acquainted with him," Sergeant Gavin affirmed. "Andy here has fought him in close combat. More than once." The sergeant winked at Andy.

"My stars, boy!" exclaimed the queen. "Whatever would possess you to do such a thing?"

"I didn't exactly have a choice, ma'am."

"From everything my husband told me about this beast, he uses flattering words with hidden motives. He's one to take up arms against. ."

Nithi took in a slow, deep breath. "He left voluntarily, but ever since then the zolt have been coming. Our prison is filling up with them, but I don't dare let them go. Who knows what they're looking for and what they'd tell their leaders. Nasty little spies."

Father put his fork down and looked into the regent's eyes. "Abaddon's objective is to rule the world." Father paused, letting that sink in. "As you know, the lands surrounding Oomaldee have been ravaged. I believe Oomaldee is the crown jewel in his plan. Frankly, I don't think he cares much about those lands he's already conquered or any others you trade with. His goal is to shut off Oomaldee's supplies and put us in a stranglehold. I fear he will target Voluspa as part of his evil scheme."

The sovereign kneaded his brow, frowning.

"But why is Oomaldee so important to him?" the queen scowled.

"That, my lady, is *the* question, and I do not yet have a satisfactory answer. I have searched for information about Abaddon's origins, but thus far haven't turned up much. His past is rather a mystery. He certainly existed long before I was born."

There's a scroll in my attic about Abaddon, Andy remembered. He looked over at Father and across at the queen, opened his mouth to speak, then thought better of it and closed it again.

No, I'd better not. I don't want to get sent home. Andy made a mental note to study that scroll upon his return home.

"Was there something you wanted to add, Son?" Father asked.

"Uh, no."

The rest of the meal passed uneventfully. Just as the servants cleared the dishes from the final course, a sous chef entered the chamber and announced, "Chef Fallan has prepared a delicious dragee to complete your dining tonight. For the adults, please enjoy this bottle of Ardo, a rare spicy wine he procured from his favorite winery in Oomaldee. It will go nicely with the Pendir cheese that has been aged in our own cellars, along with the apple spiced sugar. Enjoy!"

Dragee, huh? Andy thought.

"They may not grow their own food, but they sure know how to prepare it," Hannah proclaimed, taking another candy as it passed.

"Agwee!" Alden managed to get out, his mouth stuffed full of cheese.

Andy and the soldiers laughed and nodded, taking more for themselves.

When the meal at last ended, Montag escorted the eight back to their chambers. Everyone headed to bed as soon as they arrived, for it promised to be an early morning.

Andy lay on the soft bed and stared at the dark ceiling. Before he allowed himself to drift off, he reflected on the events of the day and the translucent sphere that plagued him. His mind remembered the little she-dwarf in the treatment room, watching her mom work. It brought back memories.

He remembered going with Madison to Mom's office on school holidays, before they were old enough to stay home alone. He and Maddy would usually color in the morning, but as they grew bored, they'd migrate out to the warehouse and play hide and seek. Climbing around on the racks of inventory always made for an exciting adventure. Andy stifled a laugh as he recalled one time when Madison couldn't find him and was getting ticked. He had jumped down right in front of her and scared her half to death. Then there was the time Mom had unexpectedly hid behind a huge box and grabbed him as he walked by. He nearly peed his pants. Madison couldn't stop laughing at that one and nearly peed her pants, too.

His thoughts moved to family game nights when he and Mom would team up against Dad and Madison. Talk about competitive! If one team started trouncing the other at Risk, things would get a bit heated. But in the end, no matter who won, Mom always insisted everyone give each other a hug and mean it. On these occasions, Mom gave him a hug for being a good partner. She always overdid it, making her hug more animated and longer than usual. He loved it!

And then Andy's thoughts turned to the conversations he had shared with Mom after he learned she had come from Oomaldee. She told him all about growing up as a servant in King Hercalon IV's castle where she had been brought after both her parents were killed in a raid when she was just three years old. She barely remembered her parents. Through all her stories, he had begun to feel closer to her than ever before.

Short of giving my life, I'll do whatever I must to save Mom, he vowed.

CHAPTER THIRTEEN

Unwelcome Bargain

A s promised, the day began too early as Father jiggled Andy to semiconsciousness.

"Hmm?"

"Come on, sleepyhead. It's time to get moving. We've got a big day ahead."

"Uh-huh," Andy mumbled, rolling over.

Aromas promising tasty vittles finally enticed him to stumble from the room he'd shared with Alden. His eyes considered opening, and as he slowly forced them, he saw everyone else was already dressed and munching on freshly baked bread, fruit, and cheese in front of a blazing fire.

Andy stretched and yawned before helping himself to breakfast. *Wow. My shoulder sure feels better.* He tested it, making a circle with his elbow.

Montag disturbed the silence several minutes later, announcing, "Please be ready to leave in ten minutes. Sergeants Mazar and Brufn will be escorting you to the edge of our realm."

Everyone nodded appreciatively.

An hour later the group of eight trouped after Sergeant Mazar through a maze of earthen tunnels. Sergeant Brufn brought up the rear to ensure no one was left behind. They had exited the lavish, polished marble palace soon after embarking and had navigated stone-lined tunnels where stairways branched off to the right and left like the branches of a large tree.

As if in answer to Andy's unspoken question, Sergeant Mazar informed them the stairways led to residential and business districts within Voluspa. Others led to the various mines.

Having reached a decision regarding his mom that his inneru could support, Andy smiled as they walked. The weight of guilt had lifted, and he felt at peace for the first time since he'd encountered that swirling sphere.

They approached a sign suspended from a bulky wooden support beam: CORUNDUM MINE. It pointed left.

"That's the mine we toured," Alden indicated.

The path led down through a shopping district with more than two dozen businesses selling all types of wares: fresh fruits and vegetables, cut flowers, mining tools, medicines, baskets, candles, and more.

"I thought dwarfs didn't farm," Andy piped up.

"For the most part we don't," Sergeant Brufn replied. "The merchants bought this produce early this morning from vendors in Oomaldee."

They climbed three flights of stairs after leaving the market area and soon came upon another sign indicating EDELSTEEN MINE.

Heading off the question before it could be posed, Sergeant Mazar explained, "The Edelsteen Mine is where our finest rubies come from."

"How many mines do you work?" the King inquired.

"We have twelve active mines at the moment. As our population grows, we open new mines and convert less productive properties to residential or business wards. Our realm currently extends under large portions of ogre territory. We make sure we don't dig too close to the surface."

Mazar and the King shared a knowing smile that piqued Andy's curiosity, but he didn't pursue.

At the end of the tunnel the group had been following for the last hour, a dirt wall blocked their path. The incline hadn't been bad at the beginning, but over the last twenty minutes it had increased to the point where everyone panted, winded from the exertion. Sergeant Mazer called a halt.

"We have reached our destination," he informed. The news was met with a collective sigh.

"Destination?" Alden asked, straining to catch his breath as he studied the wall.

"Yes, that's right."

"Umm," Andy breathed heavily, wiping his brow, "there's no place to go."

He glanced over at Father whose chest heaved as he slowed his breathing. Father winked.

"You indicated your journey takes you to the territory of the trolls. We have reached the southernmost point of that domain," Sergeant Bruhn explained.

"Thank you for your direction and gracious hospitality," Father acknowledged.

"You're quite welcome. Safe travels and a prosperous journey to you and your party," replied Sergeant Mazar, bowing.

Both officers then turned and headed back in the direction from which they'd come. After watching them disappear, everyone turned their gaze back to the King, awaiting instruction.

"On we go then," he exclaimed and started toward the earthen wall.

Andy and the others watched curiously, unmoving.

The King paused when he heard no one following and glanced back. "What are you waiting for?" His eyes danced with mischief.

Andy's mind flashed back to Daisy's approach to the mountain around Denver and he started after Father.

"I guess it's just you and me."

"I guess so."

Andy grinned, catching up.

The two walked forward, losing sight of the rest of the group. Captain Ladilas appeared next, his sense of duty compelling him through the wall. One by one they passed through the barrier and exclaimed as they entered a forest blanketed by fallen leaves and soaked with cheery, if foggy, sunshine. Birds chirped and frogs croaked in chorus, celebrating their arrival.

Andy looked back from where they had come and saw no sign of a door or any opening, only the face of a steep, vine-covered cliff.

"A dwarf door is invisible to all but those in need," Father commented to Andy, patting him on his good shoulder.

With the discovery of dwarf doors being made available when in need, committed to the memory of all, the group proceeded. The sergeants again flanked them with the captain bringing up the rear. The King and Mermin led the way with Andy, Alden, and Hannah sandwiched in the middle.

The terrain was no less steep outside the tunnel, and the group trudged ahead in silence. They approached a clearing and got their first glimpse of Mount Mur Eyah off to the right. While the fog obscured its summit, Andy could see the base of a single mountain. The sun radiating off its foggy slopes cast a golden hue.

"What does Mur Eyah mean?" Andy threw the question out to no one in particular.

From in front, Mermin slowed and turned. "Mur Eyah means 'pwovision shall be made.'"

"Why's it called that?" Hannah quickly questioned.

"There are tales told of twavelers in need, stumbling upon the slopes of that mountain. Inexplicably, their pwoblem fixed itself, almost as if magic played a part."

"How do you mean?" Alden pursued.

The company halted as Mermin continued his explanantion. "One account tells of a patwol being chased by savage werewolves and taking wefuge in a cave in that mountain. No sooner had the gwoup entered the cave, the enemy nipping at their heels, than the werewolves mysteriously lost their scent. The patwol weported they could see the werewolves lingering about the cave entrance, sniffing and clawing, but the pack never entered the cave. Finally, the pack gave up and left. This is not an isolated incident."

"Maybe werewolves are afraid of caves," Andy suggested.

"Werewolves live in dark caves, Andy. And they have an excellent sense of smell," Mermin countered.

"Oh," Andy replied, filing the story for future exploration.

An hour later, only the sounds of huffing and puffing, scuffled leaves, and nature itself broke the stillness. The trek had grown increasingly steep, the exertion and monotony dulling everyone's senses. The company rejoiced as they crested the mountain. But as they did, the birds went quiet. Andy thought he heard an unnatural noise to the right of the path. The forest seemed to hold its breath, waiting.

Is the bellicose back?

Andy drew Methuselah and assumed his ready position, motioning Sergeant Gavin on their right flank to do the same. Hannah and Alden saw Andy and silently drew their weapons. Sergeant Albin, Captain Ladilas, and the King took defensive postures, as did Mermin in the rear. They waited more than five minutes in tense silence before a group of fifty or more zolt charged from the dense foliage, brandishing swords and whirling war hammers above their beady-eyed heads.

Andy and his companions engaged. He and Sergeant Gavin slashed their way toward the middle of the enemy, protecting each other's back. Out of the corner of his eye, Andy glimpsed Alden and Sergeant Albin teamed, working their way through the left flank. Andy brought Methuselah's blade down on a zolt to his left, freeing its head from its scrawny shoulders. A stab to Andy's right brought two more of the enemy down. Sergeant Gavin had equal success as they plowed a path through the middle of their adversaries.

Andy noticed movement to his right and saw Hannah and Captain Ladilas pulverizing the right flank. Any doubts he might have harbored as to her sword skills vanished instantly; she was definitely Cadfael's daughter. A bird-man approached, ready to decapitate the captain. Hannah spun and with one quick, downward slice the creature slumped over, dead.

Andy watched as three zolt squawked and hurtled through the air, gangly arms flailing. They smashed into a thick tree ten yards away and fell limply to the ground. Tracing their trajectory, Andy realized Mermin had used magic to produce the impressive result. Father had Mermin's back, brandishing his sword and cutting down three more of the enemy. It looked as though they had fought together before.

The vulture ranks thinned as Andy and Sergeant Gavin continued slashing and jabbing. A meaty zolt charged Andy, whirling a war hammer over its head. Andy barely dodged injury, ducking at the last second. Having committed to the attack with an extended arm, the bird-man left an exposed side that Andy quickly used to his advantage. Methuselah found flesh as the enemy slid past and slumped to the ground.

As the fighting continued, Andy's shoulder began to hurt and he found it increasingly difficult to slash with any degree of power. He glanced over and noticed Captain Ladilas wearing a pained expression as well. With ten zolt remaining, the four pairs intensified their defense, taking the enemy down with determination.

When Andy saw no bird-men remained, he and Sergeant Gavin stepped over and around the dead to join the others. He sprawled on the ground, his chest heaving. After several minutes, he sat up and inspected his extremities. With the exception of a small gash to the back of his hand, he was not injured. Everyone else came through unscathed and let their guard down as they rejoiced.

Without warning, several dozen vultures appeared through the fog, landed, and instantly transformed into zolt. They moved in quickly, separating the group and binding their hands with heavy rope. The apparent leader commanded his troops to secure the captives' weapons and line them up single-file.

"March!" the leader bellowed when they finished.

Andy felt spearheads and swords poking him in the back and on his arms as they struggled up the mountain. *I feel like a pig being led to slaughter.*

After nearly half an hour, they reached the only flat clearing Andy had seen in the area. Across the muddy plateau sat a weakened, seven-headed dragon. Its four wings flapped lethargically as it sat on the thick, rotting trunk of a fallen tree. As Andy had seen in his dream, it wore a patch over the left eye on each of its heads.

The zolt shoved the group across the clearing to within ten feet of the beast. No one uttered a word.

"So you have found them, Dagon," Abaddon noted, three of his heads slowly bobbing.

"Yes, my liege," the vulture-warrior confirmed, bowing.

"Very good." Abaddon paused and scrutinized each member of the party before continuing. "Hard to believe these vermin hold the key to my longevity." Three of his heads spat on the ground.

Noticing Andy studying him, the beast laughed and roared, "A sniveling peasant boy for the chosen one." He left the words hanging for several seconds, then sneered, "Now why would a king, his wizard, three children, and a meager security detail be wandering around in the woods?"

No one responded, so Dagon approached the King and shouted, "He asked you a question. Answer him!"

"The same could be asked of you," the King responded.

"Bring him here," the dragon demanded, five of his heads motioning toward the King.

Dagon cut the King loose from the group and shoved him toward Abaddon. He fell onto his hands and knees in the mud, and Andy bolted forward until the rope connecting him to Captain Ladilas and Alden prevented further progress.

Abaddon looked at Andy and derided, "Such a shame you can't help your king."

Andy felt his face grow hot and his nostrils flared. He barely managed to hold his tongue.

The seven-headed dragon laughed and two of its mouths mocked in unison, "That's right. Hold your tongue boy, or my soldiers will hold it for you."

The King stood, his head held high, his face expressionless.

Four of the beast's heads studied him, moving up and down like snakes before a charmer.

The King didn't flinch, only stared straight ahead.

"Take it!" the monster at last commanded.

Andy bit his tongue as Dagon walked over and took his dagger to the front of the King's tunic, slicing it down the middle. Again, his father didn't flinch.

"Where is it?" all seven heads managed to roar despite the dragon's weakened condition.

The King remained silent.

"Answer me!" demanded three heads in harmony.

Dagon brought his dagger up under Father's chin and growled, "You will answer."

"Where's what?" the King asked.

"The Stone of Athanasia," two of the beast's mouths rumbled.

Father did not respond, and the servant cut into his neck with the edge of his dagger, drawing a trickle of blood.

Abaddon scowled at the King for several minutes, at an impasse. "Kill him!" the beast finally roared.

Before Dagon could act, a shrill voice sounded over the clearing. "Tut, tut, tut. You don't want to do that," it cackled. "Do you not remember what I told you? If you kill him, the stone's loyalties can never be changed."

Abaddon briefly considered Imogenia's interruption.

The servant stared at his sovereign, awaiting orders. Finally, Abaddon rolled all fourteen of his eyes and waved Dagon away from the King.

"I need energy. Convert them," two heads instructed in stereo.

Dagon shoved everyone closer to the dragon and commanded, "Kneel and pledge allegiance to your new sovereign!"

No one moved, so four zolt warriors approached and whacked everyone in the back of the knees, forcing them to collapse onto the muddy ground. With everyone now kneeling, Dagon repeated his demand. Again, no one uttered a word. Andy closed his eyes, praying he wouldn't be transformed into one of these hideous creatures or worse, turned into one of the stone statues he'd seen in his nightmares. Still, if he died, it would be with those he loved.

"Fine, you have chosen your own fates," the servant barked.

Please, no. Please, no.

In an evil rasp, Abaddon chanted a phrase.

Andy squeezed his eyes tight.

The dragon repeated his utterance, more loudly.

Andy peeked open one eye as he heard the incantation a third time.

Abaddon looked about, furious. Green vapor poured from three of his heads as the other four slumped.

"Why isn't it working?" the beast complained weakly. Andy knew the complaint would have been a thunderous roar had Abaddon not been so sluggish.

It didn't work! It didn't work! Whew! But why? Is the stone still protecting us even though it's implanted under Father's skin? Was my guess right?

"Get up!" Dagon commanded.

Once standing, five zolt shoved the company to the edge of the clearing where eight poles the thickness of mature trees were sunken into the ground ten feet apart. The soldiers cut the ropes connecting the prisoners and moved each to a post, tying their hands behind their backs and their legs together. Gags ensured no one would talk.

"Looks like you have a bit of a problem," Imogenia taunted.

Abaddon didn't reply.

"I might know a way to help you. In exchange for—" she stopped.

"In exchange for what?" two heads queried.

"Glad to see you're listening," the ghost crooned. "In exchange for the life of Prince Andrew."

Father's eyes met Andy's across the semicircle.

"Prince Andrew?" Abaddon questioned.

"Indeed. My brother discovered the boy is his son," Imogenia explained.

The corners of five of Abaddon's mouths curved up in a smile. "Really? Interesting. Very interesting." He paused a moment, considering. "But surely this news, while welcome, is not what you had in mind to strengthen me? I need a cure!"

"I know a way for you to be healed so that you are regenerated and whole again, with no marks or effects from the boy's sword."

"How?" Abaddon hissed.

"The boy's life or I won't say."

The beast considered the trade, calculating, before it finally replied, "Only after your cure works will I slay the boy."

Andy glanced at Alden and Hannah, their expressions worried.

"Is that a promise?" Imogenia pushed.

"It is as much as I will say," Abaddon rasped. "Now, the cure."

Satisfied for the moment, Imogenia's silvery form floated across the clearing, stopping in front of Andy. "You shall be mine!" she sneered.

Andy struggled against his bonds to no avail, and despite the gag, he noised, "Yuu unn uuu un!" trying to hide his terror.

Imogenia cackled and turned toward Abaddon.

"The cure," the spirit began, "is a unicorn horn. Curiously enough, that is why this group is traveling. They seek such a horn to break the curse." The spirit's voice sounded sickeningly sweet.

"Unicorns? There are no unicorns in these parts!" three heads intoned.

"Oh, but there are. The boy overheard a group of them talking not more than two days ago thanks to a dragon's tapping into their conversation."

"I see." Abaddon cleared two of his throats and sighed deeply. "And how will a unicorn horn cure me?"

"Unicorns are pure and undefiled. When ingested, unicorn horn flows through the body and mends all imperfections. Your ability to shapeshift, not to mention your sight, will be restored."

"Bring me this cure," Abaddon growled.

"I will need the assistance of two of your warriors, for I cannot carry it, as you well know."

"Gozler, Maladoca, assist her!" Dagon commanded.

Two long-armed, beady-eyed soldiers slunk forward and saluted.

"Follow me," Imogenia instructed.

What am I going to do? As soon as they return, I'm toast!

Andy glanced around the semicircle. Everyone watched him with concerned expressions. He tested the bonds holding his arms again. Secure. He twisted his wrists, but like the last ten tries, he found no room to move.

Calming his thoughts, he finally remembered the gold key still in his pouch. They hadn't taken that. A glimmer of hope formed.

Please untie my bonds, he willed.

He twisted his wrists again. It was working. He felt a little space!

That's it, loosen the ropes.

Again he swiveled his wrists, but the ropes remained too tight to squeeze out of.

Come on, faster! Does the key have to be closer to Methuselah? he wondered, his panic growing. He eyed the group's weapons where they lay in a heap on the ground at Abaddon's feet.

Calm down, Andy told himself and continued to twist his hands with mixed success. While he gained a bit more room to move, his skin grew raw. He looked around the group. Everyone wore looks of concentration and he noticed slight movement in their shoulders; they all worked to free themselves.

Andy didn't know how much time elapsed, but too soon Imogenia and the bird-men returned bearing a white, cone-shaped object about a foot long.

The ghost fumed, "Your men rushed the unicorns against my orders! For a unicorn horn to work, it must be given freely, to a maiden. They took it by force. I will not be responsible if it does not cure you!"

Abaddon laughed maniacally. "Oh, but you will, you will. For I will not kill the boy unless this miracle cure of yours works."

"Bring it to me!" the beast commanded his men.

Don't work! Please don't work! Andy begged.

The long-armed warriors handed their commander the horn and he took seven greedy bites, one with each of his mouths.

The guy's a slob, Andy thought as he watched the dragon devour the antidote.

Please don't work! Please don't work!

Everyone stared, curious. Five minutes. Ten minutes. Twenty minutes passed. Nothing.

"Unicorn horn will cure you!" Imogenia insisted after yet another ten minutes passed with no change.

Nodding four of his heads toward Hannah, Abaddon chided, "It looks like the maiden will have to retrieve another one then."

Hannah glared at the beast, her jaw set. The rest of the group watched in horror as Dagon freed her wrists, then cut the rope from around her legs. It took Hannah only a second to rid herself of the gag.

"Move!" the warrior demanded, pushing her toward Abaddon.

Hannah walked across the clearing to within ten feet of the beast.

"You will find the unicorns and bring me back a horn that will cure me!"

"And if I don't?"

The dragon flapped its wings weakly. "If you don't, I will kill your King, his wizard, and the rest of your company one by one in the most painful way possible," Abaddon leered.

"Fine. Then I'll need help. I'm not going to go bumbling about in these woods all by myself. Who knows what's out there. And I'm certainly not going with your soldiers!"

Still smiling, the beast said, "Very well. The chosen one will accompany you to ensure your safety."

Imogenia flared. "What? You can't let the boy loose!"

"Oh, but I can. He will return."

"You don't know that!"

"The boy's father is our guest. He will come back, I can assure you."

"I want Alden to join us too," Hannah insisted.

"You're hardly in a position to make demands," Imogenia reproved.

Abaddon chuckled. "If it would please the maiden, your friend will go. Release them!"

Andy and Alden joined Hannah before the dragon, rubbing their sore wrists.

"We need our weapons to defend ourselves should we encounter enemies," Alden said flatly.

Abaddon laughed again. "It's a good thing I'm in a good mood. Dagon, give them their weapons."

The trio buckled their weapons belts about their waists as Hannah inquired, "In what direction did you find the unicorns?"

"North," Imogenia huffed.

"It will take us longer to go and return since we can't fly," Hannah declared.

"Very well. You have five days before we will begin toying with our guests in ways you may find...upsetting," Dagon informed.

"Five days! That's hardly time to find the unicorns, let alone return," Alden insisted.

"Fine," Abaddon interjected, his heads wagging. "If this unicorn horn does what our ghost friend insists, what's another five days?" The dragon addressed Hannah. "You have ten days, fair maiden. Will there be anything else?"

Hannah looked at Andy and Alden.

"Food," Alden insisted.

A vulture-man waddled over and handed Andy one of their backpacks with provisions.

"One pack of food will ensure you hurry," Dagon laughed.

"We need blankets too," Alden added.

The bird-warrior, his patience expired, purged two more packs of food and threw them at the travelers.

Andy looked back at Father as they departed in the lengthening shadows of early evening. Father nodded his head and the corners of his mouth rose around the gag.

"We'll be back soon," Andy promised, a knot forming in his stomach.

CHAPTER FOURTEEN

Company

A lot of help, that Imogenia. North she says. Of course the unicorns are north. The entire territory of the trolls is north of us," Alden grumped as the trio hiked up to the top of a ridge to get their bearings.

"It's okay," encouraged Hannah. "I'm sensing something pure in that direction." She pointed straight ahead.

Andy briefly considered making a wisecrack but thought better of it. His memory of Hannah's warning about sensing something evil just before the first bellicose attack remained fresh. He'd never forget that Oscray match.

They stopped on the ridgeline between two mountains and surveyed the terrain. A bed of green, leafy treetops stretched to the horizon, rising and falling with the ground beneath. In the fading light, Andy watched shadows spring to life, the prankster ghosts of nighttime that delighted in playing tricks and striking terror in the hearts of travelers.

"Come on, we need to set up camp," Andy encouraged.

"But where?" Hannah questioned. "Trolls are nocturnal, and I for one don't care to have them find us while we're sleeping. They're quite fond of the taste of humans from what I've heard."

"I didn't need to know that," Alden grimaced.

"If we can find a cave that's uninhabited, we can start a fire and stay warm tonight without being seen," Hannah suggested.

"Works for me," agreed Alden.

Andy nodded his assent.

"Okay then, let's go," Hannah directed.

The walk down the other side of the mountain proved easier than the ascent, despite having to make their own trail through the thick undergrowth. In the quickly fading light they traipsed over rotting tree trunks and avoided boulders left by long-ago landslidesThe tree cover seemed to squelch the light quicker than usual, so Andy pulled out Methuselah to illuminate their journey.

Within a few minutes, twilight succumbed to the night and the three children began to hear noises in the near darkness.

"What was that?" Alden whispered.

"I don't know, but it sounded big," Hannah added quietly.

"Come on, we've got to keep going," Andy declared, willing himself not to panic.

The trio heard a loud boom ahead and crept for cover behind a cluster of trees. Andy put Methuselah's glowing blade down on the ground so as not to give them away. Without saying a word, they peered out and saw the shape of a giant ambling along, a club slung over its shoulder. Downwind from the creature, their noses instantly objected to the assault of strong body odor.

"Oh!" Andy whispered, fanning a hand in front of his face. "That's worse than cow farts!"

Hannah shushed him.

The troll looked in their direction and listened momentarily before moving on.

"Come on," Andy said softly, motioning his friends to follow.

Pitch blackness descended on the forest by the time they finally located an opening in the rock face. Andy's bearings had left him ages ago and he breathed a sigh of relief that they might at last have found a camp for the night.

"I'll go in first with Methuselah to make sure there's nothing in there," Andy offered.

"I'll come too if you want," Alden replied.

"What, and leave me out here by myself? No thanks," Hannah protested.

"Don't worry. I'll go in while you gather firewood," Andy suggested.

His companions satisfied, Andy stole silently into the large opening. Expecting something like the red dragon caves he'd experienced on a previous visit to Oomaldee, Andy slunk around the bend to the right. His feet crunched bones that lay scattered everywhere. He noticed his knees shaking as he paused and listened. Senses heightened in the dark, he detected faint scratchings and the scampering of tiny feet. Mice, he hoped.

He moved forward around two boulders and kicked something that sounded like metal. He moved Methuselah's light and found several old swords, daggers, pickaxes, and a chest overflowing with trinkets and coins. A metal pendant caught his eye and he picked it up to study it. The image of a square within a square had been etched into its face. The inner square's corners touched the middle of each side of the outer square. Simple symbols were engraved at each corner of the outer square. *Awesome!* Andy added it to his pouch.

Continuing on, he paused every few feet to listen. The sound of water caught his ears as he went farther in, but he heard no other noises, certainly nothing to indicate the presence of a monstrous troll. After passing another boulder, the sound of the water grew louder. He stopped at the edge of a raging torrent. The water shot out from the wall to his right, forming an arch of spray and mist that soaked the ground around him. *I could take a shower in that,* Andy thought. *Of course, it might be really cold.*

A reservoir in the rocks collected the free-spirited moisture, dumping it back into the dark abyss under the mountains. *Must be running fast from all the rain,* he reasoned. Drawing Methuselah high, the light illuminated the back wall of the cavern and Andy sighed. *No one home. Good.*

He headed back out to collect the others and they set up camp well back from the cave opening. Soon they were enjoying a rationed dinner over a small fire.

"We should turn in. We need to get an early start since the unicorns won't be around much longer," Hannah proposed.

"I'll take first watch," Andy offered.

Neither Hannah nor Alden objected, so Andy grabbed a watch candle that was in his backpack and headed forward to find a position where he could see the entrance. He decided one of the two boulders would serve as the perfect lookout post and climbed up.

As he settled in for the duration, his thoughts turned back to their ambush and capture by Abaddon's goons. He replayed Abaddon's instruction to kill Father when he didn't see the Stone of Athanasia around his neck. Only Imogenia's intervention had stopped the dragon from acting. *What will happen if we bring back a unicorn horn and it cures Abaddon? What then? He'll have no need for any of us.*

Andy's stomach twisted as he wondered, *Did Father figure this out before we left and his parting nod was actually him saying goodbye? Does he believe Abaddon will kill him?*

Before he had time to entertain more dark thoughts, Andy's nose picked up a whiff of strong body odor.

His muscles stiffened and he sat up straight, straining to see in the shadowy darkness. Without warning, his perch suddenly moved and the stench grew stronger. Below him he heard a loud yawn and then felt more movement.

A troll! I'm sitting on a troll!!

As the creature unfolded itself and stood, Andy leapt to the ground, landing as quietly as possible but not quietly enough to avoid notice. In the shadows cast by the campfire around the bend in the cave, he made out a troll twice his height. It slouched like a large chimp, had a long nose and oversize ears with hair sprouting from them, and let out a guttural grunt as it eyed him. Andy and the troll turned their heads toward the mouth of the cave as they heard banging and tromping.

Not more trolls!

The sounds died away and the troll returned its attention to Andy. It took a step toward him, blocking any route of escape from the cave. Not that Andy would have taken it, for he needed to protect his sleeping friends.

Hoping all other residents had left for their nightly hunt, Andy risked calling out to Alden and Hannah, "Guys! Wake up! We've got company!" His cry reverberated off the hard walls.

The troll took another step forward and Andy dashed toward the fire and his companions. Turning the corner, he found Alden and Hannah standing in ready positions. Seconds later, the troll emerged into the firelight, its club poised and ready for a fight. When it saw the light of the campfire, it brought a large arm up to shield its eyes from the brightness. It plunged forward and swatted its weapon about with its free arm.

Hannah and Alden avoided its downward pummel as Andy sliced its back. Undeterred by the strokes, the troll turned and moved toward Andy, a roar echoing off the walls. Alden sliced at its legs while Hannah's blade made contact with the arm wielding the club. The wounds did not slow the beast. Rather, the giant's flesh seemed to heal itself before their eyes. It raised its club again, and Alden scrambled out of the way just in time as the cudgel smashed the floor where he had been standing. Andy plunged his dagger into the brute's back, but the troll ignored him and continued waving its weapon. The trio kept scrambling out of the way of the pounding club, taking shots at the troll when it left vital areas exposed, but nothing slowed it.

"It's not working. We need to try something else," Andy yelled. "Follow me!"

The three bolted past the campfire and the troll happily followed, believing it had trapped its prey in the back of the cave with no escape. As soon as the troll passed the flames, Andy yelled, "Add more wood! Make it bigger!"

Hannah doubled back while the boys kept the beast occupied. With the light of a brighter campfire, it roared and squeezed its eyes tighter.

"Grab a piece of burning wood and follow me," Andy instructed, dodging a ground-shaking wallop.

Flaming branch in hand, Hannah prodded the creature toward Andy and Alden at the back of the cave. The sound of spraying water grew louder. When they reached the edge of the raging river, Andy raced into the spray with Alden only a step behind. Thankfully it was relatively shallow. The boys flailed their arms, trying to remain upright in the torrent, the rocks slippery underneath. After a minute both found their footing in the icy-cold spray.

"Time for a bath, you foul hunk of BO!" Andy taunted.

"Come and get us!" Alden added, following Andy's lead.

ANDY SMITHSON: DISGRACE OF THE UNICORN'S HONOR

"Come get some tasty treats!" Andy shouted through chattering teeth.

Alden's body shivered from the cold, but he managed to shoot a look at Andy. "Really?"

Andy shrugged his quivering shoulders and added, "Just trying to keep its attention."

The troll paused at the water's edge, watching the boys curiously. It turned and found Hannah only a few feet behind with a flaming branch inches from its head. It lowered the arm shielding its eyes, revealing a terrified look as it returned its attention to the boys, who continued to offer taunts.

Hannah slowly prodded the creature forward. It stepped into the river and advanced three steps nearer to the boys, then paused in the jet of water shooting from the wall. Before it could comprehend what was happening, first its right arm and then an ear disappeared in the torrent. The children watched as its other arm turned to mud and washed away, followed by a shoulder. Within minutes, their enemy had disintegrated. Only a beefy wooden club peeked out of the water as evidence of the conflict.

"Woohoo!" Hannah celebrated. "Great idea, Andy!"

With blue lips and chattering teeth, Andy and Alden forced frozen smiles. They shivered their way back to dry ground as quickly as their frozen legs would carry them. Happily, the fire was roaring and they sat down to thaw.

When the last chills left their bodies and they'd shared their fears behind masks of laughter, they decided it would be safe enough to remain in the cave for the rest of the night as long as they doused the fire.

"Come daylight, the trolls will return," Andy reasoned aloud. "We're probably safer back here than outside as long as our friends stay up front in the cave."

No one disagreed with his reasoning, so Alden and Hannah filled their drinking cups and beat a path between the river and the fire until only a flickering pile of coals remained. For his part, Andy went forward, scouting out a new lookout post on solid ground.

After relighting the watch candle, he settled in for the remainder of his shift at sentry duty. Save the scratching of tiny rodent feet, silence ruled.

Andy woke Alden after an hour, found his bedroll, and quickly drifted off to sleep. He didn't dream. Instead, Abaddon's promise to eliminate him when he returned with the unicorn horn kept marauding his brain, wreaking havoc with the peace he desperately sought at that late hour. *What can I to do to save Father and the others?* His mind raced to invent an answer, but any solution sneakily hid in the space between consciousness and slumber.

Hannah's announcement that he ought to get moving awakened Andy the next morning.

"The trolls returned about an hour ago, stinky barbarians," Hannah reported as the three downed scant breakfast rations. "I watched them transform back into boulders. We won't make that mistake again."

"Who would have thought?" Alden added.

After packing up camp, they emerged into foggy conditions. The thick mist coupled with the forest's dense foliage prevented the sun's rays from reaching the ground, leaving them to walk in gray light.

"So where should we look for the unicorns?" Alden ventured after they'd walked for several minutes.

"Where the trolls aren't?" Hannah joked.

Andy laughed.

"Seriously though, I'm sensing something unusually pure in this direction." Hannah pointed straight ahead.

"Then lead on, m'lady" Andy replied, smiling.

The morning's travel proved uneventful. After stopping for a quick lunch, the afternoon found them huffing and puffing up yet another steep grade.

"My sense is growing stronger," Hannah informed as they stood at a mountain peak and surveyed the path ahead. "We're definitely headed in the right direction."

After deciding on a reasonable route through the valley, they began their descent. The trees had not thinned since this morning, and navigating a clear path continued to prove taxing. As they paused to rest, Andy thought he heard a twig snap as if someone crunched it under foot. He glanced around for several minutes but didn't see or hear anything more.

It must be my imagination. If the bellicose was near, it would be on me by now.

The threesome continued on, and Andy chose to share his concerns about what Abaddon might be planning if they gave him a unicorn horn that would cure him.

"We've got to find a way to free Father and everyone else. And I'd like to stay alive too," Andy shared. "Any brilliant ideas?"

Alden shook his head and Hannah replied, "I've been thinking about how I'm going to get the unicorns to give me not just one horn but two."

"That's right," Alden realized. "We need one to free everyone and one to break the curse."

Hannah nodded.

"How many unicorns did you say you heard talking, Andy?"

"Three. We know the zolt stole one horn. That leaves only two others."

"Let's hope they're in an agreeable mood," Alden mused.

"Yeah," Hannah added, raising an eyebrow, "especially since they need to surrender them willingly in order to work."

Alden walked close to Hannah, attempting to comfort her as they walked.

Harrumph, Andy thought.

"Jealous?" It was Andy's inneru.

No! Go away. I don't want to think about it.

"Very well, just thought I'd see if I could help."

Andy pulled out in front of his companions, scouting what was to come. He reached a small clearing and paused to listen before Hannah and Alden caught up. Off to his right he again thought he heard a twig snap. He stared into the woods but saw nothing unusual.

When his friends reached him, he whispered, "Don't look around, but I have a feeling we're being watched."

The two stared at him.

"By who?" Alden whispered.

"Or what?" Hannah added in a hushed voice.

"I don't know, but every once in a while I hear a twig snap, as if someone's close but trying to stay hidden. I don't think it's an animal. Let's stay sharp."

Hannah and Alden nodded, reflexively moving their hands to their sword hilts. Andy drew Methuselah for good measure.

As the light began to fade, the trio scouted out another deep cave and took up residence well past the boulders crowded just around the corner from the entrance where daylight couldn't reach its skinny fingers. They dispensed with a fire and spent the night without incident.

Emerging into sunlit fog the following morning, the trio continued their trek.

"My sense is growing stronger, but it still feels like the unicorns are a ways off," Hannah reported an hour into their march.

"That could be a problem," Andy fretted. "Best case, we've got no more than seven days before the unicorns leave. Hopefully they won't leave early because of what that zolt did. Stupid bird-brain!"

"I hadn't thought about that," Alden confided.

"Hannah, how are you coming with your story to get the unicorns to give us two horns?" Andy queried.

Hannah shook her head. "I'm not. I can't think of any way short of just coming out and telling them our situation. But I have a hard time believing they'd give us a horn to heal a beast that is evil to the core and already had his goons steal one of their horns."

"Yeah, I see what you mean," Andy agreed. "I'm not having any luck coming up with a plan to free Father and the others, so you're in good company."

"What are we gonna do if we can't get two horns?" Alden worried.

Andy and Hannah paused their conversation and stared at him.

"Okay, just asking," Alden cowered.

"Failure is not an option," Andy affirmed.

The trio followed Hannah's lead as she directed them up yet another mountain ridge and down the other side later that afternoon. The trek had grown monotonous with no change in the thick foliage and oppressive fog. Periodically, Andy would hear a stick break in the woods near them, but he could never make out the source. It kept everyone on edge.

Their fourth night they took shelter in another troll cave and ate from dwindling rations that fell far short of filling any of them. Andy stood watch with his stomach rumbling, hoping the trolls wouldn't hear it complaining as they came to life.

Thankfully they hadn't, and now, halfway through his shift, Andy grew drowsy. But his sleepiness evaporated instantly when the form of a glowing, swirling sphere took shape in the blackness. It flowed out of a large rock near where he sat and came to stop just two feet away, slowly revolving its fluorescent green, red, and purple threads.

"You've had much time to contemplate, Andy," came Mom's voice. "So what say you? What would you give to save me while still breaking the curse?"

Andy glanced around, checking to make sure there were no trolls within earshot. Satisfied he was the only one awake, he repeated the question he'd last posed: "What would you have me give?"

After a minute of silence Mom's voice spoke. "A unicorn horn. It will give me everlasting life beyond the curse."

"Wait, I thought unicorn *blood* gave eternal life, not the horn," Andy questioned, remembering his earlier conversation with Mermin.

"The horn heals all weaknesses forever. It is our weaknesses that cause us to die," responded the sphere, not answering his question.

"How would you know that?"

"I have learned more in my lifetime than you can possibly know, Andy. Do not question me."

He knew he was being disrespectful. How many times had he heard that?

The glowing ball continued revolving as Andy thought through his situation. *Mom can stay alive even after I break the curse with a unicorn horn.* He let out a deep breath. While the possibility should have given him hope, it frustrated him. *So we're supposed to get a unicorn horn for Mom, another one to save Father and the others, and one more to break the curse? This is never gonna work. There aren't that many horns!*

"I'll do my best," he replied, without conviction.

"I know you will," the sphere responded before dissolving.

Andy's thoughts wouldn't leave the problem alone but kept picking at it like a scab. What if he gave one horn to Abaddon to free his father and the other to the sphere to save his mom? Breaking the curse could wait, couldn't it? Of course, they were sent on this trip to get the next ingredient, but that was before he knew a unicorn horn could save Mom...and when there were still three horns. Hopefully Hannah would be able to get both horns. How ticked would Father and Mermin be if he used one horn for something other than breaking the curse?

I think I'd better not tell Hannah and Alden my plan. Surely we can find another unicorn horn, he reasoned.

"That's a really bad idea, Andy," his inneru piped up. "You don't want to mess with the Master Chef of this potion to break the curse, let alone betray the trust of your family and friends."

Who asked you? Andy shot back. *Mom's part of my family, too! And I can't let her die! I won't! Not if I can help it!*

CHAPTER FIFTEEN

Awe & Wonder

Their situation unchanged, Andy's mind and his inneru became locked in a heated battle. He found himself getting testy as the trio huffed and puffed up yet another mountain two days later.

"Three hours ago you said the unicorns were near, Hannah," Andy whined.

"They are. My sense locked onto what I think is them when we first started out this morning," Hannah insisted.

"Then where are they?" Andy questioned. "We've only got four days left before the unicorns leave. Assuming we're successful, we've still got to get back to Father and the others within that same time or—"

"I know!" Hannah cut him off. "You think I haven't thought about that?"

"It's not *your* father's life on the line," Andy shot back. *Or your mom's,* he added silently.

"No, you're right, it's not. But he's my king, and I plan to do my part to save him and the others." The look Hannah shot Andy was sharper than any sword.

Alden chose to remain silent.

Andy strode ahead, knowing no good could come of a reply. His anger fueled his steps and he crested the mountain before the others.

He studied the terrain as his temper cooled. Not more than a hundred yards ahead he noticed a small clearing on the downslope. A white shape crossed the space and he knew they'd found what they'd come for.

Andy immediately forgot his anger. Somehow seeing one of these creatures, even from a distance, made everything real and he regretted his earlier comments. *Wow, that's awesome! I never thought I'd see one of these in person, and now we're so close. Unbelievable.*

When Alden and Hannah reached him, he brought a finger to his lips, motioning for them to keep their voices down.

"I saw a unicorn through the trees over there," Andy whispered, pointing toward the clearing.

Alden and Hannah peered through the foliage and also spotted the creature.

"Incredible," Hannah murmured reverently.

"Are you ready, Hannah?" Alden asked.

She hesitated only a second before nodding, a determined look steeled upon her face.

"Then lead on, fair maiden," Andy invited, sweeping his arm wide with an open hand.

They descended single file as slowly and quietly as possible, not wanting to startle the creature. As they approached, Andy could make out a second unicorn through the scrub. Its neck extended high as it nibbled tree leaves, much as he'd seen giraffes do on nature shows. The first unicorn stood unmoving on the far side of the clearing.

The trio stopped twenty yards short.

Hannah turned and whispered, "Something's really wrong. I sense it."

"What?"

"I'm going with you," Alden insisted.

"No, I need to go alone."

Andy watched Hannah creep forward and stop when she reached the edge of the glade. The stationary unicorn, larger than its partner by a hand, turned to look at her. As it did, Andy had to shield his eyes from the reflection of the sun off its silver mane and tail. Its coat and hooves of pure white shimmered, filling Andy with wonder as peace flooded his inner being. It felt as though he stood in a holy place.

Hannah stepped out of the trees, but as she did her eyes fastened on the ground near the creature and she cried out in anguish.

With the foliage blocking their view, neither Andy nor Alden could see what had alarmed her. Alden bolted from cover to join Hannah. His sudden appearance startled both unicorns and they lowered their horns, readying a charge.

"Stop! Please!" Hannah intervened, trying to compose herself. "He's my friend. Don't hurt him. He meant well."

The pair relented, and the unicorn that had been foraging joined its partner to study the new arrivals. After a silence that felt like an eternity, Hannah choked on her response to an inaudible question: "Yes, there's one other man-child in the trees. May he join us?"

Alden sent Hannah a questioning look.

"It's okay, they're speaking to me telepathically," Hannah whimpered, wiping a tear.

Seconds later she motioned for Andy to come forward. He met them at the edge of the glade and instantly understood what had caused her outburst. A larger unicorn lay on the ground behind the others, its eyes closed, unmoving. Only the jagged stub of a spiral horn remained on its forehead.

With her friends by her side, Hannah's attention refocused on the scene of devastation. Grief overwhelmed her, causing her body to quake as tears streamed down her cheeks. "How could they?" she croaked.

She crossed the clearing as though in a daze, the pair of unicorns allowing her to pass. She knelt next to the fallen creature and bent forward, hugging its neck as her tears continued unabated.

If I didn't know better, it seems like she's blending with their pain, Andy observed as he saw tears fall to the ground from both the attending creatures. Andy remained still, feeling like an uninvited guest at a funeral. Next to him, Alden bowed his head.

Hannah managed to regain her composure after several minutes and sat up on her knees, wiping her tearstained cheeks with a sleeve. Alden began fidgeting and pulled a pouch from inside his tunic, extracting the blue sapphire he'd received from the dwarfs. As if drawn by an invisible string, he started across the glade before Andy could stop him.

Both unicorns whinnied and tossed their heads about, but Alden continued, holding the stone out in his open hand.

Interesting…it doesn't seem like they're going to attack him.

Alden stopped in front of the fallen unicorn, knelt, and placed the stone on its cheek. He stroked its neck several times before he stood and retraced his steps back to Andy.

"Why'd you do that?" Andy whispered after Alden resumed his reverent stance.

Alden looked up at him and replied thoughtfully, "I don't know. I just felt like I was supposed to."

Andy smiled and shook his head.

The unicorns returned their gaze to Hannah, and a minute later she said, "Yes, that's Alden. Andy's my other friend."

At this, Andy telepathically heard, "Please approach."

Startled but thrilled, he advanced, halting four feet away from the pair. At close range, Andy felt dwarfed by their size and awed by their majesty. A pearly, spiraling horn protruded more than a foot from each creature's forehead and looked to be a formidable weapon if needed.

The unicorn he'd seen foraging gazed down at him with soft purple eyes. "We sense an old magic with you, man-child. What dost thou wield?"

"Excuse me?"

"Your spirit feels much older than your figure presents. What do you carry that creates this intensity?"

Andy wracked his brain. Old magic? After a minute it occurred to him, "Do you mean Methuselah?"

He reached for the gold hilt and presented it for them to inspect. He pointed out the four intricate carvings: clouds blowing with puffed-up cheeks, a giant wave, a flaming ball of fire, and a pile of rocks. He also showed them the two stones set on either side near the top, one pure white, the other pitch black.

One of the unicorns bobbed its head as the other replied, "You are a man-child of the Old One. Your presence has restored dignity to our father in death. We are honored." At this, both unicorns bent a knee and bowed before Methuselah.

Andy glanced at Alden and Hannah and found them google-eyed, their chins nearly touching the ground.

Andy heard the unicorns summon Hannah and Alden to join him, which they did. It appeared the creatures had begun communicating with all three of them.

"My name is Jada and this is my sister, Naria," the larger of the two creatures shared. Indicating the fallen creature, he added, "Our father, was known as Benica.

"Alden," Naria began, "we speak to man-children only on the rarest of occasions, for men love war. They delight in slaughter and violence against their fellows, actions we shun. Many of our kind have also fallen at their hands."

Alden nodded.

"I sense a question in your thoughts," Jada intoned, turning purple eyes on him.

"So why are you speaking with *me?*"

"You demonstrated an uncommon sensitivity to our prompting, Alden. Jada sensed each member of your company bore a blue sapphire, but only you acted to honor our father," Naria explained.

"Is that why I felt like I should give the stone?"

"Yes," Jada confirmed.

"What's the significance of a blue sapphire?" Hannah interjected, curious.

"Sapphires create tranquility and inner peace, speeding the journey of a unicorn to Isandum, the fair meadows of honor and dignity," explained Naria.

Had it been any other situation, Andy would have thought Naria had misplaced a few marbles. But given the nobility of these creatures and the senseless death of their elder, he immediately dismissed such foolish thoughts.

"So Benica will reach his eternal home quicker because of that blue sapphire?" Alden clarified.

"That is correct," Naria confirmed.

Alden shared a small smile with Hannah and Andy.

"Excuse me, but may I ask a question?" Andy ventured.

"What troubles you, Andy?" Jada responded.

"I don't mean to be rude or insensitive, but can you tell us what caused your father's…demise? Other than his horn being broken, it doesn't look like he's injured," Andy questioned as delicately as he knew how.

Hannah rolled her eyes, clearly not happy with him for asking.

Jada lowered his large head and began, "The horn of a unicorn can be likened to the crown of your sovereign, something you would know much about seeing as you are next in line for the throne of your land."

He paused, and Andy did a double take. "But how—?" he stuttered.

"Your bearing and your blade reveal your story," the unicorn continued. "Your monarch's crown is given only on a sacred occasion after the chosen one pledges a solemn oath to rule rightly. It, therefore, represents power, honor, legitimacy, even glory and righteousness.

"Upon the rare and hallowed event of a unicorn's birth, the young has no horn; except for its radiant coat and features, it could be mistaken for a common horse. The foal's parents vow before the other members of their blessing to pursue purity, nobility, grace, dignity, and honor as they raise their young. The newborn sprouts the nub of a horn at this measure of goodwill. As the foal flourishes and learns the ways of its kind—to love dignity and honor—its horn grows. So you see, the horn is the essence of our being. When the thief tore our father's horn from him, it stole that essence, and he could not live without it."

"I had no idea," Andy responded in a hushed voice.

Several silent moments elapsed before Hannah asked, "Would you allow us the honor of burying your father properly?"

"A unicorn is pure and is not of the ground. It must be returned to the elements a different way," replied Naria. "We would be pleased for you to help us send our father on by means of fire, for it will purify his body from that which defiled it."

The moment felt holy, and the trio could only nod. They set about gathering sticks and fallen branches. They stopped only when the pile in the center of the glade rose higher than Andy and threatened to collapse on top of them.

"The body must not be moved, for that would defile it further," Jada instructed. "Build a ring of wood, touching but not spoiling it."

Hannah, Alden, and Andy worked in silence for an hour, then stood back, tired but satisfied with the result of their labor.

Alden's stomach let out a loud rumble. The unicorns, Hannah, and Andy all turned and looked at him. "Sorry," he said, covering his mouth.

"I suggest you take nourishment before we continue," Naria suggested.

The trio nodded, sat down by the edge of the glade, and ate from dwindling rations.

"That's better," Alden reported after several minutes, rubbing his stomach.

"The last element we need is water," Naria interrupted. "The body must be cleansed before purification. There is a stream not far, in that direction," she motioned with her head.

What? Andy questioned, but dared not ask.

He exchanged looks with Alden. Hannah ignored their glances, devoted to the solemnity and honor of the task.

With just one canteen between the three of them, Andy lost count of the number of trips they made back and forth between the clearing and the brook. Each time they returned to the glade, one of them would slowly pour the water on the body. Naria told them it should not be haphazardly splashed but steadily and reverently poured.

On the thirty-fifth trip to the brook, Andy's brain screamed at the absurdity of drenching the beast before burning it. He didn't understand. The wetter they made the body, the less likely it would burn, right?

Andy grew weary of the ritual, but Jada's passionate insistence coaxed him on. Father's motto jogged through his brain: "Responsibility, diligence, and dignity are the keys to success." *This task requires diligence, that's for sure,* he thought. *At this rate, success should be oozing from my pores.*

On what had to be their eighty-ninth trip, his mind numb from the monotony of the task, Andy tried on a new thought: *How would it feel if that was Father and I believed this ritual would release him into a bright eternity?* The last twenty trips flew by, and before Andy knew it, Jada was satisfied.

Rather than collapsing on the ground from exhaustion as they felt like doing, the boys followed Hannah's stern look, which was much like the look Mom used to make Andy comply. *Good grief, are girls born knowing about "the look"?* Andy wondered.

"Would you do us the kindness of setting the wood aflame with your sword, Andy?" Jada asked.

"Excuse me?"

"Go ahead," Naria encouraged.

"But Methuselah has never produced a flame."

"Legend says differently," Jada countered.

"Really?"

Alden and Hannah watched the exchange with curious expressions.

"Well, okay," Andy relented, stepping over to the pile of wood that circled the fallen unicorn. He slipped in the mud that oozed beneath the stack but quickly regained his balance before pulling Methuselah from its holster. The unicorns flinched as the blade extended.

"Sorry," Andy whispered, not wanting to disturb the solemnity of the occasion.

He moved the tip of the blade over the wood and willed aloud, "Methuselah, please set this wall of wood on fire." Instantly, a pure white flame shot from the tip, igniting the stacked branches in front of him.

"Whoa!" The murmur escaped Andy's lips as he froze with wonder. He sensed every cell in his body tingling as he continued to gaze. He didn't know how long he stayed that way, for only when Jada nudged him from behind could he break concentration.

"Best move back," the stallion suggested.

Andy had seen campfires before, but this blaze didn't compare. Instead of red or orange flames, pure white slivers danced atop the wood, lapping up the wet. He brought an arm up and squinted, trying to dim the brightness as the fire spread around the ring and finally jumped to the elder unicorn in the center. Intense heat drove the living back to the periphery of the clearing. Within moments the wood and everything within the ring disappeared in the inferno.

No sooner had the body been consumed than the flames extinguished themselves and arms of coolness wrapped about the site once more. Andy wiped beads of sweat from his brow and the back of his neck as he gazed about. No scorch marks, no ashes, not even a hint of mud. In fact, the area where the fire had raged looked new and untouched. And a distinctly fresh floral scent filled the glade.

He still held Methuselah in his right hand, and he now examined its tip. No marks or any other evidence of flame, just the usual shininess of the blade.

What else can you do that I don't yet know? he pondered as the blade retracted.

Glancing about, he noticed Naria and Jada kneeling over Hannah and weeping. Hannah caught his eye as she righted herself. *What happened?* his eyes implored.

Alden took two steps forward and helped her up.

The trio stood silently for several minutes before Jada and Naria slowly rose.

"You fainted?" Andy questioned Hannah.

"She couldn't help being overcome," Naria's voice broke into his mind. "She has such a gift."

Alden held Hannah's hand, trying to steady and reassure her. At the sight, a flutter rushed through Andy's consciousness, then vanished before he had the opportunity to identify it.

"Thank you for celebrating our father and for speeding him on his way. Surely the Fates brought you to us, knowing you could restore the dignity that was stolen from him," Naria acknowledged.

"It was our honor," Hannah assured. "To be privileged to be a part of this was…" She could not go on.

"We understand. Such an experience is beyond the limitations of words," Jada reassured.

"If we weren't around to help, how would you have, you know…" Andy queried, drawing another scowl from Hannah.

"What? Can't a guy wonder?"

Naria smiled sadly. "We performed this ritual the way we did so Methuselah and the three of you could participate. This is not how it would normally be done, but the ceremony stayed true to the elements, releasing our father from his earthly bonds to begin his journey."

"What do you mean it 'stayed true to the elements'?" Andy questioned.

CHAPTER SIXTEEN

No Other Way?

"Where is Methuselah?" Naria queried Andy's mind.

"Right here," he replied, grabbing the hilt from its holster.

"Do you know what the carvings represent?"

"I didn't know they meant anything. I thought they were just decoration."

Jada and Naria shared a whinny.

"Are you making fun of me?"

Neither of the unicorns replied and Andy rolled his eyes as his two companions gave a slight smile, lightening the mood.

After a brief silence, the she-unicorn began, "The clouds represent wind or air, the wave represents water, the flaming ball is fire, and the pile of rocks is earth. Air, water, fire, and earth are the most basic components of which all things consist."

Andy stared blankly. "Okay, and…"

"We believe the right combination of the four elements rejuvenates and creates immortality for someone who has died. Without bringing the four elements together close to the time of death, the deceased's spirit ceases to exist."

"Is that why you had us soak your father's body before burning it?"

"Yes, for air was present and you gathered wood, which is of the earth. You soaked his body with water and then started a fire with Methuselah, completing the four elements. This is why we believe Father's spirit is now enjoying immortality." Naria paused. "I hope to be honored to join him one day."

"Do the four elements work with the living to make people immortal?"

"Why? Do you want to live forever?" Jada teased.

"Not me, but I know someone who would like to," Andy said. Then, forgetting that the unicorns could hear his thoughts, he added, *And I know someone I wish could live forever.*

Naria hesitated, seemingly surprised by Andy's unspoken desire. "I've never heard of that, Andy," she replied gently.

Well, it was worth asking.

"Why would those symbols be on Methuselah's hilt?" Hannah queried.

"I can only speculate," Jada replied, "but the symbols may reveal the process through which it was created."

"Are you saying that sword is…alive? And immortal?" Hannah clarified.

"In a manner of speaking, yes," Jada confirmed.

Everyone's eyes locked onto the blade Andy held in his hand.

"I know it's different from other blades, but *alive?*" Andy's mind filled with awe and wonder.

The group contemplated that for several moments, then Naria interrupted Andy's private musings. "I sense you are troubled."

Why do you say that?

"Your thoughts betray you."

What do you mean?

"I sense a mood of fear when I look at you. Your thoughts dwell on someone living forever, and your conflict reveals you love them deeply."

Welcoming an opportunity to talk about his problem, Andy demanded, *You can't share this with anyone. Promise?*

Naria bobbed her head, drawing curious glances from Alden and Hannah.

It's my mom, Andy launched into his narrative. *How much do you know about the fog and the curse?*

"Bits and pieces."

Andy quickly summarized the situation in Oomaldee, telling of his two previous visits and revealing that the King was his father. He also shared about his mother's long-ago marriage to King Hercalon, their current predicament with Abaddon, and their need for unicorn horns. For a split second Andy contemplated hiding the fact that it was Abaddon's thugs who had stolen Benica's horn, but out of his deep respect for these magnificent creatures, he laid bare all the facts.

The curse needs to be broken, but I don't want my mom to die. I can't choose between her and the King, Andy pleaded, wiping his eyes and trying to regain his composure.

Jada, Hannah, and Alden had moved to the other side of the glade to give Andy and Naria privacy. The she-unicorn now summoned them.

"Andy has explained the situation to me," Naria shared when they were together again.

Hannah quickly glanced at Andy, then exhaled in relief.

"Let me talk things over with my brother."

The unicorn siblings met in the middle of the clearing, their heads touching, for what seemed an eternity.

"Andy, are you okay?" Hannah probed.

He nodded, taking another deep breath.

Alden kicked at a small pebble, Andy rocked in place, and Hannah bit her lip as they waited.

"You have a difficult challenge," Naria said after she and Jada rejoined the trio. "Given the situation, we feel called to help."

Andy, Hannah, and Alden ricocheted looks.

"We will both give you our horns. Normally they would not grow back, but based upon a legend involving a similar situation, we believe that if Methuselah cuts them they will regrow, though it will take several years," Naria informed.

"Thank you!" Hannah, Alden, and Andy exclaimed in unison.

"To Hannah, we will entrust Naria's horn to free your king and companions despite the actions of King Abaddon," Jada declared.

Hannah ran over and hugged Naria's velvety neck.

"To Andy, we will give my horn," continued the he-unicorn, then turned aside and addressed Andy privately. "You have a choice to make: breaking the curse, which is why you have been brought to Oomaldee, or preserving the mother you love. Based upon Methuselah's appearance at this time, I believe your choice will determine the fate of the land. I won't tell you what to do, but I encourage you not to be greedy."

Andy jerked his head back at the admonition. *What do you mean, don't be greedy?*

"I think you know the answer to that, Andy. Your destiny is to rule this land. A king must make difficult choices between his personal desires and the welfare of his subjects. Until recently my father governed a blessing of seven unicorns. Barbarians attacked us and slaughtered two of our brothers and our sister before cornering Naria, me, and our mother. I watched my father choose to save Naria and me over our mother."

I...I had no idea. I don't know what to say, Andy fumbled.

"I told you this to demonstrate my point, not to ask for pity," Jada asserted. "While it's not the same situation, it's similar enough."

Andy frowned and dropped his gaze to the ground. *You're making me choose.*

"Every action we take in life is a choice between competing options and reveals what we most value."

But I don't know how to decide.

"Thoughtful consideration is the first step. I am confident you will choose well."

Andy walked slowly next to the stallion as they rejoined the others.

"You said Methuselah has cut off a unicorn's horn before?" Alden queried. "Would you tell us about that?"

Andy caught Hannah glancing over to Alden, giving him an appreciative smile. Andy rolled his eyes.

"It happened before either of us was born. Father delighted in telling old stories, and this was one of them. As the legend goes, long, long ago in the kingdom of Cromlech, there lived a king and his daughter, a fair maiden whom he loved more than life. They were the last remnants of a noble dynasty that had once been rich and powerful, owning all the land as far as the eye could see. Misfortune befell the king, however, when he chose to take a stand against rabble-rousers who strayed into his kingdom one autumn. As great fires erupt from a single spark, so discontent spread among the citizens until civil war broke out. So great was the conflict that, when the fighting ended, only a few handfuls of rebel sympathizers remained. They packed up their meager possessions and followed their new leader.

"With no one left but the king and his daughter, the castle fell into disrepair. The pair wandered about their kingdom barefoot, their silk and velvet clothes now patched and faded. One day they came upon the ruins of a grand hall, its beams charred and its stones crumbling. Stopping to investigate, the king noticed something gold glimmering under the debris. With some digging, he unearthed Methuselah. As he stood marveling at the sword's beauty, a heavy roof beam fell on the maiden, killing her.

"Beside himself with grief, the king cried out for justice and a unicorn appeared. The creature assured him his plight had not gone unnoticed, for his unwavering commitment to right had unknowingly granted him favor. The unicorn watched as the king prepared a funeral pyre for his daughter. When her body had been laid on top of it, the unicorn offered its horn as a gesture of comfort. The king accepted the generous gift and used Methuselah to gently sever the horn. Placing the token with his daughter's body, he used the sword to ignite the fire.

"As the flames spread, the king marveled to see a large bird rise up from where his daughter's body had lain. The feathers covering its body dark were orange, red, and crimson, and its tail was deep yellow and orange. The bird soared up and circled the man, singing a song sweeter than any he'd heard. His heart rejoiced exceedingly, for he knew his daughter had overcome death itself. A phoenix, the unicorn called her, for she was a maiden of unsurpassed beauty.

"The king celebrated at the top of his lungs, his joy attracting the attention of wayward subjects returning after finding their newly appointed leader underhanded and untrustworthy. They begged the king's forgiveness and pledged him their loyalty, then returned with him to the castle where they served him faithfully."

"So that's how you knew Methuselah could ignite your father's funeral pyre?" Andy questioned.

"It is," confirmed Naria.

"So a unicorn horn created a phoenix," Hannah marveled.

"That, and Methuselah," Jada clarified.

"A phoenix never really dies, does it?" Alden questioned.

"No. When their body grows old, they incinerate themselves. Out of the ashes a new phoenix emerges," the he-unicorn explained.

At that moment, Andy thought he again heard a twig snap in the surrounding woods. He glanced around quickly but spotted nothing out of the ordinary. Returning his attention to the group, he pulled Methuselah from its holster. The blade extended and glowed orange in the fading afternoon light. The unicorns lay down in the center of the clearing to make it easier for him to reach their horns. As the trio faced them, Andy stepped forward and placed his left hand on Naria's horn.

"It won't hurt, will it?" Hannah asked nervously.

The she-unicorn didn't reply, and Hannah brought her folded hands to chin level with a grimace.

Alden rested a reassuring hand on Hannah's shoulder, but from their shared expression, Andy knew his friends felt as uneasy as he did. Andy brought Methuselah up and contorted his face, mirroring his friends. *And here I thought the hardest part would be convincing them to give us their horns.*

He hesitated several seconds then lowered Methuselah again. "Is there any other way?" he pleaded.

All three children let out a collective sigh. It seemed they all shared the same question. Neither unicorn replied, and after several minutes, Hannah broke the silence.

She wiped both eyes as she lamented, "I so wish there was another way, but I don't see any. It's not right that you and Jada surrender the symbol of your honor for our sake."

"My dears," Naria began, "the fact that you understand the gravity of the situation and that you are learning the high price of redemption comforts me. To attain what is valuable requires cost; the higher the value, the greater the cost."

The trio slowly nodded.

Alden and Hannah held hands as Andy again brought Methuselah up. He hesitated only a moment before bringing the blade across and through. The she-unicorn didn't make a sound, and Andy held her severed horn. Hannah lunged forward, ready to stanch the bleeding. To her surprise and relief, there was no trace of blood. The blade had cut cleanly and the remaining stump glittered in the sunlight. She wrapped her arms around Naria's neck.

I feel like I just desecrated something holy, Andy thought as he examined the fifteen-inch section of horn. His stomach threatened mutiny.

Alden stepped over and asked, "You okay?"

"Not really—"

"You need two horns. Let's finish this," Jada interrupted.

Andy nodded, handed Naria's horn to Alden, and walked around to the he-unicorn. *Sure doesn't get any easier,* he thought as he grasped the stallion's horn. He took a deep breath, trying to calm his nerves, and raised Methuselah.

"Are you sure?"

"I am."

Andy contorted his face once more as he brought the blade across, amputating a foot-long section of horn. As it had the first time, Methuselah cauterized the wound, leaving a gleaming stump on Jada's forehead.

Thank you so much! Andy expressed silently. *I still don't know how I'm supposed to choose between breaking the curse and saving my mom, but after your sacrifice, I will do my best to decide.*

"I know you will," Jada replied.

"Something's wrong!" Hannah shouted.

Andy heard a disturbance behind him and Alden yelled, "Look out!"

Andy whirled to see ten vulture-men bursting into the glade as more materialized in the growing darkness.

The bird-men quickly surrounded the children. As Alden drew his blade, Hannah began hacking at any zolt within reach of her sword. Three adversaries fell instantly. Still holding Naria's horn, Alden sliced at another four attackers, successfully besting them.

Andy held his ground, positioning himself between the attackers and the unicorns who, in their weakened condition, struggled to stand. Grasping Jada's horn in one hand and Methuselah in the other, Andy felled two would-be thieves as the unicorns finally righted themselves and wobbled to the edge of the clearing.

As another dozen zolt materialized, Alden tripped over a fallen vulture-man and did a face-plant in the dirt. He managed to keep hold of the horn and his sword, but two goons pounced on him and tried to wrestle the horn from his clutches. Hannah rushed in and slashed the attackers, who fell down dead.

Three more zolt attacked Andy, sending him sprawling. He lost hold of Methuselah but managed to protect Jada's horn by curling himself into a ball. The goons pummeled his head, arms, back, and legs, and he felt a strong pair of hands attempting to extricate the horn.

He fought to hold on, but his grip weakened. "Help! Get them off me!"

Another burly zolt reached in, grabbed hold of the horn, and yanked. The combined strength of the two would-be robbers proved too much for Andy.

"Help!" he screamed again, growing desperate.

The second brute gave a final yank and the unicorn horn slipped from Andy's grasp. The vulture-man pulled away as Andy yelled, "Stop him! He's got Jada's horn."

He didn't have time to watch what happened next, for the zolt continued raining blows and he had to cover his head. But a loud exclamation was immediately followed by Naria's assurance, "He's been dealt with, Andy."

Andy struggled and managed to reach his dagger. Grabbing a leg in front of his nose, he sank the blade in. The creature yelped and grabbed its extremity. Andy repeated his defense and defeated two more bird-men. Three zolt fewer provided him an opening, and he scrambled up as motion slowed around him. He spotted Methuselah on the ground just three feet away and scooped it up. As the blade extended, he slashed at six attackers and quickly felled the lot. Only one remained, but it wised up andfled in slow motion.

Andy spotted two scrums of vulture-men. Certain that Alden and Hannah were at the center, he raced to thin their ranks. He slashed and jabbed with lightning speed, cutting down eight zolt to free Hannah. He helped her up and the pair attacked the third pack. After taking down another dozen enemies, they extricated Alden, who still clutched Naria's horn. Time slowed to its normal pace for Andy.

"You were amazing, Andy!" Hannah cheered, a smile spreading across her face. Andy felt his cheeks warm.

"Where's Jada's horn?" Alden shouted.

Andy quickly scanned the glade. The unicorns lay at the side of the clearing, watching.

"You said you'd dealt with the guy who stole Jada's horn. Where is it Naria? Where's his horn?" Andy questioned, his voice rising.

"Over there," the she-unicorn indicated a place ten feet away from the body of the burly goon who'd grabbed the prize. Suddenly, a vulture-man stumbled out of the darkness, grabbed the horn, and fled.

"Don't let him get away!" Andy yelled, giving chase.

CHAPTER SEVENTEEN

Pets

A ndy, Alden, and Hannah plunged into the forest in hot pursuit. The bird-man wasn't very fast, but through the darkness they saw him begin to transform, sprouting wings and feathers where his arms had been.

"We've got to stop him before he can fly!" Andy yelled, bounding over a fallen log.

Within fifteen feet of the zolt, the trio prepared to pounce. As they closed the gap to ten feet, Andy felt certain they had him. Eight feet. Five feet. And then it happened. The bird-man took off, flapping its wings wildly to get lift, Jada's horn clutched in its talons.

"No!" screamed Andy, grasping for the horn, but it was just beyond his reach. A stitch stabbed his side.

The vulture-man gained altitude and was nearly through the canopy of leaves when Hannah threw her dagger. Her aim was true, the thief let loose an ear-piercing caw, and one of its feet fell to the ground. Jada's horn wavered precariously in the remaining clawed foot. Alden brought his dagger up and hurled it. His throw also found its mark, knocking the horn free just as the zolt disappeared through the treetops.

Andy raced to where he saw the prize fall and belly flopped on top of it before anything else could claim it. Alden and Hannah reached him seconds later, breathing heavily. Andy gasped for air as he cradled Jada's horn in his arms.

Everything's okay. I got it, Andy tried to calm himself.

Once he'd caught his breath, Andy sat up and exclaimed, "You guys are great shots!" Hannah and Alden grinned.

"Let's check on the unicorns," suggested Alden.

The trio found Jada and Naria where they had left them in the darkening glade.

"Are you okay?" Hannah queried.

"We need to eat to regain our strength," Jada informed.

"Let's get them some foliage," Alden suggested. Hannah and Andy nodded and set to work. Gathering wood in daylight proved much easier than collecting leaves and grass in the dark. They chose not to use Methuselah's light for fear of attracting unwanted company, so the trio stumbled over exposed roots and fallen debris.

Andy felled several leafy saplings and dragged them back to the unicorns. As he worked, his mind mulled over the problem of freeing Father, Mermin, and the others without being recaptured. *I hope everyone's okay.* He refused to allow his thoughts to wander to possibilities he'd considered in dread. *This is a rescue mission*, he insisted to himself. *We've only got three days left to make it back and save them. But how?*

The three had been working in silence for over an hour in the dense foliage when Andy heard rustling and felt the ground shake as heavy footsteps approached. Aided by slivers of moonlight that snuck through the canopy, he motioned to Hannah and Alden and they froze. The stench that preceded it gave away the creature's identity. The trio watched as a troll that was at least fifteen feet tall ambled toward them, a club slung over one shoulder. It was humming to itself. *At least it's in a good mood,* thought Andy. It stopped and sniffed the breeze. Several tense moments elapsed before it passed their position.

"It's headed toward the clearing!" Hannah whispered, her eyes wide.

Andy leapt from their hiding place and pursued, determined to redirect it before it found Jada and Naria. Hannah and Alden followed closely.

"What are you gonna do?" Hanna asked quietly.

"I don't know yet."

The giant paused and scratched its head, then ran a large finger up a nostril as it looked around.

"Gross!" Hannah objected in hushed tones.

"Shhh," Alden cautioned.

Seconds later a thought occurred to Andy: *Trolls like treasure.* Remembering the pendant he'd pocketed earlier, he pulled it out of his pouch and bolted toward the unwelcome explorer.

"Alden, Hannah, go make sure Jada and Naria are okay. I'll meet you back at the glade once I give this thing the slip," Andy instructed as he headed for the troll.

"Wait!" Alden called, but Andy motioned them to go.

"Hey, you big baboon!" he yelled just twenty feet away from the giant.

The troll turned and looked at him, then took a step in his direction.

"Look what I've got." Andy held up the pendant and it glistened in the moonlight.

Curious, the creature took another step toward him.

"That's right, come and see." Andy retreated several steps, coaxing it away from the unicorns.

The giant took more strides in Andy's direction, but he matched it, keeping a safe distance. *Where am I gonna take this thing? And what other creatures are out here?* Andy tried to push his fears aside as he kept the troll moving.

He paused and tested the wind. He needed to lead it upwind from the unicorns. He adjusted course, moving into the light breeze. Several minutes later he heard movement ahead and quickly discerned another troll out hunting.

Great, I'm sandwiched between the two! Time to lose both of 'em.

Andy waited until the second troll had come into view of the first. When the two brutes saw each other, the one following Andy became distracted and began grunting noises that sounded like an animal in pain. The other reciprocated in a slightly higher pitch.

I'm not waiting to find out what happens!

Andy slipped behind a nearby tree and waited. The two trolls approached each other and Andy snuck downwind. He crept close to the ground, staying as quiet as possible. When he could no longer hear the creatures, he stood up and pulled out Methuselah. The blade seemed to sense the situation and didn't light up as it extended. Cool! Maybe it was alive.

Andy looked around and realized he had no idea where he was. Nothing looked familiar in the dark. He whispered, "Please show me the way to the clearing."

As it had on previous occasions, Methuselah shifted in his hands and directed him to the right. He paused several times as telltale troll stench assaulted his nose, but the blade directed him around any confrontations.

I didn't realize I'd come so far, he thought as he continued walking. *Wonder how much farther?*

His thoughts returned to the quandary about how he could free his father and the others without being captured. Then it dawned on him: *I'll bet a few trolls in Abaddon's camp could create a disturbance long enough for us to free them.* As he thought it through, a smile crept across his face. *Oh, this is gonna be good.*

He continued on and soon reached the clearing where Hannah, Alden, and the two unicorns kept watch. He still wore a grin as he approached, and Hannah questioned, "What's so funny? We were getting worried."

"I'm glad you're okay," Andy addressed the unicorns before answering Hannah.

"Thank you," the pair replied in unison.

"I think I've figured out how we can free my father and the others."

"Well, don't keep us in suspense," Alden replied, matching Andy's expression.

Andy outlined his plan.

"I don't know," Hannah cautioned when he'd finished. "There's a lot that could go wrong with trolls. We have no control of them."

"Well, I like the idea," Alden encouraged. "We haven't come up with anything better. Andy and I can keep the trolls busy while you give Abaddon Naria's horn and bargain for the release of the others. If you aren't successful—which, no offense, I doubt you will be—we'll bring on the trolls to shake things up a bit."

"I don't know," Hannah mused, slowly shaking her head.

Andy yawned, setting off a chain reaction from Hannah and Alden. With no better ideas to consider, the trio grabbed blankets from their packs and curled up next to the unicorns for warmth. In no time they were asleep.

The rising sun filtered through the fog and woke the group the next morning. After an insufficient breakfast that finished off their provisions and tearful goodbyes, the trio departed to Naria's reassuring words, "If you need help, just think our names. We'll hear you in the whisper stream."

An hour later, as they hiked up a mountain with Methuselah leading the way, Andy reminded, "We've only got two days." He felt the nearly empty backpack with his free hand and found Jada's horn. His thoughts returned to the choice he faced: saving his mom or breaking the curse. The unicorn's admonishment—"Don't be greedy"—kept bumping through his thoughts, but saving Mom still seemed the more urgent matter. Every time he nearly resolved to use the horn to break the curse, his emotions would well up and make an impassioned argument to save Mom. He didn't know what to do.

"How much farther do you think?" Alden wondered two days later.

"I don't know, but we're running out of time," Hannah fretted. "If we're not back tonight, who knows what Abaddon will do."

Andy tried not to listen. Concern had morphed into urgency several hours before and was gnawing at his stomach. Thus far he'd held off panic, but he didn't know how much longer he could.

Several minutes later they passed a rock formation and Hannah observed, "Isn't that the cave we stayed in the first night? It looks familiar."

Andy looked around, trying to place it. The angle of the cave opening and the protruding rocks just to the right of the door triggered a memory, but daylight made everything look different.

"It might be," Andy replied.

Alden stuck his head in the black opening, then went in several steps. "Yep, this is it. That treasure hoard is here," he called. "Looks like there are three trolls," Alden reported, his voice echoing off the hard walls.

"Good. Then we wait until dark and coax the brutes into following us," Andy declared.

Hannah raised an eyebrow. "You're sure this is a good idea?"

"Best one we've got. Look, I don't know how this'll turn out, but we agree we've got to do something."

"I know," Hannah nodded. "I just don't like it."

Alden grabbed several trinkets from the treasure chest and rejoined the others. "This ought to make a tantalizing enough prize. Nothing like having them come after the booty they've already claimed." He handed Andy half of what he'd helped himself to.

"Do you know what you're going to say to Abaddon?" Andy asked Hannah.

"Well, I plan to be firm and tell him if he wants the horn he needs to let everyone go."

"And if he laughs at you?" Andy probed.

Hannah shook her head.

"It's okay, Hannah," Alden encouraged. "I don't see how you can convince him, and unfortunately, we don't have any leverage. It's not your fault."

"Still, I wish I could do more."

Alden's stomach rumbled and Andy suggested, "I saw a moonberry bush not far from here. We should probably eat before it gets dark and we have company."

Foggy twilight faded into blackness as Andy, Alden, and Hannah waited outside the cave entrance. Soon they heard yawning, scratching, and thumping. Then a large silhouette emerged. Andy greeted it with Methuselah illuminated.

"Here, Lumpy!" Andy called, shaking a handful of booty.

"Lumpy?" Alden queried.

"A pet name," Andy joked.

"Pet? Are you kidding me?"

Andy laughed, then coughed at the repugnant stench.

"Your pet needs a bath," Hannah chimed in, fanning the smell away with her hand.

A second troll exited and Alden engaged it. "Hey…uh…Thumpy!"

"Thumpy?" Andy questioned, taking several steps with his oversize follower in tow.

"If you can call that troll Lumpy, I'm naming this one Thumpy. It's got a club and would probably love to use it on me," Alden joked, attracting Thumpy's attention. It followed.

"Here comes one more!" Hannah called after them. "Call it Slumpy. It fits."

"Got it!" Andy replied, guiding Lumpy around in a wide circle and adding Slumpy to their recruits. He whirled Methuselah about and shook the treasure. The creatures lumbered after, curious but silent.

Hannah darted ahead of the boys to scout out any obstacles they might need to avoid.

Lumpy and Slumpy started exchanging low grunts. Andy shook the treasure more loudly, trying to keep their attention. The communication between the two brutes grew louder and before he knew it, Andy's pets made enough noise to wake anything from a sound slumber. Between that and their ground-shaking steps, Andy wondered what unexpected surprises they might be stirring up.

Hannah darted back several minutes later to report, "There are three more trolls heading in our direction. I was afraid things could go terribly wrong with these beasts."

"The more the merrier!" Alden clowned.

"How can you joke at a time like this?" Hannah scolded. He just laughed.

Several minutes later, one of the new trolls joined the procession. Alden decided to name it Bumpy because its bald head looked as though it had tangled with a club or two.

The trio made as much noise as possible to keep their followers moving, and soon the other two trolls joined the throng.

"Just call them Thing One and Thing Two," Andy shouted over the din.

As the new brutes joined Andy's followers, Lumpy raised his club and brought it down on Thing One's head. Thing One stood dazed for a second and then retaliated, whacking Lumpy. The two beasts thumped and pounded each other until Thing One relented, rubbing its head and bowing submissively.

The rest of their "pets" had stopped to watch the brawl. When the altercation ended, Andy joked, "Think we can move on now that you've shown you're the mightiest?" He jingled the loot and waved Methuselah to regain the trolls' attention. The noise level quieted and the group of three humans and six trolls progressed once more.

"How much farther?" Alden asked an hour later.

Hannah ran ahead and returned shortly, reporting, "Abaddon's camp is just ahead. You need to keep your pets busy while I go talk to him."

"No problem," Andy replied. "They're behaving themselves...for now."

"I hope Abaddon and his goons don't smell them and come check us out," Alden thought aloud.

Hannah gave him a look.

"What?"

"Hey, can you signal and let us know how my father and the others are?" Andy asked.

His request was met with silence, telling Andy they had all been thinking it but hadn't dared speak their concerns.

"How about two coughs for 'they're alive' and three for 'we've got big problems'?"

Hannah nodded.

"You've got Naria's horn?" Andy continued.

"Right here." Hannah patted her backpack. With a deep breath she added, "Okay, here goes."

CHAPTER EIGHTEEN

Party Time

Through the trees Andy could see Hannah approaching the camp. He glanced back and saw Lumpy and Slumpy getting too close for comfort and moved ahead. Alden mimicked his movements with Thumpy and Bumpy. Thing One and Thing Two had stopped for a drink in the small brook trickling through the area and appeared content for the moment. When Andy was again satisfied with the trolls' positions, he paused to listen for Hannah's signal. The silence proved deafening and unbearable.

At last, off in the distance, Andy heard two coughs. He held his breath, praying not to hear another. When no third cough came he gave a thumbs-up to Alden who moved his pets again. Andy mirrored him.

Keeping track of the trolls made it difficult to watch Hannah and judge her progress, but he persevered. Andy knew the instant she entered the clearing, for Imogenia boomed her dissatisfaction to the entire forest.

"Where's the boy? I knew your plan would fail, King Abaddon! The boy is gone." She emphasized the word *king* with a decidedly mocking tone.

We may need Daisy to help, Andy thought as he considered the possible outcomes of Hannah's conversation. *Daisy, wherever you are, can you come and help us?*

I'm on my way, came a familiar voice in Andy's head.

Thanks, Daisy.

Andy chanced peeking through the trees and saw Gozler, Maladoca, and two other zolt warriors standing guard around the clearing. Hannah waved her arms animatedly as she addressed their adversary. He couldn't see Abaddon, but based on the direction she faced, Andy knew his nemesis remained where he'd last seen him.

You tell him, Hannah! Andy cheered silently, then noticed his trolls getting a bit too close again. The boys increased their distance.

When Andy next looked, he saw Dagon remove the gag and help Captain Ladilas to his feet. Judging by the captain's stiffness, he probably hadn't walked the entire time they'd been gone. Abaddon's chief bird-man then untied Sergeants Albin and Gavin. *No sign of Father or Mermin.*

Lumpy and Bumpy lumbered toward the boys, forcing them to take evasive measures to regain the advantage.

Resettled temporarily, Andy and Alden watched Hannah pull Naria's horn from her backpack. *No! What's gonna happen if this horn cures Abaddon while Father and Mermin are still held captive?*

Alden sensed Andy's growing panic and whispered, "I'm sure Hannah's doing everything she can to keep them safe."

Andy forced a smile.

The calm broke several minutes later with Abaddon's booming announcement, "I will rule the world and live forever!" Through the fog and trees, Andy could see the dragon standing with arms outstretched as if he was Moses parting the waters.

The trolls jumped at the unexpected outburst and looked to where the noise originated. They began grunting and pounding their clubs on the ground. Their grunts morphed into roars, and soon all six of them lumbered toward the disturbance, abandoning any interest in the boys or the treasure.

"Sounds like the horn cured Abaddon," Alden surmised.

"Yeah, time to bring on our friends and rescue everyone."

Andy and Alden advanced to within several feet of the clearing and crouched in the thick undergrowth. The trolls burst into the glade, bellowing.

"Stop them!" Abaddon commanded as Hannah dove for cover to his left.

Where's Father? Andy worried, scanning the scene. Then his eyes opened wide. Through the darkness he saw the seven-headed dragon as it had appeared the first time they battled. The beast flapped its four wings then ripped the eye patches from its seven heads and flung them to the ground.

Andy raised Methuselah, and Alden followed his lead.

Captain Ladilas, Sergeant Albin, and Sergeant Gavin ran to the King and Mermin. Even though they had no weapons, they began working to break the bonds.

Whew…he's okay. Andy sighed with relief at seeing the man he so deeply loved alive. Dirty and a bit worse for wear, but alive.

In the commotion, vulture-men materialized out of thin air and the trolls began batting practice with their clubs, clearing the space. No sooner had one round of bird-men been decimated than another wave appeared.

Hannah darted across the chaos toward the King and Mermin, her arms filled with their confiscated weapons. She quickly distributed them to the officers who cut the King and Mermin loose.

While he desperately wanted to go hug Father and Mermin to reassure himself the world he loved remained intact, he knew someone needed to deal with Abaddon. If the dragon retained its newfound power, no good could come to Oomaldee.

"I'm going after Abaddon," Andy informed Alden.

"I've got your back."

The instant Andy stepped into the clearing, Imogenia spotted him and shouted, "Grab the boy!"

Andy locked eyes with his father, and the King gave him a reassuring smile, mouthing simply, "Son!"

"Father!" Andy silently replied, relieved.

With everything going on, Imogenia's demand went ignored. Several seconds later she repeated herself with the same outcome.

Andy refocused on the task at hand and slashed at a zolt that unwisely chose to engage him. Alden made quick work of its comrade, felling it where it stood. Andy jumped over several bodies and his blade connected with two more of the enemy. He ducked quickly to avoid meeting the business end of Lumpy's club, and Alden bobbed to avoid contact with yet another zolt as it materialized. Alden sliced the bird's wing before it had fully transformed, impairing it.

Crossing the glade proved slow and taxing, and Andy briefly worried that Abaddon might escape before he reached him. Just as the thought crossed his mind, however, he sensed time slow. He slew five more zolt, leaped over three bodies, and ducked to avoid two more clubs.

Six trolls can create a lot of damage…to both sides, Andy thought as he and Alden worked their way through the middle. Captain Ladilas, Sergeant Gavin, and Sergeant Albin fought on the left side of the clearing. Hannah, Mermin, and Father worked in coordinated movements to the right of the fracas.

At last Andy neared his nemesis at full speed, whirling and twisting Methuselah about. It took the dragon a minute to register his presence, but as soon as he did, Abaddon let loose three blasts of fire, incinerating several of his own troops in the process. Andy deflected the flames with his blade, shielding both he and Alden from injury. Alden felled two more zolt preparing to assault Andy's back.

The dragon roared its displeasure at failing to stop the boys and shifted its shape. But just before Abaddon fully materialized in his new form, Alden yelled, "Get off me!"

Andy whipped around to see a vulture-man on Alden's back, its arm in a choke hold around his friend's neck. Andy grabbed the dagger from his belt and plunged the knife into the unwanted guest's back. It slumped to the ground.

"Thanks!"

"No problem," Andy called as he turned back to see a gray-haired, wolflike beast. Its shoulders came halfway up Andy's chest, and it growled as it slunk back and forth on oversized paws, its eyes locked on him.

"Andy, it's a herewolf! Don't let it bite or scratch you or you could start transforming!"

Alden's words came just in time, for the beast launched itself straight at Andy, teeth bared and saliva spraying. Andy held his ready position until the last second, then faked left. Abaddon flew past, snarling.

Andy did a pirouette, and Alden ran to again defend his back.

The herewolf's momentum landed it fifteen feet away. It sprang up and whirled around, undeterred.

"Surrender now or I will finish you," Abaddon growled in a low voice.

Andy didn't respond. He focused his attention, looking for a vulnerability to exploit, but nothing presented itself.

Abaddon readied another charge and came barreling at Andy a second time. Again Andy evaded, to the right this time. But as he did so, his foot landed on the corpse of a vulture-man and he sprawled to the ground. He scrambled to right himself, but the herewolf proved faster, landing easily and rounding on its prey. It towered over Andy. Andy scuttled back, eyes locked with the creature, Methuselah still clutched in his right hand. The beast took a step forward, then another, advancing slowly, menacingly with its mouth open. Andy could feel heat and smell bad breath.

"Get away from my friend!" yelled Alden, charging.

The unexpected distraction granted Andy an opportunity. He sat up and brought his blade toward the enemy's head. But Abaddon moved and Andy came up empty.

Abaddon swatted at Alden, driving him off.

Andy scrambled to his feet and put three yards between himself and his adversary before the beast looked his way again. Abaddon resumed pacing, considering Andy.

"Kill him!" Imogenia screamed.

Andy took his ready position. *I need to get above him. I only need to maim him; I don't need to kill. If I can just nick his ear... Oh, where's Daisy? She'd be able to take him in herewolf form.*

No sooner had the thought entered his brain than his mind heard, "I'm getting there. I'm flying as fast as I can."

Andy chanced a quick look around the glade. The fog was lighter than usual tonight, and in the moonlight he saw Slumpy connect his club with a thinning congregation of zolt, adding to the growing pile of corpses littering the ground. Bumpy and Lumpy battled more bird-men. Hannah, Father, and Mermin fought Thumpy, and Father's officers engaged Thing One and several vulture-men. Thing Two ambled toward Abaddon. With the din of the chaos around them, the herewolf didn't notice the threat. Andy watched as the troll raised its club in Abaddon's blind spot and connected with his hindquarters.

The beast yelped and its legs buckled, landing its behind on the ground. Abaddon hurriedly regained his footing and rounded on the troll, dragging one leg. Without hesitation, Andy ran, launching himself onto his adversary's back. He landed near the middle and grabbed hold of a thick clump of gray fur. Abaddon brought his head back and nearly caught Andy's leg in his bared teeth, but Andy moved forward just in time. As Andy brought Methuselah up, he felt the body beneath him shift. The long fur vanished but Andy remained focused, slicing the sword downward and removing an ear before the herewolf completed its change. He felt himself take flight as Abaddon writhed in pain. Andy landed with a thud next to a monstrous rhino with a jet black corkscrew horn, which immediately changed into a gigantic bird. Thunder clapped above the glade, halting all action except Abaddon's transformation into his dragon form.

Andy jumped up and distanced himself from his enemy. He needn't have worried though, for as soon as its red scales materialized, the dragon vanished.

"No!" Imogenia screamed.

"Andy, look out!" Alden yelled.

Thing Two smashed its club too close to Andy, jolting him back to reality. Andy turned to face the troll and took his fighting stance as Alden rejoined him.

And then it happened. As the zolt realized their leader had fled, a deafening cawing sound arose as they took flight, abandoning their fallen comrades. Humans and trolls alike stopped fighting and watched the horde disappear into the night sky.

The peace didn't last long. For as soon as the bird-men left, Lumpy whammed his club on the ground, breaking the spell.

"There's no point in fighting these brutes," Andy yelled across the clearing. "Troll wounds heal immediately."

"Then what do you suggest?" Captain Ladilas called from across the glade.

"We'll have to keep them occupied until sunup," Hannah advised.

"Why? What happens then?" Sergeant Gavin queried, distancing himself from Thumpy.

"They'll turn to stone," Mermin confirmed as he, the King, and Hannah walked around several mounds of dead zolt to where Andy and Alden were. Andy watched with surprise as Thumpy did not pursue. Instead, the troll looked around, scratched its bald head, and seemed to contemplate its situation. Lumpy, Slumpy, and the other trolls looked at each other, then sat down in silent agreement, each where it was.

Please no, Andy thought, horrified.

Bumpy grabbed a dead zolt in its huge hand and brought it up to its mouth.

Hannah shrieked and turned away.

"Bon appetit!" Andy managed, wearing a pained expression.

"What's that mean?" Alden questioned.

"I believe it means 'good eating,'" Mermin interpreted.

"You're disgusting!" Hannah cried.

Andy watched Captain Ladilas, Sergeant Gavin, and Sergeant Albin share a chuckle.

"While it may disgust you, Hannah, trolls eating the zolt is not much different than us eating cows and goats," the King encouraged. "And they'll clean it up before they start to stink."

Hannah grimaced.

Alden clearly didn't know what to say to comfort Hannah. He stood stone-faced as the sound of bones being crunched by large teeth echoed across the clearing.

"I've got to get out of here," Hannah announced, waving her hands.

"We should all get out of here. Best to distance ourselves before more trolls investigate," suggested Captain Ladilas.

No sooner had the words left the captain's lips than everyone felt the ground shake with a heavy footfall, then another and another.

"That way," Captain Ladilas whispered, pointing in a direction across from their current position and leading the way. Everyone holstered their weapons and hurried to find their backpacks. Andy realized he hadn't retrieved his dagger. *Oh well, no time to find it now. I hope I don't need it.*

Several minutes later Andy walked next to his father and engaged in hushed conversation.

"I'm very proud of you, Son. Defeating Abaddon for a third time is nothing short of amazing."

Andy grinned. "Thanks."

"When you left to find the unicorn horns, I didn't know whether that might be the last time I saw you. Abaddon didn't need to keep me or the others alive," Father remarked.

"Why do you suppose he did?"

The King raised an eyebrow before responding.

"No, don't take it the wrong way," Andy apologized.

Father chuckled then added, "It may be he has power over Imogenia if I'm alive."

"But what good would that do him? It's not like she can do anything for him."

"She may know some things he needs, or it may be he's that arrogant. He may have kept us around to show off his newfound might and instill fear once the horn cured him. I have to say, I became concerned when he was restored."

Sergeant Gavin alerted the group to the presence of another troll and everyone took cover in the thick underbrush until it passed. It headed in the direction of the glade, no doubt smelling an easy meal on the breeze.

They had not gone far when Captain Ladilas again interrupted with a whispered, "Everyone take cover!"

The continual warnings to hide put everyone on edge. While waiting in shrubbery for yet another troll to pass, Andy glanced up and saw a monstrous winged creature fly across the foggy predawn sky, casting an ominous shadow across their path.

Not another monster!

The rest of the company noticed and all drew their weapons.

Andy, why are you hiding? came a voice in his head.

Daisy? He sighed. *It's you.*

Yes, good to catch up with you. I got here as quickly as I could.

"Hey everyone, it's okay. It's Daisy," Andy announced.

"Daisy!" Alden exclaimed.

The dragon landed gracefully in a small clearing just ahead. She ruffled her wings and folded them against her body as the group joined her.

"Thanks so much for coming on short notice," Andy began.

I promised you I would come if you ever needed my help, Daisy spoke to everyone's thoughts.

The soldiers, who had never experienced telepathic communication, looked about nervously, wondering where the voice came from. The rest of the group shared a laugh.

"Do you know what happened?" Alden queried.

Yes. I monitored Andy's thoughts. I'm sorry I didn't arrive in time to help defeat Abaddon, but it appears you had things well in hand without me.

"I hate to break up this reunion, but I think we've reached the end of troll territory judging by the terrain. I believe the realm of the dwarfs begins not far off," Sergeant Albin reported.

"Let's grab a bite to eat and get some sleep," Captain Ladilas suggested. "I don't anticipate any more trolls."

"Even if one stumbles on our camp, I have to believe they'd think twice with our dragon friend here," Alden added, patting Daisy's neck.

Daisy gave a snort of approval.

Everyone agreed no watch needed to be set with Daisy around, and a short time later, with the sky nearing dawn, silence reigned across the campsite. Eight slumbering humans and their reptilian friend sprawled around a glowing bonfire, lit courtesy of Daisy.

Several hours later, Andy opened one eyelid a slit, trying to remember where he was. He heard Mermin let out a snore nearby. Daisy shifted in her sleep, smoke rings wafting from her nostrils with each breath. Everything and everyone else lay still. Then he heard Mom's voice, gentle and soft, ask once more, "Did you get a unicorn horn for me?"

CHAPTER NINETEEN

The Weight of Evil

A ndy glanced around the camp. He spotted the translucent sphere slowly revolving above the tip of Daisy's tail in the hazy morning light. Sitting up, he rubbed sleep from his eyes. His brain wrestled against the slough of slumber. As it finished assembling the jumbled pieces of reality, he sprang up, suddenly clear. He glanced down at his backpack that he'd used for a pillow, considering whether to extract Jada's horn. He decided to wait, confused by his own hesitation.

He tiptoed through the maze of arms and legs cluttering his path until he stood an arm's length away from the sphere.

"Did you get a unicorn's horn for me?" it repeated.

"Sorry, but first I need to make sure you're really my mom," he whispered.

"Andy," Mom's voice interrupted, "what do I mean to you?"

"Huh?" Over the last several days he had rehearsed a dozen questions he wanted to ask the sphere, but it trumped them all with the inquiry.

"What do I mean to you?" it repeated.

As he collected his thoughts, Andy heard Alden roll over behind him.

"Well, you're my mom."

"But what does that mean to you?"

Andy fidgeted as his mind tried to overcome its aversion to expressing his feelings. Finally he spoke, "You take us to the library and treat us to ice cream." He looked down and nudged a twig with his foot. "And you make me laugh when you play jokes on me and Madison. And you listen and cheer me up and, I don't know... You make me feel loved." Andy's cheeks reddened.

With no further questions, Andy stepped back through the labyrinth of appendages and bent down, opening his backpack. As he pulled out the unicorn horn, Alden asked, "What are you doing?"

Andy looked up. "You know the sphere I told you about?"

Alden nodded.

"It's my mom's spirit. It's back. It's over there."

Alden looked to where Andy pointed. "I don't see anything," he declared.

"If I give her Jada's horn, she'll live even after the curse is broken. She said so."

"But how will you break the curse? That's your primary objective." Alden's voice grew louder.

"Shhh," Andy cautioned.

"No, I won't be quiet. You can't give Jada's horn to whatever or whoever you think that is."

"You don't understand." Horn in hand, Andy moved back toward the swirling sphere. "I have to save my mom!"

"This is a bad idea, Andy," his inneru objected.

Andy ignored it.

"Your mom wouldn't ask you to save her if it meant not breaking the curse," Alden argued.

Reason raised its head briefly in Andy's brain, causing him to pause. He glanced back at his friend.

"She doesn't know there's only one horn left."

"Don't do this, Andy!"

The noise of their conversation roused the rest of the party.

"I have to," Andy insisted, resuming his previous course. "We'll have to find another horn. I can't let her die!"

"What's going on?" the King asked sleepily.

Alden quickly filled him in, and he stood.

"Andy!" Father called.

"Andy," Mom's voice beckoned.

"I *have* to do this!" Andy insisted, reaching the swirling sphere.

"Son!" Father insisted.

"Here!" Andy exclaimed holding up the unicorn's horn. "I love you, Mom!"

A zolt swooped down through the foliage canopy. It appeared so suddenly Andy didn't have time to react. It grabbed the horn in its talons, drawing blood, then flew away.

"Ouch!"

Gloating laughter erupted from the rotating sphere as it morphed into the translucent form of Imogenia. Across the campsite everyone heard her taunt, "Foolish, greedy boy! You didn't really think you could save your mom, did you? Your love for her is your weakness! You surrendered the horn and now the curse can't be broken." More laughter followed.

"What have I done?" Andy exclaimed, disbelieving.

"Imogenia!" another voice boomed. "What you have done is despicable and not worthy of my daughter. Preying on the love my grandson holds for his mother and exploiting it for your own gain? Revenge has changed you from the caring, loving girl I knew into something lowly and sordid."

Everyone in the clearing stood and looked up, their eyes catching sight of two ghostly forms. The King rushed to Andy's side and hugged him. The officers circled the two of them protectively, weapons drawn. Alden and Hannah darted for the edges of the campsite amid hushed exclamations while Mermin just stood and watched, unmoved by the chaos.

"Yes, I was a caring, loving girl," Imogenia continued, "before Kaysan killed me!"

"And he has been punished sufficiently. Imogenia, my sweet girl, your actions are beneath you. I think you know that."

Imogenia didn't respond.

"I love you," the man's voice continued.

"If you loved me, you wouldn't try to break the curse!" Imogenia resisted.

"Revenge is killing you inside, Imogenia. I worried about this possibility when I first consented to allowing the curse, do you remember? The curse needs to be broken out of love—not only for my former subjects, but for you."

Silence reigned across the clearing for several seconds until Imogenia replied, "I can't, Father," and disappeared. The second ghost vanished as well.

"What am I gonna do?" Andy thought aloud, rubbing his wounded hand.

I don't know what you're going to do, but I'm going after that bird-man, Daisy communicated to Andy's thoughts. He nodded vacantly as she stalked to an open area of the camp and extended her wings, taking off in the direction the zolt had disappeared.

Hannah and Alden rejoined the others, and Hannah offered, "For what it's worth, I think Imogenia's father made her think even though she's not quite ready to listen, but it's a start."

"How could I not know?" Andy questioned.

"Son, your actions came from love. Don't regret what you did."

"But how could I not know it was Imogenia deceiving me the whole time?"

"Sometimes love blinds us. What we love has power over us and can be exploited by others, but I would rather risk that and know love than know loneliness without love."

"But I don't want my mom to die if I break the curse, just like I don't want you and Mermin to die."

"I understand, Son. There have been times in my life I wanted something so badly, I chose to ignore reason."

"So you're saying I wanted to believe I could save my mom so badly that I believed even what didn't make sense?"

"Think about it, Andy. Why would your mother appear to you alone in the form of a rotating sphere?" Father queried.

"But it sounded like her."

"Yes, but why wouldn't she appear to everyone? And why a sphere?"

"I don't know. I never thought about it."

"Exactly. Because you wanted to believe, out of love."

"But what are we going to do? If Daisy can't track the bird-guy down and get the unicorn horn back, we can't break the curse."

"Let's see what happens before we worry about that," the King suggested.

"Dwagons have a keen sense of smell," Mermin interrupted. "She'll pwobably twack the smelly fowl and make quick work of it."

"I hope you're right, Mermin." Andy sighed.

An hour had passed since Daisy's departure, and everyone sat quietly in the clearing. Only the rhythm of birdsong, the occasional croaking of frogs, and the buzzing of bees disturbed the stillness. This peace contrasted dramatically with the tumult in Andy's head. *No matter what Father says, if we can't break the curse because of what I did, I'll never forgive myself! Stupid! Stupid!*

"Are you through beating yourself up?"

Huh?

"It's me. Or have you forgotten?" Andy's inneru intruded.

Oh.

"I chose to keep quiet and let you make your own choices since you didn't appreciate my interfering earlier. I thought a bit of learning would be good for you."

I guess I didn't do a very good job, did I?

"Honestly? No, you made a royal mess of things. Part of growing up is learning to take the advice of your inneru. What you put me through— ignoring me, talking back, disrespecting me." It paused, seemingly working to calm itself. A minute later it resumed, "Well, enough about me, this is about you. I'm not here to hurt you. Do you believe that, Andy?"

I've never thought about it, but yeah, I guess so.

"My job is to help you live the best life you can. I'm not second-guessing you or out to ruin your fun. When you are king one day, you won't always know what to do. You'll need to follow me. Your father consults his inneru all the time."

He does? How do you know?

"Learn to trust me!"

Andy laughed.

Hannah, who sat between him and Alden, looked over wearing a quizzical look.

"I promise I won't steer you wrong," his inneru continued. "Deal?"

Deal. Andy smiled to himself.

"What's up?" Hannah asked, drawing Alden's curiosity.

"Nothing, just talking to…myself."

Father approached. "Any word from Daisy?"

"She hasn't said anything to me," Andy replied. "Let me see if I can contact her."

Daisy?

Can't talk now! the dragon replied to Andy's thoughts.

Andy's eyes grew large.

"What's wrong?" Alden asked as everyone gathered around.

"She said she can't talk right now. The way she said it worries me, though. It sounds as if she's under attack."

"She's much bigger than the bird-guy. She shouldn't have any problems subduing it," reasoned Captain Ladilas.

"I know. That's what worries me. She didn't sound like she had things under control." Andy's mind started inventing all manner of horrifying possibilities.

"Remain calm," his inneru suggested. "You don't have the facts."

Andy took a deep breath and let it out slowly. *But I don't want anything bad to happen to her!*

"Worrying isn't going to change things," his inneru suggested.

Mom has said that before.

"Yes," his inneru agreed.

"What should we do?" Andy asked the group.

"Sitting around isn't accomplishing anything," Captain Ladilas commented. "That dragon of yours has a serious sense of smell. She'll find us even if we're moving. I suggest we get going."

Everyone but Andy agreed, and the consensus finally won him over.

They had just started out when Andy heard a familiar voice in his head. *Uh, Andy, I need a little help.*

"Stop! Daisy's talking to me!" Andy reported, causing everyone to halt. They all watched him as he conversed with the dragon, looking for the slightest clue to tell them what was happening.

What's wrong?

I've got some good news and some bad news.

Give me the bad news first.

I've been captured.

Captured? How is that possible?

I'm not sure, but I'm under a chain mail net. They've done something to the metal. It feels heavy and oppressive, to my very bones. I've never felt weak like this before. I can't escape.

Where are you?

I'm halfway between you and Mount Hope, just outside the Forest of Giants.

We'll rescue you, Daisy! Just sit tight. Oh, sorry. Bad choice of words.

If anything happens to Daisy because of me...

Before he could finish berating himself, Daisy interrupted again. *Would you like to hear the good news?*

Oh, yeah. What's the good news?

I got the unicorn horn back.

You did? Oh, Daisy! You're the best.

I'm holding on to it, but I don't know how long I can last. These vulture-guys will grab it back if— Hold on, there's a giant coming.

Andy didn't wait for Daisy to finish. He'd heard enough. "Daisy's been captured! We have to save her!"

As he filled everyone in on his conversation, Mermin scratched his head thoughtfully. "Sounds like the net might be steeped in dark magic," he speculated. "That's the only thing that could subdue a dwagon."

"Dark magic?" Father questioned.

Mermin nodded, frowning.

"What's that mean? What'll we do?" Andy insisted.

"Only what is pure and light can bweak dark magic."

"Can't Methuselah cut Daisy loose?"

"Perhaps, but Methuselah has seen battle and shed blood. Yours is a blade of justice, Andy, not puwity. I suggest you ask the unicorns to join us. If it's as I suspect, we won't be able to wemove the net without them."

Jada! Naria! Andy, Alden, and Hannah called together in their minds.

The trio expressed such urgency, the unicorns answered immediately.

"What is it, children?" Naria questioned.

After explaining the situation, the unicorns quickly agreed to meet them near where Daisy indicated.

Even walking at a brisk pace the trip took nearly all day. Andy periodically called Daisy in his thoughts and his alarm grew, for each time it took her longer to reply and her responses grew increasingly labored.

The sun cast long rays of foggy light before they neared the dragon late in the afternoon. They approached stealthily, moving invisibly between the thick trees at the edge of the Forest of Giants. Alden, who led alongside Andy, spotted her first and held his fist up, signaling everyone to stop.

Daisy lay on the ground with a chain mail net completely covering her like a blanket. Two giants stood to one side watching while a dozen vulture-men circled her, periodically poking and prodding with spears. Andy and Alden nodded to each other, immediately recognizing the giants from an earlier encounter with their kin.

Captain Ladilas and the two sergeants disappeared, quietly scouting the surrounding area.

Daisy? We're here, in the trees. How are you? Andy asked.

Oh, I've been better, Daisy brightened. *I think they're going to lift the net near my claws and try to grab the horn soon. They've been waiting for the magic to wear me down so I can't move anymore. I'm so tired, Andy.*

Hang on just a few minutes longer and we'll get you out of there!

We have arrived, Jada informed Andy, Alden, and Hannah. *Just let us know when you're ready for us.* The trio scanned the surrounding area but didn't see the unicorns.

The captain and his soldiers reported back minutes later. "It appears they've used the giants to manage the net," Captain Ladilas began. "It's not clear whether they are working together or not. We didn't see any other bird-men outside the camp, but you know how quickly that can change. Once we eliminate the zolt, we'll deal with the giants based on how they react."

The group of eight raced from their hiding place, taking the bird-men by surprise. In moments, all twelve zolt were either knocked out or dead, depending upon the fight they'd put up.

The giants stood idly by, watching but not reacting to the loss of the bird-folk. When the excitement ended, Captain Ladilas approached one. From a safe distance he asked, "Will you help us remove the net?"

"Maybe. What'll you give us if we help?" it replied.

"What would you like?" The King stepped forward, ready to negotiate.

"Some nice juicy dragon steaks." The second giant grunted its hearty approval.

The trio looked at each other, eyebrows raised.

"No, we are rescuing our friend, not eating her," the King declared.

"Then I guess we'll have to help ourselves," the giant replied. "We were promised dragon steaks for our help. I've been looking forward to that all day. Not our fault the beast wouldn't die quickly."

At this, the two giants stepped toward Daisy.

"I wouldn't do that if I were you," Captain Ladilas cautioned, taking a ready position. The King, Mermin, and the two sergeants followed suit, halting the brutes.

"Come on," Andy whispered to Hannah and Alden.

The three strode to the dragon. "We'll have you out in a minute," Andy encouraged.

I...hope...so, she struggled.

Each of them grabbed a corner of the net. Expecting it to lift easily, they stopped short, unable to pry it from the ground.

The giants began laughing. "They'll never get it up, Zank!"

"Yeah, I can smell the steaks already, Tank!" the other grunted daftly.

"What's going on?" Alden questioned.

"It's the magic," Mermin surmised, continuing to hold the carnivores at bay.

"Jada. Naria," the children called.

The two unicorns strode from the trees.

"Well, I'll be. Hey look, Tank!"

"What happened to their horns, Zank? They look stupid without them."

The unicorns ignored the hecklers and set to work, each placing a front hoof on opposite sides of the net. They closed their eyes in concentration and the metal began to spark, causing the kids to back away. The net took on a reddish glow as it heated up. Naria and Jada placed their other front hooves on the netting and the sparks began to arc wildly. If this were a celebration, the display would have produced a festive mood. Hannah raced to stamp out several sparks that flew into the nearby grass. Alden and Andy followed suit.

Daisy, how you doing?

I'm hot, she replied groggily.

The scene resembled popcorn popping before Daisy's restraint vaporized.

The two giants stared blankly at the spectacle, then started forward again, clearly intent on capturing their dinner before it escaped.

The officers slashed at the giants' hairy legs, sending them dancing an off-balance jig and crashing to the ground.

The dragon began to rouse and within a minute sat up. *Wow, thank you for rescuing me! I've never felt anything like it. I felt completely weak, drained of all energy. I began to wonder if I'd ever be free.*

Jada and Naria approached, their heads hung low. *We've not seen dark magic like this before. You saw how the net sparked when we touched it?*

The trio nodded.

"It weighed a ton!" Alden exclaimed.

You felt the weight of evil burned deep into the metal, Naria explained.

It sparked violently because purity repels evil. The two cannot coexist, Jada continued.

Realization dawned on Andy, and he voiced his thoughts. "This is what it means to fight evil, to fight Abaddon." He felt sick. *How are we ever going to defeat him?*

CHAPTER TWENTY

Saltito

It took Daisy several minutes to regain her ability to stand and walk. All the while, Alden and Hannah kept watch over her, speaking words of encouragement. Her first wobbly steps she fell over, taking Sergeant Albin with her. She finally stabilized herself with her wings, much like a tightrope walker with a pole, and made it to Andy. She raised a clawed foot, drew Andy's hand from his side, and handed him the unicorn horn she had so faithfully guarded.

Daisy! Thank you so much! It cost you a lot.

It means much to you. I was happy to do it.

Andy could only nod in reply.

Hannah and Alden joined Andy and Daisy as Jada and Naria approached.

The she-unicorn announced, "It looks like our job here is done. We will take our leave, but our offer still stands. Should you need us, please call."

"Thank you so much, both of you," Hannah replied, stroking Naria's neck then giving her a hug.

"Yeah, thank you," Alden replied. "I don't know what we would have done without you."

"Evil is not an adversary to be overthrown on your own. It will take the combined efforts, and sacrifice, of many before peace and justice reign once more," Jada advised.

Andy took several rapid breaths, wishing the looming situation could be behind them.

An hour later, in the growing darkness, a rustling through the trees sparked shouts from the three soldiers, who still held off Tank and Zank's pursuit of Daisy. Four more giants appeared.

I think that's my cue, Daisy interjected, *before they try for dragon steaks one more time. Call me if you need me.*

Count on it! Andy replied as she launched.

"Clear the area!" Captain Ladilas shouted.

Everyone scurried about the clearing, grabbing possessions. It reminded Andy of cockroaches scattering when someone turns on the lights. The giants, about as sharp as marbles, stood by and watched, unsure what to do.

Andy held Methuselah up, lighting the way through the foggy darkness. The eight had agreed it would be safer if they ate as they walked, and so Andy munched on crusty bread and cheese as he walked next to his father.

"You're rather quiet," Father assessed between bites.

Andy's eyes met the King's before he replied, "I was thinking about the golden goose delivering the clue and the moral to not be greedy."

"Go on," Father encouraged.

"And I thought about what King Nithi told us about the Whitehearted Potentate being willing to wipe out all the greedy dwarfs because he was convinced those who loved jewels weren't truly free."

Father nodded. "And?"

"While I think that guy overdid it, he may have had a point. I think you're not truly free if you're greedy toward anything."

"I see," the King replied.

"I was also thinking about what Jada said."

"Which was?"

"He said a king has to make difficult choices between his personal desires and the welfare of his subjects. He also said every action we take in life is a choice between competing options and reveals what we most value."

"Jada is wise. So what have you learned?"

"I can now see how I was greedy by wanting so badly for Mom to live after the curse is broken." Andy paused for a minute before continuing, letting the realization sink in. "I think Mom is like the jewels the dwarfs loved. It was okay for me to want to save her, but I allowed that desire to control me. And that's when I made a bad choice that nearly cost us breaking the curse, not to mention hurting Daisy."

Father smiled. "Son, you have learned a lesson most people never do. Its value equals or surpasses that of the unicorn's horn."

They chatted a bit more until Captain Ladilas announced, "We've cleared the Forest of Giants and I don't anticipate any more unwanted company. Let's make camp and get some rest."

The trip the next day proved unremarkable and they reached the city of Oops by early afternoon. Andy saw Castle Avalon's turrets rise above the tree line an hour later when Hannah interrupted his thoughts. She put her hand on his arm and softly said, "I sense something."

"What is it?" Andy queried, looking to Alden for clarification. Alden shrugged his shoulders.

"A cold prickly feeling, and it's as intense as when the bellicose first attacked you!" Hannah replied, scanning the area with wide eyes.

Andy and Alden followed her gaze, seeing nothing out of the ordinary but drawing their weapons anyway. Andy filled in the adults, who also drew their weapons, and picked up the pace.

Half an hour later, they crossed the castle drawbridge as a guard announced their arrival. As the wooden bridge was being raised, Andy glanced back. Just beyond the span stood the bellicose staring at its prey.

"I knew it couldn't be dead!" he announced.

His seven companions also turned to look, and a ripple of fear rolled through them.

"I want extra soldiers posted around the perimeter of Castle Avalon!" Father instructed the watchman.

"Yes, Your Majesty! It shall be done immediately!" the guard declared and sprang into action.

The group headed up to the dining hall, no one uttering a word.

"You're back at just the right time!" Marta exclaimed, running to Alden and Andy and giving them a collective bear hug. Her celebration instantly shifted the mood.

"We completed preparations just this morning for the king's celebration of Prince Andrew," Lucee informed. Cadfael stood beaming next to his wife as Ro attempted to climb Hannah.

"Big sissy back!" the toddler announced at the top of his lungs, to everyone's laughter.

Hannah scooped him up and showered his fat little face with kisses, to which he giggled and squirmed delightedly. Charis and Larissa gave Hannah more hugs, clearly happy to see their sister back safely.

"The festivities will take place tomorrow evening," Ox informed.

"What would you have done if we hadn't made it back by then?" Andy asked.

"Sent out a search party for ya!" Merk joked.

Hans approached. Stopping next to Andy, he observed, "Looks like your nose is just slightly bent. I do good work if I do say so myself."

Andy laughed and hugged the healer. "Good to see you too, Hans." Sensing an unspoken question, Andy smiled and replied, "Yes, the trip brought my father and I closer. I'm glad we could go together." Hans returned the smile, patting Andy on the back.

"Am I missing something, or will you be needin' another dagger?" Cadfael questioned Andy, jokingly shaking his head. "Yours seems to be missin' from your belt."

Andy grinned. "Hey, things got a little intense out there. What can I say?" He caught a wink from Father as he spoke, and Alden, Hannah, and Mermin grinned.

When much of the excitement had died down, Razen approached Father and called him away to other matters. Only then did Andy notice Captain Ladilas and the two sergeants had silently slipped away. The letdown that follows a memorable event knocked on Andy's mind as everyone dispersed. Shaking himself from his reverie, he joined Mermin heading up to his library.

"May I join you?" Andy asked.

"Please."

"I need to put the unicorn horn in the book before anything happens to it," Andy explained as they climbed the stairs.

"A wise idea."

Andy followed Mermin into the room, located the invisible book, and brought it over to the table. He set his backpack down and pulled out the unicorn horn. Opening the cover, Andy read the first page:

Well done.
You are beginning to learn what it means to rule.

Yeah, and it's not easy, he thought.

He pulled on the white loop handle, opening the compartment behind. There lay six red dragon scales and the vial of venom, just as he'd left them. Then he realized a problem—Jada's horn measured fifteen inches but the book only ten.

How am I going to fit this inside?

Mermin noticed Andy's hesitation from across the room and came to investigate.

"Pwoblem?"

"Yeah. Jada's horn is taller than the book. Any suggestions?"

After a moment of thought, Mermin recalled, "Didn't you mention once that the key changes size based on the need?"

Andy nodded, remembering how the gold key had shrunk to fit a smaller keyhole when he and Alden had been trapped by vulture-people at the inn in the village of Oohhh. "You think the horn will change size?"

"I don't know, but it's worth a twy."

Andy angled the horn toward the book. To his delight, as soon as he inserted its tip into the compartment, it started to shrink. The horn fit with room to spare.

"That's so cool!" Andy remarked, returning the invisible book to the shelf. "Thanks, Mermin! I wouldn't have thought of that."

Mermin only smiled and nodded.

The rest of the day passed uneventfully, and as he dressed in his blue T-shirt and jeans the next morning, Andy found himself wondering how much time he had left in Oomaldee before being sent home again. His last two visits had ended abruptly after he'd recovered an ingredient. He hoped this time would be different, especially in light of recent events.

I wonder when I'll get to stay for good… But what'll happen to Dad and Madison? He now knew Mom's fate, and it felt like a big foot kicked inside his stomach whenever he thought about it. He had no idea how Dad and his sister fit into the picture, and it left him feeling…uncomfortable.

Father, on the other hand… Andy couldn't help but loose the smile begging to cross his face when he thought about the man he loved so dearly.

"Andy! Good morning!" Father boomed across the dining hall the instant he appeared.

Andy reached the King and felt arms engulf him in a welcome hug.

"I can't tell you how proud I am of you, Son," Father praised softly in Andy's ear as they held the embrace.

Andy's heart did a happy dance, and for the first time he quietly affirmed, "I love you," coaxing a grin from Father. They finally broke apart and seated themselves in their usual positions at the long communal table.

Mermin quietly chuckled at the display of affection and commented, "I can't wemember the last time I've seen you so happy, old friend."

The King returned the expression, then reached over and tousled Andy's hair.

"You ready for the celebration tonight?" Father asked.

"Is there something I need to do to get ready?"

"Yes, you should go see Kalpit, the tailor. He'll make sure your new robes fit perfectly for tonight. We can't have the prince looking unkempt," Father replied.

"Excellent! I'll do that right after breakfast."

"You also might want to pwactice a few dance steps?" Mermin suggested.

"Dance steps? There's gonna be dancing tonight?" Andy's voice betrayed the dread suddenly overwhelming his thoughts. "But I can't dance. I have two left feet."

Father and Mermin shared an appreciative laugh before the wizard declared, "Then you will learn. Today."

Okay, now would be a great time to be sent home!

"That's right," Father realized, "you've never attended a formal celebration here."

"Your father's quite the dancer," Mermin shared. "Light on his feet, he is."

"Dancing makes me happy," the King replied.

Their comments didn't change the frown smothering Andy's face.

"Tell you what, I'll rearrange my schedule," Father offered. "You get your robes properly fitted, and then I'll give you a dance lesson later this morning."

Andy brightened.

At the appointed hour, Andy knocked on the door of the King's chambers for his first dance lesson.

"Come in, Son. Come in," Father welcomed. "I'm glad you got my message. I thought you'd appreciate a little privacy."

Andy nodded.

"We should have enough room in here," Father declared, waving his arm and indicating the open floor to the right of his overstuffed bed. Mermin perched on a chair at the edge of their makeshift dance floor and three musicians—one with a harp, one with an oboe, and one with a lute—lined the stone wall to his right.

"I didn't know we had musicians!" Andy exclaimed, getting his first look at them.

Father and Mermin laughed. "This is Bigul," the King introduced an older man of slight build sitting in front of the harp. "And Alaap." The plump woman holding an oboe smiled warmly and nodded. "And Liber," he finished, indicating the bald man with fat, rosy cheeks poised to strum the lute cradled in his arms.

"I've seen you all around," Andy acknowledged, "but I didn't know you played music."

The King refocused his attention. "I asked Mermin to assist since it's usually easier to watch the first time through."

"I get to dance the lady's part," Mermin joked, standing and curtseying.

"You do that so well," Andy laughed.

Father's face beamed as he began his instruction. "Some people see dance as just moving about with no story or purpose." The King cleared his throat and winked at Andy, who rolled his eyes playfully. "I, on the other hand, view dancing as expression, being free of one's usual constraints. I connect with the music and let my emotions take control."

I can get that, I'm sure everyone expects Father to act a certain way. Dance is probably one of the few opportunities for him to be himself, Andy thought, then nodded.

"The dance I want to show you is called Saltito. Mermin...shall we?"

The wizard cinched up his flowing blue robes as he and the King stepped to the center of their dance floor.

"If you please," Father requested the musicians, who struck up a lively tune.

Father stood next to Mermin and bowed, then took the wizard's hand. In unison, Mermin and the King stepped left then right, forward then back, followed by one hop on each foot. They slid forward left, forward right, then repeated the first steps four times. After two repetitions, they spun around and retraced their steps with each repetition. On and on the dance went, until Andy's brain could hold no more.

How am I gonna be any good at this by tonight? he panicked.

When the wizard and Father finished, the King commented, "You don't need to master this for tonight's festivities, Son. I wanted you to see what the whole dance looks like so you can appreciate your progress as you learn."

"That's a relief," Andy sighed, as Father laughed.

"I want you to have fun with this, Andy. Remember, I've had over five hundred years to practice."

"Oh, right." Somehow that perspective helped calm him.

"So, let's take it one part at a time," Father suggested.

"Okay."

Following this approach, Andy had learned the fundamentals by the time his stomach grumbled two hours later, causing everyone to adjourn for lunch.

Father had other matters to attend after the noon meal, but Andy and Mermin returned to the King's chambers for more practice. Three hours later, the beginnings of confidence began announcing their presence in Andy's brain, and he smiled as he and Mermin shared the dance's final bow. *I didn't even look at my feet that time!*

Mermin and the musicians clapped.

"Well done, my pwince," Mermin affirmed. "You'll do fine tonight. Best get weady, our guests will begin awwiving shortly. You—"

Mermin didn't have a chance to finish his sentence, for there came an urgent pounding on the door. A servant rushed in and announced rapid-fire, "Sorry to intrude, sir. Is the King here? There's a…a…a black, hairy beast thing loose in the castle!"

CHAPTER TWENTY-ONE

Cotillion

A ndy didn't wait for Mermin, but burst from the King's chambers and took the stairs two at a time, stopping at the dining hall where shouts rang out.

The bellicose gazed about the room dagger in hand, sniffing the air, then halted as soon as it eyed Andy.

Unarmed, Andy wished, *If only I had Methuselah!*

No sooner had he thought it than the hilt materialized in his hand.

No way! You transport yourself, too? You're so cool!

The blade extended and Andy slowly approached, his eyes locked on the bellicose. Onlookers instantly hushed and parted like the Red Sea.

Before Andy got close enough to begin circling his adversary, Father sprinted into the room having bolted up the grand staircase behind the beast. He growled loudly, "Oh no you don't! You'll have to get through me before you ever touch my son!"

Father's bellow startled the bellicose, and it whirled to face the disturbance.

"Father, no!" Andy yelled, racing to intervene.

But before Andy could separate the two, the bellicose leaped on the King, tackling him to the floor.

"No!" Andy screamed.

Andy expected to hear gut-wrenching shrieks from Father. In the instant it took his brain to register what was happening, however, his ears and mind attempted to reconcile a disconnect. He heard yelps, but they came from the bellicose not Father.

The King wrestled the beast, grabbing it around its thick, furry neck and strangling it with his bare hands. Andy had never seen such a fierce look of hatred as the one on Father's face in that moment. The beast writhed and squirmed, straining to push Father away. It finally broke free. Scrambling to its feet, it grabbed the weapon it had dropped when it made contact with the King, then bolted for the stairs and back out the door.

Andy heard a collective sigh go up from the onlookers. He retracted Methuselah's blade, sprinted to Father, and extended his hand to help him up off the floor. "What just happened?" he questioned, disbelieving.

Father's face now wore a confused expression and he replied, "I'm not sure, Son." He took in another deep breath. "All I know is I wasn't going to allow that beast to harm you."

"Didn't the bellicose's touch burn?"

"No, not at all. In fact, judging by its cries, I think I burned it when it touched me."

"But how?"

The King looked at Andy and shook his head. "No idea."

"Are you okay?" Mermin interrupted, finally reaching them.

"Yes, I'm fine," affirmed the King, patting the wizard on the shoulder.

Andy glanced toward the back of the room and saw Razen appear. The castle operations manager exchanged an assuring glance with Father before admonishing the staff in his high-pitched, nasally tone, "I think we've had enough excitement for the moment. We have a celebration to host."

Relieved but still a bit shaken, Andy took that as his cue to go change. "You're sure you're okay, Father?" he questioned as he, the King, and Mermin ascended the steps to their respective chambers.

"Oh yes, Andy. If anything, I feel energized from the altercation. I surprised myself. I never knew I could feel so protective. When the bellicose threatened you—"

Mermin chuckled and remarked, "Sounds like a father who loves his son."

By the time Andy made it back downstairs, a ten-piece orchestra had begun playing, setting a festive mood. New royal blue banners hung around the perimeter of the room. Each one bore the King's coat of arms: with the woven images of a fox above chains, separated by a line that looked like turrets.

"Well, don't you look handsome!" Marta crowed as soon as she saw his new outfit. She wore a freshly pressed blue dress with a white apron and had braided her bright purple hair with small white flowers.

"Thanks," Andy replied, feeling his cheeks warm. He leaned in and gave her a hug. The flowers in her hair smelled like baby powder, and the scent reminded him of a fragrance Mom wore, He smiled.

Charis and Larissa dashed by in new dresses of baby blue and white gingham. They chased Ro, who squealed in delight.

"Andy," Hans chimed, approaching from behind. The healer grabbed Andy's shoulder and drew him into an embrace.

"Wow!" Andy exclaimed at seeing the tall, slender man. He had shaved off his pepper gray stubble and Andy hardly recognized him.

Hans gave a hearty laugh and replied, "It's not every day you get to celebrate a new prince in the kingdom. I figured I'd clean up a bit more than usual."

"Well, you look great!"

Hans bowed with a flourish. "Thank you, *my prince.*"

"Oh, stop it," Andy blushed, waving the gesture away.

Andy joined the King. "Son! You look dashing in your new robes. Another excellent job by Kalpit."

"I like them. They feel…comfortable."

"Our first guests are arriving!" Razen announced moments later above the din. "Your Majesty, Prince Andrew, if you'd follow me."

Andy had never seen the vulture-man smile, and certainly not as broadly as he did tonight. *What's up with him?*

Father wrapped an arm around Andy's shoulder and the pair followed the steward through the growing throng of servants and other castle staff, stopping on a royal blue carpet some twenty feet from the grand staircase.

Razen summoned a group of six young girls wearing identical royal blue dresses with freshly starched lace aprons and headscarves. Each held a basket of flower petals. It quickly became clear they had been drilled with instructions, for they stood artificially still and gazed up at Andy and the King with wide eyes.

The first guests appeared on the stairway, the governor of Oops and his wife. At Razen's nod, one of the maidens sprang into action, showering Andy, Father, and their guests with a handful of petals.

"Thank you!" Andy said, batting the confetti away.

"You remember Governor Woodgate and his wife, Lady Elizabeth?" the King introduced.

"Congratulations, Your Majesty! We're so happy for you," the dignitary greeted.

"I don't think we've ever been formally introduced," Andy replied.

"Prince Andrew, you must be so proud to know you are the heir," the governor's wife presumed.

Andy nodded and smiled, at which Razen ushered the dignitaries into the dining hall. The sequence repeated itself as more than two hundred officials, dignitaries, and all manner of other notable persons filed through.

Viceroy Stoneshield and Regent Bellum both reported that the actions taken after the last war council were proving effective and no further citizens had been turned into vulture-people.

By the time the last guests straggled by, Andy's feet had grown sore, his arm tired, and his smile plastic. The flower girls lagged. If one ran out of petals, Andy would whisper in her ear when Razen wasn't looking and relieve her of further duty, which always drew a worn-out but grateful smile. Two or three of the girls chanced to give Andy hugs before dissolving into the crowd.

When most guests had joined the party, the King shook one foot then the other, attempting to regain feeling in his feet.

"You too?"

"These receiving lines are always brutal," Father affirmed. "But it's part of our job."

Andy nodded.

"What say we join the festivities?" Father suggested.

"Gladly."

Andy drank a glass of water and helped himself to appetizers brought around on trays by white-gloved servants. He spotted Cadfael across the room and approached. The beefy man cleaned up nicely. The fringe around his balding head lay flat and properly groomed, and he wore a white linen tunic with a wide ruffle over his muscular torso.

"Andy!" Cadfael boomed. Taking a serious tone, he added, "I'm sure everyone has said it many times already, but congratulations. I will be honored to serve you, my prince."

"Thank you, Cadfael. That means a lot. I am honored to have you on our side."

As they spoke, a maiden in a white dress appeared in Andy's periphery. He turned to look and stopped mid-sentence. Cadfael noticed and chuckled as Hannah approached. She had pulled her golden hair back in a braid and wore a crown of flowers. Instead of the functional work attire Andy was accustomed to seeing her wear, she wore a long white cotton dress with poofy sleeves. Overtop of that she had layered a white corset with a skirt that extended to below her knees.

She looks amazing!

"Congratulations, Andy!" she said as she waltzed over. "Are you enjoying your big night?"

Razen cut Andy's reply short as he announced from atop a chair, "If everyone would clear the floor, we will begin the dance portion of our festivities."

Everyone complied, and shortly Razen reappeared in the clearing. "His Majesty," he introduced.

The King strode onto the dance floor. "Thank you, Razen. And thanks to everyone who worked so hard preparing our celebration tonight. Your effort means a great deal to me and tells me you love me and my son."

Hearty applause erupted. Cadfael and Lucee, who had joined her husband and daughter, compelled Andy forward. The crowd parted and he joined the King.

"Prince Andrew!" one of the onlookers yelled.

"We love you!" chimed in another.

Several more exclaimed their sentiments until the magistrate waved his arms for silence.

"Thank you again. Prince Andrew, is there anything you'd like to say?" Father inquired.

Andy snuck a quick glance and caught Father's wink, then took a deep breath. "I don't know how much you've all heard about how I came to learn I am King Hercalon's son, but it's been an unforgettable experience. I feel so lucky."

Several listeners sighed happily.

Andy glanced at Father once more, then around the room. All eyes locked on him.

"As your prince, I will do my part to defend our land from our enemies. I love you all and don't want bad things to happen."

"Hear, hear!" someone shouted, precipitating more applause.

Father quieted the gathering, then added, "As you all know, I love dancing, and no celebration in Oomaldee would be complete without it."

A murmur of chuckles rippled through the onlookers.

"So tonight, I want to share the first dance with Prince Andrew and the partner of his choice."

"Me?" Andy questioned.

"Select your partner, and I shall do likewise. Then we'll dance the Saltito together."

"With your permission," the King said to Cadfael, "may I have this dance with your wife?"

Lucee glanced at her husband who nodded his approval, and she took the King's hand.

Andy, who had not lost track of Hannah in the crowd, locked eyes with her over the throng. He felt his stomach tense as he mouthed hopefully, "Dance with me?"

Hannah blushed. Then, encouraged by her father, she glided forward.

Andy and Hannah shifted uncomfortably next to each other until Father motioned for the musicians to begin. Hannah kept glancing from her mom to the floor and back to Andy.

Focus. Remember the steps. Don't make a fool of yourself, Andy coached himself.

As the dance began, he bowed to Hannah. Despite his brain's coaxing, the instant Andy's hand met Hannah's he felt his cheeks warm. A smile he'd tried to suppress now spread broadly across his face. He wiped his brow with his free arm and heard a giggle escape from his partner.

Father and Lucee stepped left then right, forward then back in unison, followed by one hop on each foot. Andy and Hannah mimicked their movements.

Forward slide left. Forward slide right. Both couples repeated the first steps four times, moving forward, then spun around and retraced their steps after two repetitions. Then hop, then spin, then slide left. Andy chanced a glance at Father, who beamed with enthusiasm.

As the dance neared its conclusion, Andy realized he was focusing on Hannah rather than his feet. He laughed, drawing another giggle from her.

The music stopped and everyone applauded. Both couples bowed, thanked their partners, and clapped. Lucee put her arm around Hannah's shoulders and gave her a squeeze before leading her back to Cadfael.

"You looked like you were enjoying yourself, Andy. Couldn't help but notice your cheeks got a bit rosy," Father remarked with a twinkle in his eye. As they left the dance floor, other couples took their place and the musicians started up again.

"Yeah," Andy grinned. "Of course, you looked pretty happy, too," he added, changing the subject. "What were you thinking about?"

"Your mother." He paused before adding, "Your mom is a very good dancer."

"Really?" Andy questioned. He had never seen her dance, and was finding it hard to picture.

"We used to tear up the dance floor," Father added with a chuckle.

Andy smiled.

As the night wore on, Andy grew weary of all the fuss people made over him. He recalled Father's words: *"Ruling well is about the people, not you."* All the same, there was only so much praise a guy could take.

Andy spied Alden as he appeared from the hallway leading to the kitchens and headed his direction.

"I haven't seen you all night!"

Alden wiped his brow. "I've been helping my mom in the kitchens. This is the first break I've gotten. What'd I miss?"

Andy recounted the highlights, including his dance with Hannah. He hoped he didn't betray the pitter-patter his heart he felt even now.

"Alden, we need more wine," Ox informed, approaching from behind. He rattled off a list of vintages that needed restocking before adding, "Andy! Congratulations again. I've been tied up in the kitchens, but I'm glad I saw you on your special night." The burly man not-so-gently patted Andy on the back.

"Thanks, Ox," Andy replied, recovering from the jolt.

"Well, I best head down to the wine cellar," Alden said after Ox left.

"I'll go with you. Save you a trip."

"You sure?"

"Absolutely. I'd love a diversion about now."

"Okay, suit yourself."

The boys made their way down the grand staircase and through the mingling crowd that filled the entry hall. Andy politely acknowledged every well-wisher, much to Alden's amusement.

"Where is the wine cellar?" Andy questioned as they continued down the stairs, passing the servant's quarters.

"Right here," Alden indicated, stopping at the dungeon door.

"It's in the dungeon?"

Alden smiled. "Nope, that way." In the blackness, Andy couldn't see where Alden pointed, but his nose picked up a musty odor.

Did something die in here? I don't remember it smelling this bad since Abaddon took over the dungeon that time. Andy shuddered at the memory.

Alden quickly lit a torch on the wall and walked twenty paces to the left, stopping before a wooden door Andy had never noticed before.

"The wine cellar," Alden declared.

Alden fitted a key into the lock and the door creaked as he pushed it open. In the dim light, Andy could barely make out the flat ends of miniature wooden casks lining the walls from floor to ceiling. Each container looked to be an eighth the size of the barrels Andy usually saw.

"Wow! I had no idea."

Alden laughed. "Come on, let's get what we need."

Within several minutes, both the boys struggled toward the entry, each bearing two casks.

"They're heavier than they look," Andy observed, exiting the wine cellar.

Alden set his casks down and locked the door behind them. Andy's nose again objected to the musty odor as Alden extinguished the torch and replaced it on the wall.

In the blackness, the boys heard the scuffling of feet approaching on the stairs.

"Who could that be?" Alden puzzled in a whisper.

"Let's wait and see."

CHAPTER TWENTY-TWO

Deliveries

C oncealed by the darkness, the boys crouched on the far side of the wine cellar door, listening to the footsteps grow louder. A minute later, the torchlit silhouette of a short man with beak-like nose and bulging eyes waddled to the dungeon door and disappeared into its depths.

"Come on," Andy whispered.

Alden nodded, following closely.

Thanks to the gold key Andy kept in his pouch, the boys found themselves on the landing in the stairwell leading down to the cells. Andy felt naked without Methuselah, and he gave a thought, instantly causing the blade to appear in his hand.

Alden's eyes opened wide,. "Whoa! How'd you do that?" he whispered.

The blade extended, but this time it exuded a dim glow rather than a brilliant beacon.

"It *is* alive!" Alden mouthed.

Andy grinned, then motioned, indicating to pursue Razen.

Silently, they made their way down the main hallway lined with cells, passing Sir Kay and Sir Gawain. They motioned the statues to keep quiet when they began to stir, then stopped before entering the large open area where they'd practiced sword fighting. All the while, the musty stench grew stronger.

A rat scuttled across their path, startling Andy as he prepared to look around the corner into the tapestry-lined area. He strained to hear footsteps and breathed a sigh of relief when his ears detected them. Methuselah's light dimmed further as Andy and Alden crept around the corner, and Andy's peripheral vision caught Razen disappear through a tapestry. They pursued in stealth, pushing aside the wall hanging to discover a tunnel they had never seen before.

"Do you suppose this is where those vulture-guys who regularly parade through the dungeon disappear to?" Alden pondered quietly.

Andy shrugged his shoulders before continuing pursuit.

Up ahead, the boys heard the sound of stone sliding across stone and saw dim light escape from a secret opening into the tunnel. Andy and Alden slowed their pace. The stench grew stronger as they approached, and Andy's eyes watered.

"My liege," they heard Razen say.

Ignoring the vulture-man's greeting, the boys heard Abaddon's hushed growl, "Father, I've summoned you from beyond the grave, for I need your help."

Andy whirled his head around to Alden, eyes wide.

Razen's and Abaddon's shadows danced on the tunnel wall, making the two look larger than they were. Andy could not make out a third shadow.

"So I was informed," another voice replied. "Highly unusual and *highly* disruptive."

"I'm sure it was," Abaddon replied without apology.

"You've gotten mixed up with the wrong crowd, my son. Evil sorcerers, dark magic. Your hatred has changed you. Not to mention your appearance—a shapeshifter? Imagine my astonishment. Is revenge really worth all this?"

Evil sorcerers? Hatred? Revenge?

Andy again looked back at Alden, neither knowing what to make of the conversation.

Abaddon interrupted, "I didn't summon you to hear your rebuke. I called you to assist in procuring a second Stone of Athanasia."

"A second one? But why?"

A long silence followed before the dragon responded, "Methuselah."

"The sword of legend? It has appeared?"

"Three times the blade has..." Abaddon hesistated before bellowing, "The boy who wields it must die!"

Without warning, a duet of worry-filled voices sounded in the tunnel: "Andy? Can you hear us?" Then everything went dark.

Andy landed with a thud in the middle of the family room, drawing a shriek from Madison who had been watching television. He tried to orient himself.

"No! Oh…I was about to find out more about Abaddon," Andy harrumphed.

"Thank goodness you're okay, Andy!" Mom sighed, touching down on the floor next to him and giving him a hug like an anaconda.

"It's been seven hours since you left us at the water park, and we were getting worried," Dad intoned, reaching behind him for the arm of the recliner and lowering himself into it.

Madison sat up ramrod straight on the couch and looked about, a gopher scouting the landscape. "Why are you dressed like that?" she interrogated.

Andy looked down at his new black robes with the crest of King Hercalon on the left sleeve and tried to explain. "They're my new dress robes. Father threw a huge party tonight—" He stopped, realizing it would make no sense to his audience.

"Well, you look better than you did the last time you disappeared," Madison quipped.

Dad cleared his throat. "We've explained the situation to Madison."

"You're my half-brother?" his sister chimed in. "Maybe that explains why you're so weird."

"Maddy," Dad growled.

"I saw a note in that little trunk a couple weeks ago addressed to Prince Andrew. I figured it was just one of your little dweeb friends, but flying off on a dragon?" his sister continued.

Andy couldn't help but smile at Madison's attempt to camouflage how impressed she was.

The doorbell rang, interrupting the reunion.

"Who could that be at this hour?" Dad questioned, rising to answer it.

Andy followed, curious. Dad shooed him away from the door, so he took up a position by the front window. Moving the curtain back, he spied a Sir Gawain's Delivery Service truck parked by the curb.

"I'm sorry to disturb you at this late hour," the delivery man apologized. "I thought I'd finished all my stops, but on my way back to dispatch, I noticed this letter wedged between the seats."

Andy abandoned his post and joined Dad at the door. The driver wore a confused expression as he handed over a large envelope.

"Not your typical letter," the man observed.

Dad accepted the envelope and said, "Thank you for your trouble. I appreciate your diligence."

Andy did a double-take. *Did he just say diligence?*

Back in the family room, Mom asked, "Who's it from?"

"Not sure. Looks like a child judging by the packaging."

When Dad turned the envelope toward Mom, she rose to examine it more closely.

"What is it?" Madison insisted.

Andy noticed a coin crudely affixed to the upper right corner. It bore King Hercalon's image.

"What is it?" Madison repeated.

"It's from Oomaldee," Andy confirmed, drawing a questioning look from his sister. "I'll take that," he added, holding out his hand.

"But it's addressed to me," Dad countered.

Andy sat up. "Really? What's it say?"

Dad opened the envelope and handed it to Mom.

She studied the coin. "This is the first time I've seen him since…"

"You okay?" Dad asked, his attention focused on the letter.

Mom nodded unconvincingly.

Madison's eyes ping-ponged between her parents.

Dad scanned the letter and noted the signature. He announced, "It's from King Hercalon." He read to himself, nodding several times. He grew still as he turned to the second page.

Andy's curiosity begged to know what Dad found so engrossing. "Well?"

Dad looked up as he finished, and Andy detected tears in his eyes. He quickly covered, explaining, "King Hercalon shared some of his story and thanked me for our diligence in raising you as we have. It's a very moving letter."

Dad caught Mom's eyes and the corners of their mouths turned up a tad.

"What's that?" Madison interrupted the moment, pointing at a gold object peeking out from under the couch.

Andy glanced down. "That would be my sword," he explained, pulling it out from where it had rolled on impact.

All eyes zeroed in on the object, and Andy clarified, "Well, it's the hilt."

Mom and Dad's eyes grew large.

"It's okay, really. I know how to use it. The blade only extends in Oomaldee."

"May I see it?" Mom requested.

Andy held it out for Mom and Dad to inspect. Mom gasped the instant she saw the detailed carvings.

"What's wrong?" Dad questioned.

"It's Methuselah!" was all Mom could get out, pulling a hand up to cover her mouth.

"You recognize it?" Andy marveled.

Mom nodded slowly.

"How?" she asked, her eyes locked with Andy's as he handed her the hilt. The instant she gripped it, the blade extended and, startled, she dropped it.

Andy reflexively jumped to avoid being cut.

The Andy Smithson series continues with more adventures to retrieve secret ingredients needed to break the long-standing curse plaguing the land of Oomaldee.

Other books in the Andy Smithson series:
Andy Smithson: Blast of the Dragon's Fury
Andy Smithson: Venom of the Serpent's Cunning
Andy Smithson: Disgrace of the Unicorn's Honor
Andy Smithson: Resurrection of the Phoenix's Grace - Coming 2015
Books 5-7 yet untitled

Reviews
Be sure to let others know what you thought about
Book 3 in the series. Please submit a review at Amazon.com.
It would mean a lot to the author.

http://www.lrwlee.com
http://www.twitter.com/lrwlee
http://www.facebook.com/lrwlee